Edison's Phonograph

DAVID HARRY
TANNENBAUM

Library of Congress Control Number: 2021944471

ISBN: 978-1-943267-84-2 Trade Paperback

Printed in the United States

Red Engine Press

Disclaimers

Everything in this book, except for some of the establishments frequented by Detective Leslie Hodges, is purely fictional and any similarity to any person, place or artifact is purely coincidence. The Edison Botanic Research Laboratory that is associated with the Edison and Ford Winter Estates in Fort Myers is a real gem. If you haven't already toured the facility, I suggest you treat yourself to a very pleasant and educating day. I have taken literary license with the creation of the first phonograph by Thomas Alva Edison, one of our country's preeminent inventive geniuses. He, and he alone, is the inventor of the "speaking machine" as he called it. To my knowledge, a second "original" phonograph does not exist. Certainly, all of the "facts" in the story pertaining to the Edison Museum, or its employees and officers, are totally fictional.

Lee County Acronyms

ASA   Assistant State Attorney

BOLO   Be On Lookout

CIA   Criminal Investigation Assistant

CFS   Call For Service

DFU   Digital Forensics Unit

DOA   Dead On Arrival

ROR   Release on Own Recognizance

RTIC   Real Time Intelligence Center

SOU   Special Operations Unit (SWAT)

TOD   Time Of Death

The Seminal Society

Edison	Chladni	Newton
Phonograph	Acoustics	Scientist
1847 - 1931	1756 - 1827	1643 - 1727

Galileo	da Vinci	Wolkenstein
Science	Artist	Composer
1564 - 1642	1452 - 1519	1376 - 1445

T A. EDISON.
Phonograph or Speaking Machine.
No. 200,521.   Patented Feb. 19, 1878.

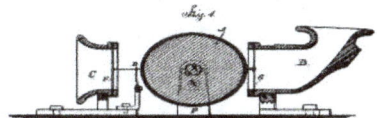

Lee County Sentinel

Obituary

Aug. 25, 2020

Sarah "Scotty" McDermitt, born in Westfield, NJ on May 3, 1944, passed away Aug 23, 2020 in Fort Myers, FL. She was the last surviving sibling of Ester and Jack Southerland. Scotty's Great-Grandmother was Sarah Davis Johnson who worked at Menlo Park, NJ as a mathematician for Thomas Alva Edison.

Scotty married Airforce Lt. Roland McDermitt, now deceased, in 1965. She leaves two children, Roland McDermitt II, of Pittsburgh, PA and daughter Linda McDermitt Murphy, now of Miromar Lakes, FL. and one grandchild.

Scotty graduated from Princeton University with a PhD in Applied Mathematics and before retirement was a tenured professor at Rutgers University in NJ. She was an accomplished amateur photographer and for the past several years was a docent at the Edison and Ford Winter Estate in Fort Myers, FL.

A private memorial service will be held later in the fall. In lieu of flowers, please make donations in memory of Sarah McDermitt to your local chapter of the American Cancer Association.

ONE

SCOTTY MCDERMITT HAD NO WAY of knowing this night would be the last she would spend on earth. Even if she had known, there is a high probability she wouldn't have done anything different, except perhaps say a prayer of thanks that the excruciating pain she had been living with for the past month would finally be gone.

Her shift as a docent at the Edison Botanic Research Laboratory Museum began earlier than usual due to the illness of a colleague. Scotty clocked in at 10 a.m. instead of 2 p.m. as had been on her schedule. That same schedule called for her to lock up after the janitorial staff finished, which meant that she wouldn't leave until 11 p.m. at the earliest and perhaps not until after midnight, all depending on how many of the cleaning staff showed up for work. This had been an extraordinary day with the end-of-summer outdoor COVID-19 rules-compliant donor VIP party and all. Supervisory logistics pertaining to the alcohol remaining from the party required a senior member of staff to be on premises with the custodians. Director Blair had asked Scotty, as he often did, to perform that function and to lock up. Scotty willingly accepted, promising to wear a mask throughout.

She was sitting in the director's office sending a text to her son when one of the cleaning crew, a guy she knew only as Hurly or Burly, she had never been certain which, stuck his head in the door. "Mrs. M," he called, "about finished here now. You lock up and I'll walk with you out to your car."

Looking up from her cell phone, Scotty saw the tired eyes of a man struggling to hold it together. "Oh, Hurly, you startled me. Let me finish this text, and I'll be right out."

"No hurry, ma'am. Be outside just in front."

Scotty finished her message, gathered a few items from the desk, dropped them into her purse, walked over to the wall where the alarm box was located, used her key to set the alarm, then swiftly opened the door, stepped outside and pulled the door closed behind her. Out of habit she turned and tugged on it to make certain it was locked.

True to his word, Hurly was waiting at the curb. He took a last drag on a cigarette, crushed it and threw the remains into a trash can. "I know these darn things aren't good for me but can't seem to kick it."

"What brought this on?" Scotty asked, when she realized Hurly was following her to her car instead of heading in the direction of his truck. "You haven't escorted me in over a year if my memory serves me. Now don't go getting me wrong, I do appreciate you doing this, but it's not necessary. No one is ever out here this time of night."

"Don't mean to scare you or nothing, but one of my men saw a couple of people in the parking lot earlier. Might be nothing. Never know these days."

"That is so kind of you, Hurly. I do always enjoy having a man around." In that instant the memory of her deceased husband Roland, a robust man who dropped dead of a heart attack in the prime of his life, flashed through her mind. For the briefest of moments, she transposed Roland for Hurly and reached out to touch her escort's arm. Her fingers grazed Hurly before she realized who she was with. She quickly yanked her hand back.

"You okay, Mrs. M?" Hurly asked, mistaking the quick retraction movement for a stumble.

"Why, yes. Of course, I'm okay. Why do you ask?"

"Oh, just that…I don't rightly know. Well, here we are."

"Thank you for looking after me. After all, a woman can't be too careful these days. Good night. And you drive carefully."

"You do the same Mrs. M. Be sure and get home safe now. This museum wouldn't be the same without you."

What Hurly didn't know was that the instincts of his men were right on. A hose had been connected from the end of the tail pipe up into the interior of her car. Crude, but effective. There was no chance of Scotty recognizing the smell and being in a position to pull over in time to avoid tragedy.

Fifteen minutes later, suffering from nausea and a pounding headache, a disoriented and lethargic Scotty turned south onto Interstate 75. Seven minutes after that she swerved off the road, went down a steep embankment and smashed head-on into a tree. A car behind her immediately pulled over, the driver and passenger running down the hill toward the horribly wrecked car. The passenger went directly to the tailpipe, yanked the hose off, pulled the other end from under the car and slipped the whole mess into a canvas bag. The driver from the parked car, meanwhile, peered through the demolished driver's side window, reached in, seemingly checking for a pulse. There could be no doubt Sarah "Scotty" Mc-Dermitt was dead.

On the way back up the hill the passenger yelled to a man running down the embankment, "Call 9-1-1. You can tell them not to hurry. Old lady's gone."

TWO

BOBBY JAMES' SHIFT WAS ALMOST finished. It had been a relatively quiet tour, allowing him to savor the before-shift Zoom party thrown for him in celebration of his twenty-second year as a Lee County Sheriff's Deputy. Normally the Highway Patrol would respond to an accident on I-75, but they were busy a few miles north directing the cleanup of several tons of tomatoes dumped from a truck when its axle broke.

One look at the accident scene immediately ended any residual high James may have still harbored. Looking down the slope from the roadway he knew, even without reports from several bystanders, what he would find when he got to the driver.

"Take your time, Sheriff," a guy had yelled, "that old lady is beyond help." James didn't slow his pace, knowing from long years of freeing people from desperate situations, there was always a chance. He also knew that laymen seldom got it right.

Not this time. One look inside the smashed car removed any doubt. Unfortunately, in this instance the man had been spot on. Minutes later, the fire captain assured him no gas was leaking and the steam under the hood was from the busted radiator. Satisfied there wasn't any danger of an explosion, James stood aside waiting for the medical transport and the tow truck. The firetruck remained on scene, but the ambulance was released.

James walked through the small group of folks who remained along the roadway, a few wearing masks, taking names, noting what they had seen. The stories of the two drivers who had seen McDermitt go off the road were essentially identical. A green Mazda was in the right, or as he thought of it, the 3 lane and suddenly moved halfway into the middle, or 2 lane. This movement caused one of the witnesses who had been driving slightly behind the Mazda, but in the 2 lane, to hit his brakes and move left into the 1 lane. This in turn caused the other witness to brake hard.

The Mazda then swerved to the right, crossed back through the 3 lane, continued onto and over the berm and down an embankment. No one saw the car hit the tree. Not surprising given they were moving over seventy miles per hour on the Interstate at night with low visibility.

So exactly why was James, on his day off, now standing beside the desk that Detective Leslie Hodges called her office waiting for her to finish a call? The Pit was the name most deputies called the area where the detectives worked and that's exactly how James viewed this part of the Sheriff's Office. The Pit. The question that bothered him continued playing in his mind as he waited. Several times he was on the verge of leaving, but that didn't feel right either.

Hodges wasn't his first choice. Not because she had a bad reputation, she had no reputation. She was a thirty-three-year-old rookie detective. "As green as they make them," the coordinator had told him when he asked about her. "Cop up in Tampa a while. Her husband went down in the line of duty, and she's down here to start over. Word on her, she's smart, keeps to herself and is a hell of a lot tougher than she looks. All the detectives are on assignment. It's her or nobody."

Hodges' call ended and she stood, all five seven of her. She pulled her COVID mask up, brushed her ash blond hair off her face, and James found himself looking straight into the greenest eyes he had ever seen. He had expected the height, as well as the eye color because he had brought up her personnel file on the computer. But he wasn't prepared for the deep southern accent with which Hodges said, "Pleased to meet you, Deputy James."

Mississippi Delta, unless his usually infallible ear was playing tricks.

Nor was he prepared for the bone crushing grasp of her handshake. "And to what do I owe the pleasure of this visit?" Leslie drawled, relying on her photographic memory to know she had never before encountered this man, either in person or on paper.

"To tell the truth, ma'am," he began, "this is kind of unofficial. Don't even know if I should be here at all. Just wanted a sounding board. This is my day off. Came in hoping to see Collier."

"Collier's working a case with two or three others. Be tied up a while I should expect."

"That's what I was told. So here I am. Don't know if you can help me."

Leslie sat down, not offering a seat to James. "I can't help you because I'm a rookie? Or is it because I'm a woman?"

James hadn't been prepared for the sudden coldness from those previously soft eyes. Nor for the tightness across her forehead. He wasn't one to back down from a fight, but that's not why he was here. "Didn't mean to offend you, sorry 'bout that. But, well, tell the truth, the age thing. How long you been a detective anyway?"

"Didn't you see it in the file?"

"How'd you…"

"Notified when someone not in my chain of command accesses my personnel file. In answer to your question, three months. Been wearing the uniform for eleven years. Three in Gulfport, Mississippi and eight in Tampa."

"I knew about Tampa. Guessed about Mississippi from your voice. What brings you to Fort Myers?"

She glanced away. When she refocused, James noticed a momentary clouding of her expressive eyes. "My husband was a detective up in Tampa. Shot in a bank robbery gone bad."

"Sorry to hear that. Must be tough. I am really sorry."

"Life goes on. Change of scenery. Took the detective exam and here we are. So, what's so important you're here on your off day?"

"As I said, this may be nothing." James unfolded an Incident Report and laid it on her neat desk. "Here's the IR. It's brief."

A moment later, Leslie, having scanned the document, looked up. "Appears to be straightforward. Ten days ago, a woman in her seventies ran off I-75, hit a tree. DOA. Estimated TOD was 11:50 p.m. What am I missing?"

"Got a call yesterday from a Fort Myers detective name of Cruzic. He caught a call from the Edison Museum. Someone had entered the place early on the 23rd, about 4:15 in the morning.

Leslie glanced down at the open report, but James answered her question before her eyes spotted what she was looking for. "Accident was just before midnight on the 22nd."

"So why call you?"

"Sarah McDermitt, the deceased, was a docent at the museum and locked up that night. Her key was used to set the alarm at 11:17."

Hodges sat quietly allowing James to continue. "The alarm was unset at 4:15. I suppose you already guessed why I was called. McDermitt's key was used to disarm the system several hours after she had died."

"You say that was nine days ago. Why didn't the museum report it back then?"

"Alarm company was archiving McDermitt's use of the key and as I understand it, their computer reported an irregularity to the museum because of the key being used after McDermitt's death."

"Museum report anything missing?"

"That's just it. They did nothing. It appears the alarm company sent the report also to the insurance company as per instructions. Someone at the insurance company, not realizing nothing was reported missing went ahead and filed a police report. To answer your question, nothing seems to have been taken. Whoever it was went in at 4:15 and reset the alarm at 4:35."

"If nothing is missing, why are you here?"

"That's what I've been asking myself. Making a mountain type of thing." James paused, gathering his thoughts. "I have a bad feeling about this. Bothering me, all's I can say. Called the tow folks. No keys came in with the car. According to the ME report, no keys were found on her person or in the car. Keys didn't walk away."

"Cause of death?"

"Trauma to the neck. Tree branch ran right through her. No mistake about that."

Hodges thought for a moment, then said, "Still no reason to think…"

"Here's the thing of it," James rushed on, gathering momentum, "the witnesses I spoke with said that by the time they managed to pull off the road and get back to the scene another car was already parked there. Two people were observed coming up the slope and getting into the parked car. One of the folks coming up the hill told the guy going down the hill to call 9-1-1."

"I suppose you're questioning why the person who yelled to call 9-1-1 didn't do so himself?"

"Bingo!" James exclaimed, surprised at how fast the skinny rookie detective caught his drift. "That, and the old lady was cherry-pink when the coroner arrived. She was so bloody when I first saw her I almost missed it. They cleaned her before putting her in the wagon. You know, this wasn't my first rodeo. Seen more than my fair share of death on the highway and it's never pretty. Over twenty years and you never get used to it. For days I seen pictures of that old lady in my head. That's when I realized it was her skin color that was rosy and not the blood."

"That's not on your report."

"Didn't think it important at the time. As I said, it took a while. Someone using her keys after she died got me thinking. That was yesterday. I'm here today, and even now I'm not sure of anything. It's in your hands now detective." James checked his watch. "Sorry to drop this on you and run, but I promised my son we'd go fishing. Got to get home and round him up. You know how to find me if you need me."

Procedure required Hodges to run the facts past her boss, Sergeant Oakmore, before beginning an investigation. As she saw the situation, there was nothing other than a few potentially unrelated facts suggesting a crime had been committed. Not wishing to come off like the rookie she was, she decided to run a few traps before going to Oakmore.

Logging into the county database allowed her to examine Scotty's autopsy report. In addition to car manuals, a list of personal items showed only reading glasses, purse, water bottle, Kleenex packets, and a lipstick. The contents of the purse were listed separately and did not include car keys, but did list a wallet with two credit cards, driver's license and various insurance cards, a pharmacy bottle from a Dr. Haywood Sayeth, labeled "Roxanol" with three pills remaining. There also were several pictures of what Leslie assumed were Scotty's grandchildren, and another lipstick, compact case, cell phone and a small shawl. Deputy James was correct, no keys.

Cause of death was listed as trauma to the neck just as James had stated. But what James hadn't reported was that the blood carboxyhemoglobin was, in the words of the medical examiner, "abnormally high". The ME further noted, "High CO-Hb coupled with cherry pinkish skin leads to speculation of likely CO involvement prior to the car leaving the roadway."

"Dr. Van Deere," Hodges said, an hour later, "so very good of you to return my call. Did you have a chance to review the file on Sarah McDermitt?"

"I did," Van Deere, a woman in her late sixties responded, her tone flat, non-committal. "What is it you wish to know, Detective?"

"Your note about carbon monoxide. High levels according to you. High enough to have killed her?"

"I cannot conclude that with any degree of certainty. High enough to have impaired her cognitive ability and thus her driving. Yes."

"You listed cause of death as trauma, not carbon monoxide poisoning."

"Correct. A tree branch severed her right carotid artery. The heart was pumping at the time, so technically the trauma caused her death."

"Are you suggesting that she would have died of CO poisoning had her artery not been severed?"

"That's the same question I already answered. I cannot be certain."

"Why the uncertainty? Pardon me if I don't follow."

"With carbon monoxide poisoning often fresh air will be enough to reverse the concentration. I can say that if the levels remained as high as I believe they were, then without mitigation, McDermitt would certainly have perished from the carbon monoxide had her carotid not been severed."

"Is it unusual for an accident victim to have high levels of carbon monoxide in their blood, or do you see this often?"

"Years ago, it was much more prevalent than recently. In older cars it's more likely than in new models. McDermitt was driving a 2019 Mazda. Can't imagine the CO came into the car from a faulty exhaust system."

"Is there anything else I should know?"

"I hate to say, I almost missed it, what with the red skin tone from the CO poisoning and all."

"Missed what?"

"Jaundice. Her feet were more yellow than red."

"Liver problem?"

"That's what I thought at first. No, she had advanced pancreatic cancer. I can't imagine her living another month, six weeks at most. Must have been in terrible pain. Explains the Roxanol though."

"Anything else?"

"Can't think of anything."

"Thank you again for returning my call."
"You're most welcome, Detective. Goodbye."
Time to brief the boss.

Sergeant Hudson Oakmore, squat and slightly over-weight with a tight, hard-to-read face, was a man of in-finite patience, one of the main characteristics of an above average detective. His biggest problem, some in the agency call it a strength, is that his patience is near zero for fools. Leslie Hodges was too new for him to have an opinion one way or the other. Since her detective exam score was the highest he had seen in many years, he was willing to suspend judgment. "So," he said after listening to her story, "you want to convert a single vehicle crash where an old woman runs her car off the road from an accident to a homicide?"

Hodges hadn't expected her boss to cut to the chase so fast. Instead, she had expected to field a ton of ques-tions, for which she was ready. "I suppose it boils down to that. Yes."

"Why else would I approve taxpayer money for an investigation? We don't usually become involved with bad driving—or heart attacks—or whatever else it could have been. ME's report doesn't indicate a suspicious death."

"I spoke with the examiner. She's clear on the cause of death. She's also clear about the high level of carbon monoxide in the bloodstream. What's not so clear is how it got there. I'm thinking if a high CO level was the rea-son the car went off the road then we have a homicide."

"Listen, Hodges. I'll grant you the CO levels might have been high and might even have blacked the old lady out. Alright. That's still a long way from homicide. Could be a problem with the car. Hell, could be a lot of things."

"True."

"Now hear me out. I've no book on you. Not yet anyway, so I don't know to go with your instinct or not. I've known Deputy James for more years than I care to remember. A hard ass if ever there was one. But the guy cares. He's probably pulled more bodies out of cars than anyone else around here. If something's bothering him, we owe it a look-see. Here's the deal. Pull a CFS. Your first stop is the car. You have a green light to take this where it leads providing you first make absolutely certain there's no chance the exhaust could have found its way inside the vehicle without human intervention."

"Yes, sir," she replied, knowing a Call For Service report was the first step in any deputy investigation.

"When you're satisfied it wasn't something faulty with the car let me know. If there was something faulty with the car, we'll pass it on to Tallahassee. Let the state deal with Mazda. Their corporate lawyers'll eat you up and spit you out. Not a pretty sight."

"Who should I be partnering with on this?"

"Go it alone for now. Everyone's tied up solid. When you need help, we'll see what we can do."

On the way back to The Pit, Hodges' exhilaration at scoring support from her boss was short-lived when she realized Oakmore hadn't thought enough of the CFS to assign her a partner. Her stomach knotted when it dawned on her that she now had in her hands all the rope required to hang herself.

THREE

THE *U-WRECKUM WE-CRUSHUM* SIGN ON Treeline Avenue was hanging lopsided, one of its mounting brackets having been severed in the last hurricane. The massive lot, hidden from motorists by a thick stand of giant arborvitae, sat a mile north of the Southwest Florida International Airport, the main commercial airport serving the Fort Myers area. A crushed gravel driveway wound its way back to the yard and as Hodges approached, she watched with fascination as a red Chevrolet was lifted by a huge flat magnet hanging from a crane and swung into the jaws of a crushing machine. Before her vehicle came to a stop in front of what passed as an office, the Chevy had been transformed into a metal square smaller than a sofa. The magnet was already lifting a second car, this time a late model Honda Accord.

"You Detective Hodges?" a small man called out as she approached the entrance, his face long ago sun-hardened into orange leather. "I'm Honker. Me and my brother over there own this place. Been here long before the airport. Now they plan to run me out. Granddaddy worked the swamp back then. You'll find everything in order you care to look. I ain't done nothing wrong."

"I'm not here about your books, Mr...."

"Just Honker. Been called that since I was bite-size for a gator."

"Honker. I'm here for..."

"Yeah. You called 'bout the Mazda. That's what they always do. Call 'bout one thing and bust me for another."

"Hey. Play it straight with me, I'll return the favor. I'm here for the Mazda — and only for the Mazda. For now."

"Got your drift. Good thing you called. We was fixin' to feed it to Max. My, you sure are a skinny one, you are. Need to be spending more time at the trough and less time asking questions, want my opinion."

Hodges had no need for his opinion but refrained from telling him so. Instead she asked, "Has anything been removed from the car?"

"Only the dead body." Honker laughed at his joke and quickly stopped when he realized the woman across from him was squinting hard at him with the coldest looking eyes he had ever seen on a woman. Assassin eyes. "I mean, we were fixin' to prep it for demolition just today when you called. So, no, nothing's been removed. There's not much that's salvageable other than the tires, back seats, fuel tank and transmission. Oh, we did drain the tank. Price of gas is down now 'cause of that dang virus, but it'll be back up. Still worth siphoning it off."

"Show it to me?"

"The gasoline or the car?"

"The car. Gas is yours."

"Over there," Honker said, pointing to a car sitting off by itself halfway across the yard. "Want to look at it yourself, or you need help?"

"Tell you what. Give me ten minutes alone and then send someone over to answer questions. That work for you?"

Honker, glad she wasn't poking around the office files, was relieved. Matching paperwork for all the vehicles on the lot would prove embarrassing at best. "Anything you say, Detective. We aim to please."

The front end of the Mazda was a mess and mostly unrecognizable. The dashboard had been pushed back and split open where the engine had slammed back against the firewall. The rear end of the car, on the other hand, appeared untouched. Within five minutes of poking around the Mazda, Hodges realized there was nothing more she could uncover herself. She was uncertain how to ask questions about carbon monoxide without tipping off the possible murder investigation. Problem was, she couldn't move forward without conclusive proof of intentional poisoning. Looking at the mess of broken metal and glass, sideways engine, caved-in interior Leslie had no idea how she could ever satisfy her boss.

Honker intercepted her halfway back to his shop. "Just coming to see how you're do'in out here," he said, the cracked, hardened skin around his mouth giving way to what passed as a smile. "Thought you might need help."

Overlooking the guy's nervousness, she responded, "I could use a hand."

"Are you looking for a specific thing, or what? We get hundreds of wrecks in here as you can see. Almost never does a detective show up to examine the cars. Something up?"

"As a matter of fact, there is," Hodges said, deciding to play it straight. "Autopsy report shows high carbon monoxide concentration. I was wondering if the car malfunctioned in any way to let CO into the passenger cabin?"

"My father always talked about that back in the day. I've not seen that much now." He pulled a hand-held radio from his pocket and spoke a few words. "Brother will be over in a few minutes with the lift. First, we'll look at what we can see from the top, then we'll look at it from the bottom. If fumes got in, we should see a crack or something. As I said, not a normal thing now."

Honker opened the trunk, pulled out the carpet and set it carefully aside. He poked around the corners and crevasses, then pronounced, "Trunk's tight as..." He paused, thought better of what he was about to say, then continued, "...as a drum. Nothing leaked in through here. I can promise that much. Firewall, if anything." He went around to the front passenger side. "Firewall's pretty well crushed but...but truth is, fumes don't come in from there anyway. The only other place would be underneath. Rust maybe. This car's too new for that. If there was a hitch on back, I'd suspect someone launched a boat and ran the back end into saltwater. But there's never been a hitch. Maybe there's a hole under there anyway. You never know where a car's been."

While waiting for his brother to arrive with the lift, Honker bent over what remained of the right front fender, reached in and grabbed a loose hose.

"What's that in your hand?" Hodges asked.

"The air conditioning hose. It was off the pipe goes up into the car's air unit."

"Could it have come off in the accident?"

"Anything can happen when a car going at seventy hits a big ol' oak tree. But…"

"But what?"

"Stay here, don't touch a thing. I think I found what you're looking to see." He again said something into his radio, then turned to Hodges, "If you're thinkin' someone did something wrong here I think you just might be right. Brother's bringing a couple of ladders, give us a good look see. You might could have your camera handy."

Within five minutes, a guy who looked to be twice the size of Honker and not wearing a mask jumped down from a work truck and fetched two small ladders from the bed. Without introduction he set them both up against the right bumper. Honker invited Hodges to climb up on one while he positioned himself on the other. "Take a picture of the firewall right over there," Honker suggested. "That tells it all."

The picture taken, she asked, her own mask now snugly in place. "What the hell am I lookin' at?"

"See that hose hanging over there?" Honker pointed to the hose he had earlier held in his hand. "That goes from the air temperature control unit, that's the box over there in the corner, and fastens onto this inlet fitting." Honker moved his greasy hand so Leslie could see what he was referring to. "The inlet fitting blows air into the cabin."

"I don't see any fitting."

"That's because there's a piece of plastic hose wedged on there. Turn on your video so you can record me taking this thing off. You'll see what I'm saying."

With the video running, Honker twisted the plastic hose off the inlet pipe. Then he took the open end of the original hose and slipped it back onto the inlet pipe. It fit exactly.

"What's your take?" Hodges asked, the video still rolling.

"Someone removed this here air conditioning hose, the one I just slipped back on. Replaced 'er with a plastic hose."

Leslie studied the hoses and noted, "The one you just took off, the one in your hand, is short, less than a foot I'd say. I don't see anything it could connect to."

"The impact severed it. See down there where the end of this here hose was hanging? See that indent in the firewall? Something hit there and cut the hose."

"Where's the rest of it? And what's it mean?"

"Gone's all I can say."

"Where did it go? I mean why connect the hose you have in your hand to the air conditioning?" Hodges knew the answer, but she wanted it to come directly from someone who might later be called to testify in a murder trial.

"You asking where the other end of that hose went? I'd be guessin'."

"Your best guess?"

"To the tail pipe."

"Would there be a way to prove that?"

"Let's pick 'er up and see."

Hodges allowed the video to continue rolling capturing the crane moving into position. When everything was ready, Honker, not realizing Leslie hadn't stopped recording, and who now fancied himself the director, called, "Lights, camera, action." The Mazda slowly rose to a point where they could walk underneath.

"Lookee here!" an excited Honker called a moment later.

Leslie followed his finger and saw what she took to be black goo covering the end of the tail pipe.

"That stuff you see there's melted plastic. Same's this here hose. No question the missing end of this hose was fitted over this here tail pipe. And you can quote me on that."

Leslie produced an evidence bag and held it open. "Here, slip that hose you have in your hand into this." When Honker complied, she said, "Now would you please cut off that tail pipe end and I'll get you another evidence bag."

While supervising the operation, she silently prayed she would soon be hearing Honker testify in court to what he had just discovered.

FOUR

THE MCDERMITT CASE HAD NOW become a full-blown murder investigation and the best Leslie could reasonably hope for would be to get assigned as an assistant to a senior detective. But Oakmore surprised her by saying, "We're jammed. You caught it fair and square. You'll be the youngest, I mean in terms of time on the job, in memory to lead a homicide. For now, on paper I'm your partner. Just don't let us down."

Who the us was in that sentence Leslie had no way of knowing. She was thrilled, nonetheless. Aware that all eyes in the department would be focused squarely on her didn't diminish her high. She hadn't been in Lee County for sufficient time to distinguish who was with her from those rooting against her. She'd been around law enforcement long enough to recognize the truth in that thought. Careers, she knew, for detectives were made — and lost — on homicides. They had just given her more rope.

Where to begin? One of her instructors had put it bluntly and to the point. "Just friggin begin!" he had crudely told the class. "It almost doesn't matter where, just do something. Ask yourself the first question comes to mind. Go search out the answer. While you're diggin' another question'll pop up. Go where the facts lead. When you find yourself down a rabbit hole, back your ass out and go find another tunnel. If they're all dark you missed one. Start the hell over."

"Good advice," Leslie thought. "What's my first question?"

She thought about why Deputy James came to her in the first place. A call from a Fort Myers break-in report he had told her. Generated by the use of McDermitt's alarm key hours after she died.

"Cruzic?" she said into her cell when the Fort Myers detective came on the line, "This is Detective Leslie Hodges over at Lee County. Got a few minutes to answer a couple of questions about that break-in over at the Edison Museum a few weeks back?"

"Won't take but thirty seconds," the man responded. "Nothing happened."

"Somebody went in using docent McDermitt's key as I understand it."

"Yeah. Whoever it was, turned off the alarm, looked at a phonograph and left. Nothing was broken. Nothing was taken. Alarm was reset. Big nothing burger."

"Only it wasn't McDermitt. She was dead four hours. Any idea on who it was? Or why?"

"Haven't given it a moment's thought since then. Oh, that's not right. Called a friend of mine over at County. Thought it strange the intruder used a dead woman's alarm key. Bobby, that's my friend, suggested the key might have been a duplicate. I started to follow up, but Edison said to drop it. I dropped it. End of story."

"Mind if I follow up with Edison?"

"Can't see as it's even worth a phone call. But, hey, go for it if that's what floats your boat. Hey, you new or something? Hadn't heard your name before."

"Started a few months back. This my first…" She started to say homicide but thought better of it. "…case."

"Anytime you wanna have a drink, shoot the shit, don't hesitate to call. You know where to find me."

"And if you happen to remember anything more call me."

"Sure thing. 'Cept there's nothing to remember."

"Just call if you think of anything. Name's Hodges."

"Oh, hey, now you said your name again I remember. You're the newbie. Got you chasing break-ins. Hang in there, kid. Soon you'll graduate to interviewing domestics. My husband-hit-me kind of thing. When you pull something important, call me."

Leslie was tempted to tell him he'd be the last person in the world she'd call for help, but it was too early in her career to burn bridges. For now it was go along to get along.

Her next call was to the museum office where she spoke to a man by the name of William Blair. He identified himself as Managing Director, but when asked about the break-in he quickly referred Leslie to the CEO, a woman named Jayne Nikolson.

Nikolson's voice message said to leave a number and the call would be returned within the day. In fact, she called back twelve minutes later. In answer to Leslie's question concerning the break-in report, she replied, "I told the officer who called me — I believe his name's Cruzic — nothing really happened. I'm sure it's in his report."

Playing along, Leslie asked, "Was it a false alarm? What triggered the report?"

"Someone went into the museum and used a docent's key to disarm the security alarm. Unfortunately, the docent had been killed earlier that night in a tragic car wreck. But, like I said, nothing's missing. No damage done. Sorry to waste your time."

"What makes you certain nothing was stolen? Did you take a complete inventory or what?"

"Didn't need to. It's all on the surveillance video. Why can't you just accept I know what I'm talking about?"

Perturbed by what Hodges perceived as a runaround, she said, "I'd appreciate if you'd email a copy of that video."

"Gone. Don't have it."

"Gone? As in erased? Or gone, as in tossed out?"

"Erased."

"Who erased it?"

"Why's that your business, Detective? I don't understand why I'm being badgered over nothing."

Instead of arguing, Hodges changed direction. "Did you view the video personally?"

"Of course, I did."

"What did it show?"

"I said, nothing."

"Sorry, Ms. Nikolson, it showed something. Someone came into the museum after hours and used an alarm key belonging to a deceased woman and turned off the alarm. That was something. Whoever came in eventually left. Did that person reset the alarm? That also was something. For you to maintain nothing happened is not accurate. You follow me?"

"Are you finished?"

"Not until I see the surveillance video. I need to see what you saw."

"That's impossible. The disk was erased."

"When was the disk erased?"

"After I viewed it."

"Did anyone else view it?"

"Bill Blair. We saw it together."

"Was it on a computer or what?"

"One of those memory drive things. Able Security sent it over."

"When was the memory erased?"

"After we viewed it."

"Why?"

"I don't know. Nothing was taken. The stuff on that drive was of no value to us so it was erased. Is there a crime in that?"

Leslie started to tell Nikolson she hoped not. But caught herself. Instead, she said, "I'm very sorry to have bothered you, but tell me just one more time so there's no misunderstanding. Was anything of value removed from the museum?"

"I told you, absolutely not."

"Was anything disturbed or destroyed?"

"No, I said. Nothing of any consequence happened."

"But someone came into the museum and spent time there. Yet, you say nothing happened."

"May I remind you, that's what a museum's for. People coming in, looking around."

"Not at four in the morning."

"I suppose not. Nothing was taken. Nothing's missing."

"As CEO, do you spend much time at the museum, or how does that work exactly?"

"CEO for us is a paid position. I open each day and unless we have a special occasion Bill Blair closes. Bill handles the books and is responsible for daily operations. I oversee him and raise money to keep us operating."

"It must be interesting what you do. I'd love to hear more."

"Maybe we can do lunch and I'll fill you in."

"You can do me a big favor and call the security company and have them send me a copy of the surveillance video from that night."

"I certainly will not! You're making a big deal out of nothing!"

"Am I now?"

"You certainly are! And I plan to have a word with your superior. Good day, Detective Hodges."

That wasn't how Leslie had mentally scripted the call. Not by a long shot. Clearly, something on that file caused someone discomfort. "Look where they don't want you to look," Junior, her deceased detective husband, had often said. "If crimes were easy to solve, we wouldn't need a trained detective force. I spend my life chasing rabbits down blind holes. That's where the answers are, down one of those holes." Junior, her guiding light.

The only way Leslie knew to get her hands on the surveillance video without the cooperation of the museum was to file papers with the court to obtain a search warrant for Able Security. That required Sergeant Oakmore's approval, which was not going to be easy. Powerful people served on the museum's Board and many of the city's elite were major donors. Oakmore, a naturally cautious man, would tread slowly.

Leslie knew from her training that most search warrants in Lee County were obtained without the need for court appearances with the detective filing the paperwork on a secure server and the Duty Judge reading them in his or her office. It was efficient and relatively quick. But this was a high-profile case, so she wrote out the script in anticipation of Oakmore requiring an Assistant State's Attorney review prior to moving forward.

ASA: Your Honor, we're here today to obtain a search and seizure warrant asking Able Security Systems to turn over to us surveillance video footage of the Edison Museum from 11 p.m. Saturday, August 22nd to 5 a.m. Sunday, August 23rd.

COURT: And what evidence do you have supporting probable cause that what you might possibly find would have a high likelyhood of showing there was a crime or criminal activity?

ASA: Your Honor, a woman by the name of Sarah McDermitt was a docent of the Edison Museum. She had on her person a key to the alarm system. Mrs. McDermitt died in an automobile accident just before midnight on the 22nd. She had set the museum's alarm approximately thirty minutes earlier using her alarm key. At 4:15 the next morning, approximately four hours after Mrs. McDermitt's death, someone disarmed the museum's alarm using the deceased's key. Furthermore, we have evidence that Mrs. McDermitt's death was a homicide. Mrs. McDermitt's keys were not found in her car at the time of her death. There is a high probability that her keys were stolen by the person or persons who killed her and that that person or persons broke into the museum and was caught on the surveillance video.

COURT: Why not just ask the museum to allow you access to the security files in question? I can't imagine them not cooperating.

ASA: They refused, Your Honor. I was told the file they had was destroyed.

COURT: I don't understand. If the files were destroyed how can you gain access to them?

ASA: We believe the file that was destroyed was a copy of the file maintained by Able Security System.

COURT: Then why waste my time? Ask the museum for permission to review the security company files. What am I missing here?

ASA: The detective asked that very question and was denied. We believe the copy was destroyed for a reason.

COURT: Destroyed? Did they provide a reason for the destruction?

ASA: They did not. Nor did they provide a reason for the denial of access.

COURT: I find little likelihood of anything being seen on surveillance files of an empty museum between the hours of eleven and five in the morning that would prove sensitive to the museum, so I hereby find probable cause for a search warrant and one is hereby granted.

Satisfied she had her bases covered, she printed the script and walked to Oakmore's office, expecting a hard time. He glanced at the paper and out of character, quickly said, "Hodges, you're leading a homicide investigation. Do what you need to do to move forward. Going the ASA route is a good move. Just don't embarrass me all's I ask."

FIVE

THE NEXT MORNING, INSTEAD OF sending the papers and file over electronically to the prosecutor's office and allowing them to run with it, Leslie decided to go in person. It was time to see up close and personal just how the Lee County administration of justice system worked. It was one thing to sit in class and have others tell you how it should work. It was, she knew from painful experience, quite another thing to see first-hand how the sausage was actually made. And never the twain shall meet.

COVID-19 signs were everywhere she looked, both inside and outside the building, warning people to maintain proper distancing and requiring the wearing of masks. "Have you had any flu-like symptoms?" a uniformed woman guard asked, pointing an electronic thermometer at Leslie's forehead.

"No," Leslie answered.

"Temperature's normal. Hand sanitizer's over there. Good to go." The guard turned her attention to a man waiting patiently several feet behind her.

Leslie's first stop was the Court Clerk's Office which advised her to find an available prosecutor and get buy-in. "Dear, with the COVID and all, unless you round up ASA support that paper'll go into queue. It could be weeks before its heard. They're all so overloaded as it is."

"Any suggestions of who to use?"

"You can try that new guy one floor up. Just had a case dismissed so he might have a few minutes. Name's Smith."

"Good try, Detective Hodges," Allen Smith, one of the many Lee County Assistant State's Attorneys, said after reviewing her pre-scripted hearing outline. "Looks like this ain't your first rodeo. Truth is, it all depends on the judge you draw. Gonzales will grant the warrant about a third of the way through. Stymington will make you haul the museum in here. He's a stickler."

Allen, a stocky black guy with wide-set eyes was, as the clerk had said, new to the State Attorney's office. Although not as new as Leslie, he was still cutting his teeth and didn't cherish having his career impacted by making requests that weren't granted. His boss, he knew, kept score. He had just lost one motion; losing two in one day would set him apart in a way he didn't envision doing him any good.

When Allen expressed reluctance to move forward with the warrant motion, she replied, "This is a murder investigation. We catch a face on that video, we go a long way to tracking down a murderer. I can't imagine a judge, any judge, not allowing us to view a few hours of boring tape. Hell, it's the inside of a closed museum for God sakes. If there's nothing there then no secrets are lost. If by chance, there's something they're covering up then it's a win."

"Simple as that, you think?" Allen said. "Trust me. Judges have their own thoughts on these matters and go-ing against an institution like the museum with so many big donors and political powers is never a good idea."

"Is there anything in life free of politics?" Leslie snapped. Regaining her composure, she said, "Sorry for the outburst. Uncalled for I know. I repeat. If nothing happened then nothing happened, and no harm's done. That said, we could catch a murderer — a murderer of an old woman no less. Isn't that what you're here for?"

"Even if you get the warrant it's a long way to landing the perp. Anyone who went to all the trouble to get her alarm key knows the camera's always on. Chances are their face'll be hidden."

"All the same, it's a lead in a murder case. That's got to be worth something."

"Tell you what. Those two judges are the only two hearing motions today. I'll file it and if we draw Gonzales we'll go through with it. If we draw Stymington, I'll withdraw. Fair enough?"

Leslie reluctantly agreed. Smith filed the papers twenty minutes later while Leslie waited in his cramped office reviewing what she knew about the case and what she needed to find out. The second list far outweighed the almost nonexistent first.

Smith returned with a broad smile. "Great news! Drew Gonzales. Set for 3:00 today. See you in Court Room Six at 2:45. Don't be late. Might need to have you testify about the CO poisoning and the tail pipe."

Leslie walked into the courtroom one minute early. If there was a prize for long sad faces, Leslie Hodges could have draped the gold medal ribbon for first prize over the head of Assistant State Attorney Allen Smith and laid the medal on his impeccable suit.

"I can't believe this," Smith mumbled as she approached, "Gonzales went home sick and Stymington is hearing her docket. It'll be delayed 'til four."

"I thought you said you'd pull it."

"Tried. Clerk won't allow it without Gonzales' approval. I'm about to get my head handed to me."

"It's a murder investigation. Doesn't that count?"

"Probable cause counts. Can I persuade you to pull it?"

"Sorry, no. If we wait, the file could be manipulated. Surprise is critical. We do have probable cause to believe the video may contain evidence leading to the conviction of a person, or persons, for homicide. What more can the court require?"

"From your lips to the judge's ears. Ok, let's get up there. Better to be early than late. Frankly, once you're on the tiger it's best not to get thrown off."

Thirty minutes later, a jubilant Attorney Smith turned to Hodges. "Can't believe he never even asked those last few questions. It was all over when you told him about the plastic found on the tail pipe. Good piece of work by the way."

"You're the one deserves the kudos. You set it up perfectly."

"Using your script. You're good at this, you know. A natural. Ever consider law school?"

"All I've ever wanted to be in my life is a cop. A detective to be exact. Can't imagine that will change."

"Well, you're good at it, I'll say that much. Hard to believe you've only been on the job a short time."

"My late husband can take credit. Best teacher I ever had. If we catch the perps, I'd love working with you on the homicide case."

"Can't happen. I'm far too junior to be assigned major felonies. Highest I'll get for years is burglary and maybe domestic violence. Can't believe someone as…as green as you caught a homicide investigation. Never heard of it. And believe you me, over here we hear all the stories. More than I need to know, actually."

Leslie's smile broadened. "Thank you for believing in me. I know you took a big chance. I owe you one. You need someone tracked down, I'm your person."

"It's actually the other way around. You could have found someone else to work with. Lots of lawyers here live for the fight. They like going head-to-head with the judges. I'm just not there yet."

"You did a great job. Thanks. Gotta go. Have a warrant to execute."

———————

Protocol required Hodges to notify Oakmore, who then assigned a senior detective by the name of Fischer to accompany her. She knew Fischer by reputation only, having spoken to him directly once on her first day when he came by her cubicle and said, "Welcome aboard. Need work to keep you busy? I have more than enough for all of us."

Fischer spent most of his time out of the office and took the daily briefings by phone, a courtesy extended to only a few. The book on Fish, as he was known in the office, made him out to be smart with an exceptionally high conviction rate, a low boiling point for screwups, a stickler for detail and particularly tough on rookies. In his early sixties he may have lost a step or two, but he had maintained his trim figure with only the trace beginnings of a belly.

Fischer's text message said:

Meet you at Able Security in 20.

Unlike the movies where showing up with a search warrant triggers a barrage of angry talk and arm flailing, Able Security Systems had a well-thought-out protocol, starting with temperature taking and hand sanitizer spraying and progressing to warrant verification. That took all of three minutes. Then thirty seconds to confirm the surveillance location was one Able monitored. After which the receptionist said, "Tech guy'll be with you in a moment. Please wear your masks while in the building."

"Be certain he doesn't access those files before we see what he's doing," Hodges advised.

Fischer's barely preceptive nod of approval told Leslie all she needed to know. "You're the lead on this," he had said when they met out front a few moments ago. "Go for it. Let's see what you're made from."

"Been 'round this barn a time or two, Miss," the receptionist answered, her words muffled under her colorful Able Security Systems mask. "Company values its business license. Tech won't know what files you want until you personally identify them."

"That's good to know. Appreciate it."

The tech guy turned out to be a woman named Alice Tyson. She was about the same age as Hodges but stood no taller than four-eight. Unlike Leslie's broom-like profile, Tyson was built more on the order of a fireplug. Her company mask hung around her neck and she quickly pulled it up over her mouth and nose when Leslie flashed her identification.

"Come with me," Tyson instructed, leading the way through a door and proceeding down a bleak hallway to one of several offices. A computer sat on an otherwise empty desk with the only chair in the room positioned in front.

"Hold up the warrant," the techie demanded, her fingers on the keyboard ready to input information. "I need to know what location and time frames you're looking for."

"Oh, the museum. Familiar with that one." She typed in the necessary information and a moment later said, "Okay, that's all I need from you. They got four cameras. You bring your own thumb drive?"

Hodges hadn't thought to do so but was pleasantly surprised when Fish reached into his jacket pocket and produced a drive still embedded in plastic. Before handing the device to Tyson, he removed the wrapper, wrote his initials on the cover with a marker and added the date and time.

"Take less than two minutes to transfer," Fireplug said. "Four files, one for each camera."

"Almost forgot," Hodges said, "I'll need your name, address and phone number."

Tyson handed Hodges a card. "It's all right there. You're aware I can only vouch for the fact I gave you the files for a certain property between certain hours. I have no knowledge of what is or isn't on those files."

A sudden thought crossed Hodges' mind. "Does that mean the files may have been erased or tampered with?"

"If they had been erased there would be nothing transferring right now. As for tampering that would be unusual. There it's done. I hope you find what you're looking for. Log shows we sent a copy of these same files to the museum back on the 27th and to an insurance company."

"Thank you." Fischer said. "Appreciate your co-operation."

"Just doing my job."

———————

An hour later she and Fischer were at his desk, the contents of the thumb drive having been uploaded into the county database, the device itself properly tagged and logged into evidence. "And what is it exactly you expect to see on video?" Fischer asked the serious-looking string bean sitting at the computer beside him and who was about to log into the master file so they could together review the surveillance video.

"That woman Nikolson says nothing's on here, yet she destroyed the file. I'm hoping to see a face."

"From your file notes I take it you plan to link whatever face you see to the homicide you're working?"

"Thinking along those lines," Hodges confessed

"Probably going to be a bust. It should only be so easy." Fischer's tone held out little hope for success.

The shakiness of the video suggested the recording equipment was old. Instead of being smooth like a movie, the images appeared to have been taken seconds apart with jerky movement. One man, ski mask covering his face, entered the museum at 4:18 a.m. went right to the alarm box, key in hand. He then proceeded to the phonograph display, opened it with a key, picked up what appeared to be the original Edison phonograph, looked underneath it, then put it back down and relocked the case The man then retraced his steps back to the alarm box, turned the key and proceeded to leave, carefully locking the door behind him.

Hodges played the images from all four cameras and they all were in corroboration. The first one, from camera M1, had been the best one. Cameras M2, M3 and M4 were focused on other parts of the museum, but camera M4 caught a glimpse of the man as he entered and left the museum.

"So, Fish, what's your take-away?" Hodges asked, hoping to gain the benefit of his many years studying crime-scene video.

"I haven't seen herky-jerky videos like that for years. I make the perp at six-four, six-five. On the heavy side. Looking for something specific and didn't find it. What'd you see?"

"He certainly didn't take anything. Nikolson was right about that. He looked underneath making me suspect he was there to confirm something. Other than that, I think your take-away is as much as we're likely to get."

"So why destroy the disk?" Fischer asked.

"That's what got all this started. I mean the warrant and all. Why spend time destroying the video? Throw it in a drawer — or in the trash."

"Sometimes, you know, things are exactly as you see them."

"Meaning?"

"Meaning nothing of any importance was on the disk. Clearly nothing was taken from the museum. Disk is useless to them. They destroyed it out of habit, like some folks shred everything they throw away."

Feeling defeated, but not ready to give in, Hodges replied, "I hear you. Just suppose someone at the museum recognized the perp. If that's so, then the video is important to us even though nothing was stolen."

Fischer's phone rang. He listened a moment then turned to the gangly ball of nervous energy pacing the floor. "Hope you're happy. Stuck your arm in a hornet's nest. Now you pay the price."

Hodges stopped pacing. "What the hell you talking about?"

"Hud wants you in his office ASAP. Seems the museum's lawyers have been beating the ear of the mayor. And shit's sliding down the proverbial hill. If you own a slicker now would be the time to wear it."

"You sure as hell hit a nerve!" Sergeant Hudson Oakmore said to the rookie standing at attention in his doorway. "At ease, young lady. I see Fish bailed on you. That's his loss. He'd be leading this homicide investigation now if he…he…well, never mind. Anyway, I took the liberty of viewing that tape. Far as I can see there's no reason for the museum folks to get their undies in a knot over this. But maybe it's not nothing. Regardless, as they like to say around here, when you grab hold of the tiger's tail you better as hell not let go. So, my advice to you, young lady, is get yourself a good grip and see where this ride leads."

SIX

"ONE THING I'VE LEARNED, HONEY," Junior had said one night when he and Leslie were enjoying a Scotch and discussing what to do about an uncooperative witness to a bank robbery, "is to tackle it head on. Go right for the jugular. You got one shot, make it good."

"But sleep on it first," had been Leslie's advice to her husband and also to herself late yesterday when she had found herself pumped and ready to go in the parking lot of the Edison Museum at dinner time after having left her boss's office.

It was now 9:30 in the morning. Not so early as to interrupt Jayne Nikolson's opening routine at the museum, but not so late as to interfere with her lunch plans.

"Have a moment to talk?" Hodges asked, positioning herself directly in front of Nikolson's desk, her mask in place. "I'm Detective Hodges. We spoke…"

"I know who the hell you are and I've nothing to say to you!" Nikolson's mask was around her neck and she didn't bother to pull it up.

"But you, or your lawyer, had a lot to say to the mayor. So, say it directly to me. I'm here to listen."

"If you insist! How dare you get a search warrant for our surveillance tapes? I told you nothing happened!"

"I asked you for them and you refused."

"There's nothing on there. Nothing!"

"Now that I've seen them, I tend to agree. Except…"

"Except what? There's nothing there."

"Except," Hodges paused for effect, using the time to gather her thoughts. "Except, then why did you destroy your copy? And if there's nothing to see, why complain to the mayor? That's what I'd call dropping a bomb to kill a flea. If there wasn't a flea in that video, then why the bomb?"

Nikolson's lips quivered. Leslie remained quiet, anticipating the explanation she had come for. But it wasn't to be.

"I asked you a question, Ms. Nikolson. Why the bomb?"

"If you must know, it wasn't me. It was Blair. He's outraged."

"That's William Blair, Managing Director? The guy you said has day to day operational control."

"I see no reason why..."

"You're a public organization. His name's no secret."

"Yes. William Packard Blair. Now please, I have a full morning. I'd like to get back..."

"I heard my name," a voice from behind Leslie said. Leslie turned to see a tall, slender man wearing an expensive well-tailored suit, white shirt, broad-striped tie, and recently polished black shoes. Seeing the distress on Nikolson's face he asked, "Is something wrong here?" His mask, like Nikolson's, was hanging loose around his neck.

"No, everything's fine," Nikolson answered, her face remaining tight. "Just answering a few questions."

"Didn't sound so fine from out there?" Blair said, bringing his six foot-three frame further into the office. "I'm Bill Blair."

"I understand from Ms. Nikolson you're the managing director? Mr. William Packard Blair to be exact. I'm Detective Hodges with the Lee County Sheriff's office. Pleased to meet you."

"Sheriff's office? What's that all about?"

"That break-in a few weeks back. Just have a few questions."

"Nothing was taken. Nothing even broken. What is there to investigate?"

"Just routine follow up is all."

"Follow up to what?"

"Routine's all."

Blair started to say something, changed his mind and turned to leave. "Okay. Nice to meet you detective. Have a nice day."

"Now that you're here," Leslie called after Blair, "as I was saying to Ms. Nikolson, I'm here trying to understand what's troubling you about me seeing the surveillance tape the night of the break-in? You complained to the mayor. What has you so agitated?"

"Nothing is missing. What's the purpose? I understand you went and got the video anyway. Satisfied? There was nothing as we said."

"I agree. Saw nothing. But you went to the mayor over it. That's a bit much for something so... so trivial."

Blair's eyes set hard. "I didn't want this in the press. Museum doesn't need bad publicity. COVID's hurt us bad enough. Donors get a whiff of something missing, funds will dry up in an instant."

"How does nothing being stolen equate to bad publicity?"

"Search warrants are never good. You could have asked us."

"I did. I asked for a copy and was told it had been destroyed."

"It had been," Nikolson quickly interjected. "The flash drive was erased. At your..."

"Detective," Blair interrupted, "do what you must and please keep your voice down. Don't want the patrons asking questions. With this virus and all, everyone's jumpy." Blair turned on his heel and left the office, closing the door behind him.

Hodges studied Nikolson a long minute before asking. "What's bothering you? Nothing was stolen. At least not on the video I saw. So, what is it?"

"What do you mean by that?"

"By what?"

"Implying something may have been stolen at another time."

"I didn't imply that at all. But now that you mention it, has there been anything stolen, say in the last month?"

"No."

"In the last year?"

"That's not your business."

"So, there has been something stolen in the last year."

"I didn't say that."

"Well, has there or hasn't there?"

"No."

"Okay. Then you won't mind if I speak to your insurance company. Who do you use?"

"Not on your life!"

"A court allowed us to obtain the surveillance records. A court will allow us to access your insurance records as well. Oh, I forgot, this museum is a charity. I wonder if the state has access to your insurance claims. You want me to make that phone call, or will you…"

"Great Southern. Guy by the name of Jack Silver's CEO."

"So, I ask again. Has anything been stolen in the last year?"

"I've already answered that question."

"What will Silver say when I ask him the same question?"

"I can't control what Silver answers. Now please. I have things to do. A very busy museum to tend to."

"Do me a favor and call off the mayor. Make my job easier."

"And why would I want to make your job easier?"

Leslie took a step closer, her voice low in volume, but menacing in tone. "Because that's the best way to make your life easier."

"Here," Nikolson said, digging in her drawer and shoving a card across the desk. "Don't say I never gave you anything. And this is your lucky day. Silver's plane is set to land in one hour at Page."

Great Southern Insurance Company

Museum Indemnity Specialists

Jack Silver CEO

1800 555-4653

Great Southern is one of those international businesses that are so specialized that almost no one outside the business ever hears its name. Jack Silver, the founder, and his wife Patricia, according to what little Leslie was able to find on them, seem to live on their jet plane. Their specialty is high value artwork and museum-quality antiques, and they travel the world to support their clientele.

Leslie arrived at Page Field ten minutes before the Great Southern jet touched down and was waiting by the terminal door when the stairs were lowered. "Mr. Silver," Hodges said to the masked man when escorted up the steps to the private jet, "nice of you to allow me a few minutes."

"It's not my time," he replied, his voice hinting of South Texas, "it's Jayne's. We have a business lunch scheduled and she is allowing you to encroach. Make it worthwhile." He stepped backward several steps. "Mind if I take off the mask? We'll maintain distance. The air in here in here is highly filtered."

Hodges' quick assessment of Silver was along the lines of: ageless, tall, debonair, well-dressed and accustomed to wealth. "Not a problem," she replied, removing her own mask. "I am investigating a…a break-in at the Edison Museum on the…"

"The early morning hours of the 23rd. I'm familiar with that. Go on."

"Was anything reported missing?"

"Nothing missing."

"In the last year, has anything gone missing?"

Silver sat back, the focus of his eyes leaving Leslie's face for a moment before returning. "That's a difficult question to answer. Nothing has been reported missing. Stolen or otherwise. However,…here's where it gets a bit fuzzy. What we have at the museum are originals. Not all the items, but many. They are appraised when they come in and every now and then are reappraised just to be certain they remain intact."

"Intact? Meaning just what?"

"Originals can be funny. Their value is in their originality. They were first in their class so to speak. It is often tempting to substitute a fake, or a later model for the original. The fake remains on display with the patrons none the wiser while the original fetches a huge price and resides in a private collection hidden from public view."

"Are you telling me the phonograph now in the museum is not the original?"

"Not an easy answer. There were two so-called originals. Edison inscribed them with a '1' and a '2'. The one in the Fort Myers museum has always been the Two. Only a few people know that fact."

"Is the so called Two still there?"

"Yes. For insurance purposes, the Two remains at the museum."

"Please clarify, if you will."

"The phonograph in the museum has a '2' on its bottom. There's speculation it's actually the One, with a bit of forgery to make it appear as the Two. The reason that's important is that the Two also has the original foil recording mechanism inside. There is speculation that within the last year that original recording cylinder has… shall we say, grown legs."

"Speculation? By whom?"

"Let's just say, interested observers. Bystanders if you will?"

"Bystanders and not stakeholders?" Leslie pressed.

"If by stakeholders you mean the museum, then no. No one at the museum believes anything has gone missing.

"Nothing stolen?"

"If anything had been stolen it wasn't by anyone from the outside."

"One of the employees?"

"If, and I emphasize, if, something went missing then it only makes sense that someone from the inside did something to make that happen. We've studied surveillance footage and can't find when it was removed. Our conclusion is nothing's amiss."

"Did the museum file a claim?"

"They did not. In all honesty there's always doubt as to whether a museum wants to know. If they find the original cylinder gone, they are obligated to inform the public. That will decrease the value of the piece dramatically and depress their revenue."

"So, they're opting to keep quiet about the foil recording being missing."

"I didn't suggest anything's missing. I'm told you saw the video of the break-in. What do *you* believe the perp was looking for?"

"The number on the bottom? You said that would be a '2'. Correct?"

"Correct. If the '2' is still there, the Seminal Collectors will leave it be. They want only Firsts. Their desire for the phonograph is directed to Edison One. It's Edison One they covet, along with the recording cylinder belonging to the One."

"Seminal Collector? Who the hell's that?"

"That's a story for another day. Don't have the time to go into that now."

From Silver's suddenly changed manner Leslie knew she was now on borrowed time. "So, do I have this right? The foil medium, cylinder I believe you called it, of the second disk is valuable because it was actually the first sound ever recorded and played back."

"Not as clear cut as that. First ever perfectly played back. No scratches, just Edison's voice. That foil medium, call it Cylinder Two, is perhaps the most valuable artifact in the world, if you go by dollars per ounce."

"Assuming Cylinder Two is missing from the museum, do they have an idea who took it?"

Without hesitation Jack Silver looked deep into Leslie Hodges green eyes and said, "Sarah Scotty McDermitt."

SEVEN

ACCORDING TO THE OFFICIAL FILE, as compiled by Deputy Bobby James, Scotty McDermitt's daughter, Linda Murphy, age 50, unmarried, resides in a gated community called Porto Romano at Miromar Lakes. Leslie had never been in that neighborhood and knew only that it was a few miles south of the airport and not all that far from the junkyard she had recently visited. Using the universal police gate code, Hodges drove through the entrance gate at 2:17 in the afternoon, after leaving Jack Silver at Page Field and first driving a mile north on the Tamiami Trail to treat herself to lunch at the Ginger Bistro. In her mind the Bistro has the best Chinese food anywhere.

Over lunch, she contemplated calling ahead to let Murphy know she was coming, but recalling her experiences as a police officer, first in Gulfport and then in Tampa, telegraphing her visits only served to agitate to the point where they often refused to talk thinking they needed a lawyer.

While waiting for the gate into Porto Romano where Linda McDermitt Murphy lived to swung open, Leslie watched an attractive brunette rein in a small white dog lunging and barking at a golf cart waiting to cross the roadway so the lone golfer could resume her round. On closer inspection, she noticed that the dog owner, presumably because of social distancing, was allowing her dark hair to grow out with a beautiful white filling in behind. Perhaps one of the more positive outcomes of the virus.

"This about my mother?" Murphy inquired the moment Hodges identified herself. "I need to talk to you.

Was meaning to call. Hey, love that aqua blouse. Goes well with your eyes."

"Thanks. May I come in, please? It's hot out here." Indeed, the temperature was in the low 90s and the humidity wasn't far behind.

"Oh, certainly. Give me a moment to find my mask." The door closed, then reopened with Murphy's lower face now covered with a white cloth mask. "Please don't mind the mess, I'm getting ready to move. Dog's been getting into everything. Put her in a kennel for a few days."

"Where to?"

"Don't know. Now that mother's gone, no need to stay here. Plan to do some traveling before I settle."

"Lucky you. I'm saving my money. Maybe someday." Leslie thought about all the times she and Junior had walked the beaches at Clearwater, holding hands and dreaming, promising each other someday they'd have a place on the water, watching sunsets together. Unfulfilled dreams.

"So why are you here?" Murphy's voice brought Hodges back to the present.

"Maybe we should begin with why you wanted to call us?"

"Believe it or not, I don't have a key to Mom's place. I know I could get a locksmith but…but frankly I've not been in a hurry to go through her things."

Hodges knew all too well how painful it had been — and still was, even more than a year later. "How can the Sheriff's Department help?"

"Her car keys have the front door key with them. I was waiting for the coroner to release her belongings. For some reason they're holding everything, but I'm told there were no keys. I was hoping the deputy who found her, I think his name is James, has them."

"I'm sorry to tell you," Leslie said as gently as she could, "he doesn't have the keys. They seem to have gone missing."

"Then what do you suggest?"

"Have you tried getting in?"

"All locked up tighter than a drum. I have the alarm code, but not the key. She always sets the alarm when she leaves."

"How about I call for a locksmith and I'll go with you?"

"I'd like that. It seems so…so creepy going in alone."

Hodges called the office clerk who gave her several numbers. A few minutes later she told Murphy, "Best I could do is an hour and a half. In the meantime, how about telling me about your mother?" In fact, the locksmith could have met them in fifteen minutes, but Hodges preferred to gather as much information as she could while Linda still wanted something from her. Who knew what they'd find at the house to interrupt their conversation? And who knew when the inevitable lawyer talk would begin?

Hodges, as a result of her conversation with Linda, was able to enter the following information into Sarah "Scotty" McDermitt's file. Two children, Linda Murphy in Florida and Roland McDermitt II, 53, in Pittsburgh; one granddaughter, Cathy 23 in Pittsburgh. McDermitt held a PhD in Applied Mathematics from Princeton and was a tenured professor at Rutgers until retirement in 1998. Docent at Edison Museum beginning 2001.

"I assume her file should read Dr. McDermitt," Hodges said when they pulled up in front of Scotty's house an hour and twenty minutes later. "After all, she held a doctorate." The mother's house was very similar to the daughter's, only it was in a different section of Miromar Lakes, across from a magnificent lake complete with a sandy beach, hammocks and sail boats.

"Scotty only ever wanted to be called Scotty. Doctor wasn't her thing. Even in class, she insisted her students call her Scotty."

"She was a docent at the museum. What's that about?"

"I don't exactly know. It happened shortly after her mother passed on. That's when she got the phonograph. She said it had been passed down from her great-grandmother Sarah Davis Johnson. That's all she would say about it, other than she did say it would be mine when she passed. She was sad I had no daughter — or son for that matter — to inherit it."

Leslie was about to follow up when the locksmith pulled his truck to a stop directly behind her car. "Shouldn't take but a minute or two, have you inside. Mind showing me your ID?"

"Mind wearing a mask?" Hodges said, flashing her shield.

"Oh, sorry 'bout that. Have one in here somewhere." The guy poked around his front seat apparently unable to locate what he was looking for.

Hodges popped open her trunk, extracted a box of masks and gave him one, saying, "Here. Courtesy of Lee County Sheriff's Office."

"Thank you," the locksmith said, pulling the mask on and proceeding to the front door. He made a big production of opening his tool bag, taking out a couple of picks, and swiftly opening the door in less than thirty seconds.

Linda, expecting the alarm to be chirping on its countdown, quickly went to put in the code. Except there was no chirp. "Someone's been in here," she announced. Scotty never went anywhere without setting it."

"First things first," Leslie replied, turning to the locksmith. "Any evidence of someone picking the lock before you?"

"Nothing I noticed, sorry. But it could have been."

"Okay. Please put a new lock on it and give the keys to Linda here. Don't leave until you see me first. And please don't touch anything in the house other than the door." Addressing Linda, she said, "Let's take a tour of the house, touch nothing. I want you to identify anything that is either missing or out of place. First, we'll do what's visible, then we'll tackle the drawers." She produced two pairs of vinyl gloves and two pairs of paper booties. "Put these on, please."

Hodges turned her cell phone to video recording, and they began methodically examining each room. The only thing Linda identified as missing was the phonograph bequeathed to Scotty by her mother. "So, what do you know about that phonograph?" Hodges asked, not understanding why, of all things, a mother wanted her daughter to have a phonograph.

"Not much, really. There's been a family story about my great-grandmother. She was born Sarah Davis; I think around 1852. Married a guy named Herbert Johnson. Sarah was a mathematician. I think that's where my mother got it from. Family history says she worked for Thomas Edison in Rahway, New Jersey. My mother said something about her calculating the circumference and needle sizes for recording and playback. The missing phonograph was given to my great grandmother, or so the family folklore has it, by Edison himself. She showed me a '1' scratched into the base."

"And you believe the phonograph your mother received from her mother is the original from Edison?"

"I have no reason to doubt her. Scotty was a lot of things. Not truthful was not one of them. That being said, there were several generations before her."

"Did she ever have the phonograph authenticated?"

"If she did, I don't know."

"Insured?"

"Don't know. One more thing. Another old family legend. When Edison gave my great-grandmother the phonograph, he made a recording on a foil disk acknowledging her work."

"Where is that disk?"

"In the Menlo Park museum, far as I know."

Hodges phone sounded with her boss's unique ringtone.

"Gotta go," she said to Linda, "duty calls. Be sure you get the new key before you leave and change the alarm code. Don't touch anything and I'll text you when it's okay to come back in here and then I'd like an inventory of everything left behind by your mother. If you wish to file a claim for the phonograph I have it noted as missing when we entered."

"My brother Roland's in charge of her estate. I'll pass your contact info to him. I'll leave all that to Rol."

"I do need to speak with him. Thanks for your time, Linda. And again, I'm sorry for your loss."

EIGHT

THE SILVERADO CASE WAS WHAT Hodges had begun to call the heisting of generators, air compressors and other large industrial equipment from construction sites. Silverado in honor of the blue truck seen at the site of the thefts. This had been her case since her first day as a detective. While the heists continued, she was no closer to finding the perps now than she had been then.

The MO was the same in each heist. The Silverado drove away from the theft site loaded with stolen property. Even when police gave chase within minutes, the truck, pilfered property and all, would disappear as if by magic.

Leslie had spent considerable time thinking about construction site thefts. The ones during the night seemed to have a different MO, so she concentrated on the daytime robberies. The troubling question was why they were unable to track the truck even using air surveillance coupled with intersection traffic cameras.

The message from Sgt. Oakmore was that a blue Silverado with two 10,000 KWH generators in the bed was going west on Corkscrew Road. Leslie was on Ben Hill Griffin Parkway less than a mile north of Corkscrew, her car's blue lights flashing and siren blaring, closing in fast. A few minutes later her screen tracker showed the Chevy truck turning onto Tamiami Trail heading north in the direction of Fort Myers. She was minutes behind, but when she approached the intersection and swung north the tracker suddenly went blank.

Leslie had developed a theory and now was the time to put that theory to the test.

She slowed, silenced her siren, flipped the lights off and proceeded north on the Tamiami Trail at normal speed, searching for storage units where vehicles could be stored. Spotting one, she drove in, parked her car, and flashed her badge at a woman sitting staring into a computer screen. "Did a blue Silverado just drive in?"

"You have a search warrant?" came the automatic reply.

"I'm not searching anything. I'm not even going to ask you which unit it went to. All I want to know is did you see a blue Silverado. Yes or no? It's that easy and I'm out of your hair."

"No."

"Okay. If you do, call me." Leslie dropped a card in front of the computer screen and left.

She repeated this same maneuver at the next two storage facilities with the same result. Nothing!

On her fourth try, at a place quaintly called The Storage Company, a man looking to be in his late sixties, replied "What if I did. What of it?"

"How long ago?"

"Didn't say I did."

"If you had, how long ago would it have been?"

"'Bout ten, maybe fifteen minutes."

"Did it leave?"

"I ain't sayin'"

"Thanks." And she was gone.

Once back on the road, she continued north, found a small strip-shopping mall and pulled in. Holding her cell close to her face she waited for Prosecutor Allen Smith to answer. When he came on the line, she said, "Your lucky day, Mr. Prosecutor. This is Leslie Hodges. Your new favorite detective. You up for another warrant? This one's easy."

After being briefed, Smith replied, "Not as easy as you might think. Here's the thing. It's after hours for the judges. I'll have to round up the night duty judge, might take a while. But I'm game if you are. How fast?"

"ASAP."

"Dictate the facts and I'll file the papers. Keep in mind, the only thing I can ask for is the blue truck. You find it, you can seize it. This warrant will not allow you to seize random stuff. Got that? Just the truck."

"I understand. My theory is they park the truck in a rented storage unit for a night or two and then move the stuff out. I'm thinking they prearrange the storage places before the robberies. An accomplice opens the pre-rented door before they arrive, so the truck just drives in and disappears. That would explain why we can't track them."

"Sold me. Now we'll have to sell the judge."

Leslie hung up and arranged for two deputies to meet her at the storage facility in an hour. She then drove back to the facility, parking across the street.

"You live a charmed life," Smith said fifteen minutes later. Judge had no problem. Truck only and anything in it. It's in your file. If there's anything else in the unit, leave it and call for a new warrant."

"Just how green you think I am? Hey, on second thought, don't answer that."

"Just playing lawyer. How else can I impress you?"

"I'm duly impressed Mr. Prosecutor."

"And how's your murder case coming? Getting anywhere with the museum?"

She told him about her conversation with the museum CEO and what Jack Silver had said about people collecting Firsts.

"It's funny you talking about Firsts. I was thinking of running on up to the Ringling Museum in Sarasota. Care to join me? Bet they have a few Firsts up there."

"I'd love to," she heard herself answer even though her mind pronounced this a bad idea.

"Saturday work for you? Labor Day weekend. Neither of us works weekends. I even have Monday off."

"Speak for yourself, Mr. Lawyer. Mine's a 24/7 job."

"I checked your work schedule and you have the weekend off."

"That's been changed. Crime never stops. Rookie draws the short straw. I'm on-call for Saturday and Sunday."

"That still leaves Monday."

"Up and back same day. You got that? No overnight."

"Wouldn't consider anything else. What time you want to leave?"

"Does ten work?"

"It does."

"Meet you where?"

"In front of your house."

"I suppose you looked that up as well."

"As a matter of fact, I did."

———◆———

The rest of Friday, all of Saturday and a good portion of Sunday passed on surveillance duty at the storage unit. Leslie used the time to review the museum surveillance video several more times, annotate her interview with Scotty's daughter, and make a list of next steps, one of which was interviewing the witnesses to Scotty running off the highway.

Hodges struck pay dirt at 2:53 p.m. Sunday afternoon when a silver Ford pulled into the lot, dropped a man off, and sped away. The man glanced around several times, satisfied himself that he was alone, and proceeded to the unit under surveillance. Leslie notified her backup, saying into her mic, "Let's wait until he drives the truck out of the shed."

The arrest was made without incident, but it took another five hours to clear the scene, photograph and catalogue everything found in the vehicle, and load the Silverado on a flatbed for delivery to the county garage.

NINE

ALLEN SMITH WAS PARKED IN front of Leslie Hodges' small house on Alabama Road at 9:43 a.m. If asked why he was early he would be unable to answer precisely. "Just because," was as close as he could get to the real reason. He liked the skinny lady with the magnificent green eyes and the air of friendliness about her. She acted as though she was your best friend but there was a red line; cross it at your own peril.

"Nice ride." she said opening the passenger door to the low-slung blue Ford Mustang convertible. "I suppose with the top open this way we can dispense with the masks."

"Hadn't thought of that. Bought myself a law school graduation present. Only I had to wait seven months to save up for the down payment."

"University of Florida-Levin," Leslie said. "Valedictorian. Impressive."

"Now, who's into the files?" Allen teased.

"Public record, actually."

"Need breakfast? Coffee? Anything before we hit the road?"

"I'm good to go."

Twelve minutes later he turned north onto Interstate 75 and Leslie said, "Just please obey the speed limits. Wouldn't help my career to be arrested."

"Wouldn't dream of anything else," Allen said, allowing the car to settle back to seventy-five. "We've plenty of time. I scored a couple of tickets for the one p.m. house visit and the three p.m. museum tour. Thought we'd get some lunch."

"Seems you have this well in hand."

"I try. Hey, tell me about what happened with the blue truck. Catch the bad guys?"

"Sure as hell did! Went off like clockwork. Thanks to one of the deputies who had the idea to park our vehicles in a couple of the empty units and wait. Search warrants sure change the landscape. Those employees fell all over themselves to help. Storage guy got on the company computer, ran the plate number through their system and found six other company locations registered to the same vehicle. We sat on it for twenty-four hours. Boss authorized two teams. Around 9 a.m. on Thursday two men showed up and began unloading the truck. They're both now in county jail. Monday, you can go back to the judge and get warrants for the other units. Where those two are going they won't be needing any of that equipment they stole."

"You really love what you do. I can see it in your eyes."

"Beats driving up and down the highway chasing speeders. Or standing in the rain in front of a church directing traffic."

"Yeah, that's why I went to law school. Got tired of busting drunk drivers. Thought it'd be more fun actually putting them away."

"Didn't know you were a cop."

"There's lots about me you don't know."

"You like being a lawyer?"

"Don't really know yet, to be honest. Cutting my teeth filing motions, small stuff. But I'll get there. Lot to learn."

"How long were you a cop?"

"Eight long years. Over in Orlando."

"Florida native?"

"Born in Winter Park. Hey, isn't this when you're supposed to ask if I've ever been married? Any children kind of thing."

"Not my business. You need to tell me, then tell me. You don't, you don't."

"I know you were a cop in Tampa. Before that?"

"Born and raised in Gulfport, Mississippi. On the force there four years before moving to Tampa. Six years in Tampa."

Sensing a red line, Allen changed the subject. "I've been meaning to ask, what ever happened with the surveillance tapes? I suppose I'd know if you got an image of the killer."

"Nothing so dramatic. Nothing's missing from the museum, but we do know the guy who broke in is tall and stocky."

"Surely, you have more than that. What was he looking for? I assume it was a man. How did he get there? How did he leave?"

"You know, truth is, I think I know what he was looking for, but even that's fuzzy. The rest of it I've not had time. Was going to do it yesterday but Silverado's been eating my lunch."

"What's your thought on why the perp was in the museum in the middle of the night?"

"Looking for a First. The first phonograph to be exact."

"That's a good place to look," Allen smiled broadly. "I'll hand him that much. Go where the money is."

"You quoting Willie Sutton?"

"He never said that. Sutton robbed banks because he got a kick out of it. The money, he said, was the measuring chips."

"You're full of useful information. Here's something to ponder. The phonograph in the museum is marked with a '2'. I believe Scotty has a phonograph marked with a '1'. I'm thinking they may have been switched." Leslie held back telling Allen that Scotty's phonograph went missing. "Oh, shit!" she exclaimed. Thinking of the stolen artifact triggered the fact that she should have had the alarm panel in Scotty's house dusted for prints before allowing Linda to change the code.

"Oh, shit! That's never good to hear. What?"

"Oh, nothing. Just something I forgot to do. Sorry about that. Now, where were we?"

"You were telling me about the perp looking for a first something."

"Oh, yes. Guy by the name of Jack Silver, CEO of the insurance company which insures the museum, told me about First Offers. People who want to own the first of anything. First telescope, first telegraph, first phonograph. I suppose the first coffee cup, if there is such a thing. Apparently, if you're a collector of such things sky's the limit for what you'll pay for a First. Ever hear of someone called a seminal collector?"

"Can't say as I have. Seminal? As in original, ground-breaking, first? That type of seminal?"

"That's the way I understand it. I think they collect Firsts, but don't know anything further."

"Must be nice to have such money," Allen mused.

"If it's so great, why then do so many rich folks get themselves in so much trouble? I'm not certain money buys you what you think it does."

"Never thought of it that way, Leslie. But if you need a guinea pig to try out your theory, I'm your man. Here's our exit. Time flies when you're having fun. We've plenty of time. Let's go down to the water, maybe walk the sand for a few minutes, pick up some lunch. You up for it?"

Leslie hadn't walked on sand since Junior's passing and wasn't excited about doing it now. Not wanting to spoil her host's day, she agreed, flashing what for her passed as a smile. There had to be a first time, and this was as good as any.

At one o'clock they along with four other masked couples were standing on round pavers spaced six-feet apart in a semi-circle in front of Ca' d'Zan, the House of John, waiting for their tour guide. The brochure Leslie held stated clearly that the mansion was of Venetian Gothic design, but she had the distinct impression of being somewhere south. Mexico maybe. Or closer to home, Cuba.

The group went up the massive staircase with Leslie and Allen bringing up the rear. Allen's eyes were focused on the magnificent woodwork framing the stairs. "I've never seen wood this rich-looking,"he exclaimed to no one in particular. "And look at that pool table! And the room it's in. Now I know what you mean about rich people. They just live differently than the rest of us. And to think this was all built on the backs of clowns, midgets and bearded women."

"Don't forget the lions and elephants," Leslie added. "And tightrope walkers. Ever go to a circus?"

"Just the ones came around once a year and set up on a vacant lot. Mostly Ferris wheels and a few rides. Throw a basketball through a narrow hoop and win some stuffed animal. Hardly a circus."

"In Gulfport, the Ringling Circus came to town and it was all so...so exciting. Loved the clown car where a zillion clowns fell out."

"What was your favorite act? The elephants or what?"

Leslie answered without thinking, "The high-wire guy with the long pole. Always looked as though he was about to fall and kill himself. Held my breath."

"Wish I could have seen it. Sounds dangerous."

"It was. And the horses. The white horses looked so proud. As a little girl I wanted a white horse so much."

"Did you ever get your horse?"

"We had horses. Two when I was very young. Came from my grandfather. He delivered milk and the horses were gray and pulled the cart. My father took over his route when his father died. Got himself a truck when I was eight or so. When I asked about a white horse my father said horses were for working, not playing. He said he never wanted to own a horse again as long as he lived."

To view the actual circus museum, they drove across town and spent the next three hours totally immersed in Tibbals' recreated miniature circus, hand-crafted from thousands of pictures, playbills and waybills. Complete with train cars, over nine hundred miniature animals and birds, cooking and eating utensils, and mess halls.

"Fascinating," Allen exclaimed on the way out. "Speaking of Firsts, we saw a lot of Firsts. That cannon where a man was shot across the tent was a First."

"So were many of the train cars, as well as some of the equipment used by the clowns."

Smith was puzzled as to what Firsts were associated with clowns. "You thinking about paint? What?"

"I'm thinking the car itself. And stilts, stuff like that.'

"I didn't think of that. Perhaps. How about dinner? You hungry?"

"I will be by the time we get back home. Let's drive first, eat later."

TEN

DINNER WITH ALLEN WAS AN enjoyable ending to a pleasant and entertaining day. It also was the first time since the death of her husband that several hours had passed without Leslie thinking about him. When she woke Tuesday morning guilt feelings surfaced with a vengeance and she did what she always did when that happened. Emersed herself in the details. This time by opening the McDermitt file and burying herself in work.

Starting at the beginning with Deputy James' accident report, she noted every fact she could glean. Three witnesses, in two cars, had seen the Mazda go off the side of the highway. Both cars stopped to lend a hand. First car, single male, Chris Wang, 47, Naples, FL. Second car, husband/wife, Samuel and Dorothy Feinman, 73/68, Estero, FL.

All three witnesses saw another car parked on the berm. Wang said the parked car was a green Audi; both Feinmans said it was a gray Lexus. Dorothy Feinman never left her vehicle, but both Chris and Samuel did. Both men observed two people climbing up the berm from the wrecked car, one of them carried a canvas bag. Samuel reported one of the men instructing him to call 9-1-1 but to tell them not to hurry, the driver was dead.

Before leaving for her office, Leslie texted museum CEO Nikolson requesting permission to contact Able Security for surveillance footage of the parking and street areas from 7 p.m. to 6 a.m. for August 22nd and 23rd. Leslie wasn't certain what time Nikolson arrived in the morning. Surprisingly, the CEO replied within the hour saying she would have Able Security arrange electronic delivery. Leslie attributed Nickolson's cooperation to Jack Silver from Great Southern having spoken to her on Leslie's behalf

She watched the original break-in video several more times. At one point stopping the video to take a screen shot of the image of the perp. She then cropped out everything that could reveal the location of the picture. She repeated the process with two other images.

At 1:10 an encrypted email arrived from Able Security instructing Leslie how to decrypt the files she had requested. By 3:30 she had tediously reviewed the images and hadn't seen either a green Audi or a gray Lexus. She did note what appeared to be a gray Audi, but it was at the far limit of the surveillance camera and only a tiny section of trunk was captured.

"Hello, Mrs. Feinman? Dorothy Feinman?" Leslie said into her cell at 3:40.

"Yes. This she. Who is this?"

"My name's Deputy Leslie Hodges. I'm with the Lee County Sheriff's office. You witnessed an accident two weeks ago on I-75. I hate to bother you, but I do have a few questions."

"Hold, please." In the background Leslie heard Dorothy call out, "Honey. Some woman deputy from the sheriff's office wants to talk about the accident we saw. You know the one where that poor lady was killed."

"I told the Sheriff everything I saw. What more do they want?"

"I don't know. Why don't you come over here and talk to her? I didn't see anything. You did."

A moment later. "Hello. I'm Sam Feinman. Dotty said you're the Sheriff."

"Sheriff's Deputy. My name's Leslie Hodges. I have a couple of questions. I know I'm interrupting your afternoon, but can you give me a few minutes?"

"I answered all the officer's questions that night. It was awful. Just awful. I'm still having bad dreams. Is this necessary?"

"I'm afraid so. How about if I come over to your house? I see you're in Estero. Let's see, it's 3:45 now. How about, say in an hour?"

"I have nothing more to tell you."

"I have a picture I want to show you. Shouldn't take but a few minutes."

"Long as you're gone by five," came the reluctant reply. "Happy hour. Neighbors coming over for hamburgers."

"Promise. See you soon."

The Feinman residence was another gated community, this one just east of the Tamiami Trail and was designed for folks over fifty-five. Winding lanes wrapped around several lakes with a golf course woven among it all. Royal palms led the way in, each lawn perfectly manicured. Not a bad place to spend retirement years.

After telling Leslie to please wear her mask and call her Dotty, Dorothy exclaimed, "You're so young. A baby. My, I have grandkids older than you. And you're so skinny! My gracious, I'll go fix you a hamburger. Take just a minute."

"Please don't Mrs....Dotty...I'm really not hungry. And I promised your husband I'll be gone by five."

"Let her be, Dotty," Sam interjected. "She can take care of herself. She can't eat with that mask on anyway. Now what was that you wanted to show me?"

"First, please review this report carefully. If you now remember anything you didn't tell the deputy that night, I'd like to hear it." Leslie handed Sam several sheets of paper, assuming he was more comfortable with paper than using a computer screen.

Holding the paper close to his face, Sam took a moment before saying, "That's about all there is. No. Actually not. Here it says one man was carrying a canvas bag."

"That's right isn't it?"

"As far as it goes. Yes. But in one of my dreams I saw what was in the bag. Then I remembered why I knew. I saw what he did."

"And what was that?"

"When I first got out of my car — you have to remember I was backing up on the side of the highway and watching to be sure no car swerved over — there were not many cars on the road that night, so we were lucky. Anyway, I finally got back to where she had gone off the road and I had to wait for a few cars to pass before I got out. Dot stayed in the car. She has weak ankles and was afraid of the stones and stuff. I started down the slope and saw two men. One was at the driver window and the other, the one with the bag, was back by the trunk. I made my way down the hill toward the front thinking I'd help get the driver out. But I stumbled and caught myself from falling. That's when I noticed the guy with the bag, he had gloves on, reached under the car and pulled up a long hose. Plastic-looking hose like a lawn hose. He shoved it in the bag. In my dream it was a snake I saw."

"What color was the hose? Black. Clear? What?"

"It was dark so I couldn't see that well. I know it coiled."

"Try to visualize it?"

"I've tried many times. Maybe clear and dirty. Maybe gray. I can't be sure."

"Okay. The other guy. The one who went to help the driver. What more can you tell me about him?"

"I guess, nothing more. He reached way inside and I had the impression he was turning the engine off so it wouldn't explode. But I don't know. He came up the hill a bit wobbly and walked right past me yelling for me to call 9-1-1. "They needn't hurry," he said. "She's gone." I still get shivers. It sounded so...so callous."

Leslie showed Sam the three images of the perp from the museum. He studied them a while before saying, "I'm sorry. At first, I was ready to say, yes, that's him but I don't think so."

"Why don't you think so?"

"Guy coming up the hill was skinny. Like you. Tall, like the man in the picture, but much thinner."

"How tall do you estimate?"

"I'd say at least six-six. Maybe six-seven."

Dot interrupted. "Are you sure I can't get you something to eat, my dear? I have nice cookies."

Leslie stood. "One last question. The car he — they — were in, the one you parked in front of, you both said it was a gray Lexus. In hindsight, as you think about it, is that still what you believe?"

Dotty glanced at her husband but said nothing.

Sam said, "Gray Lexus."

"And Dotty is that your statement as well?"

Again, she glanced at her husband, who said, "Listen, Dot isn't the best with cars. She thinks it was an Audi. Every time we pass an Audi in the supermarket parking lot, she points to it and says that's what the car looked like."

"Here," Leslie said, thrusting a partial image of the back of a car across to the Feinmans, "I know this is sketchy, but could this be the car?"

"Yes, I think it is," Dotty acknowledged.

"And you, Sam?"

"Could be. But this is not a Lexus."

"No. It appears to be a gray Audi," Leslie responded, pleased that one of the two puzzle pieces she had was now more or less confirmed. A small piece to be sure, but a piece, nonetheless. Enough small pieces and a picture just might appear.

At least that's what she told herself as she fell into bed later that night, but not before glancing over to what would have been Junior's side of the bed and throwing him a mental kiss.

ELEVEN

LESLIE'S WINDSHIELD WIPERS COULDN'T KEEP up with the sheets of rain pouring down over her car as she slowly made her way to the office on Wednesday morning. The outer bands of a tropical depression was what the TV weather lady had called the forecast for the next few days. From past experience, that meant more traffic crashes. More crashes meant more deputies required on the streets. That translated to the likelihood she'd spend some or all of her day in a rain-drenched slicker investigating lifeless bodies found in bad places.

Her cell phone rang. She ignored it, preferring to keep her eyes on a barely visible road requiring all of her concentration. A moment later the text message alert sounded. Stopped at a traffic light, she saw the text was from Jack Silver. "Call when you can," the message read. She pulled into a shopping plaza and parked across from a mostly empty hair salon.

Silver answered on the first ring. "Glad you called back. There's a break in the weather for about an hour and a half. After that, it's closing fast."

"Hold it. What're you saying?"

"I have someone for you to talk with pertaining to your museum investigation."

"Give me his name. I'll call him."

"Doesn't work that way with him, I'm afraid. He's agreed to meet with you on condition it's a hundred percent off the record. No notes, no recordings, no arrest, just listen."

"I need permission to do that."

"Get whatever you need."

"Where do I meet with this guy?"

"Pittsburgh."

"Pittsburgh?"

"Be at Page Field within the hour. Airport's closing at ten. Need wheels up by then. Be here or not. Your choice."

"But…"

The line was dead. There wasn't time to plead her case in person, so she called her boss, Sergeant Oakmore. "Nice piece of work," he said coming on the line. Thought we'd never catch those generator thieves. You know, I think we've now retrieved every last stolen item. Locating that Silverado did it."

"That's not why I called. It's about the McDermitt homicide. Got a potential lead."

"It's not in your notes."

"Just came in," she responded, surprised Oakmore was keeping such close tabs on her. "Time sensitive."

"Go for it."

"Involves travel."

"So?"

"Pittsburgh."

"Pittsburgh? Go ahead, I'm listening."

Leslie then briefly told him about Silver and who he was, all the while watching the dashboard clock tick off the minutes. By her calculation, and even using her lights and siren, she'd barely make the ten o'clock deadline. "Look, Sarge, the ride up there is free. I may have to stay over a night or two until the weather clears. But if I'm not at Page in twenty minutes it's too late."

"The book on Silver puts him as the go-to man for upscale artwork insurance. No history of him working with authorities, so why now?"

"My guess is he's protecting an investment. Probably doesn't want to pay off on an Edison claim."

"You said they haven't filed a claim."

"Edison hasn't filed a theft report. Don't know about insurance claims."

"Let me cut this short, Hodges. Here's the thing about Silver. He's connected to all the major art dealers in the world. If you cultivate a relationship with him that'll work for you — and us — going forward. It's worth the time and expense. Just remember, you have no authority outside Florida."

"Can I carry?"

"I'll check. If you can't I'll text. Take your piece with you. Unload it before getting on the plane. And, be careful. From my experience with upscale art, you're playing in the big leagues. They dress up all fancy, but don't let that fool you. They're ruthless and play for keeps."

As Silver predicted, the rain was easing, and the sky was blue-streaked. Clearly this was temporary, the so-called lull before the storm. Leslie pulled into the parking lot with only a few minutes to spare. On the other side of the fence a plane stood in isolation, the door closed.

A masked TSA agent met her at the terminal door, checked her temperature and then her credentials, inspected her weapon and finally satisfied, escorted her onto the tarmac. The plane's door opened and a staircase lowered.

Oakmore's words of warning rang in her ears as she took the steps two at a time up to Silver's jet. She noted the Bombardier Global 6000 plaque as she stepped into the plush interior and was greeted by a stunning woman who appeared to be in her early fifties wearing a blue mask with a stylized GSI embroidered in gold on the right side.

"Welcome aboard, Detective Hodges," the woman said, "I'm Priscilla Silver. Friends call me Precious. I understand you'll be traveling up to Pittsburgh with us today. Please make yourself at home. There's a nice library in the hallway over there, and anything you want to eat just ask Pam. Jack's on a conference call and will be tied up for an hour or so. A little problem in Ankara. Something seems to have gone missing. I have paperwork to catch up on, so you'll have the front cabin all to yourself for a while. Buckle up, weather window's closing fast."

Revised age; late sixties. Still gorgeous, with a stunning figure to match.

A moment later a slender woman wearing a custom-tailored uniform came by to check her seat belt. "I'm Pam. I'll be assisting you today. If there's something you need quickly, I can get it now. Otherwise, you'll have to wait until we're in the air. It's going to be a bit bumpy for a while, so settle back."

"I'm okay. Weather seems to be clearing."

"Only temporary. We just managed to get in an hour ago between rain bands. This will close down right behind us."

Leslie wasn't aware, but the jet was already slowly moving, working its way to the main east/west runway of the tiny airfield. Pam sat across the aisle from her as the plane gathered speed. Within minutes they were off the ground, the jet quickly banking to the north. Outside, ugly, dark storm clouds gathered. Below, the Gulf of Mexico churned itself into a frenzy.

Pam called to her, "Just so you know, your seat folds back into a bed anytime you wish to take a nap."

"Hope our trip's not that long," Leslie quipped.

"Some people prefer to lie back in turbulent weather. Just giving you that option. Pilot has requested we remain seated for the next hour. So, unless it's critical, I won't be serving you."

"That's okay. I don't need anything. Thanks."

"Normally, our flight time to Pittsburgh is right around two and a half hours. My guess, today we'll be climbing higher, so it might be closer to three."

"Do you work full time for Silver?"

"For Great Southern Insurance, actually. Yes, we do."

"We?"

"My husband and I. Today's he's the captain and I'm supporting the cabin."

"The way you said that I assume he's not always the captain. Who relieves him?"

"I do. We're a team. Live aboard. We have a small cabin in the rear. Travel the world with the Silvers. We always have a co-pilot upfront with us, as well."

"How long you been with the company?"

"Three years next week. Get to meet some great people. And some who...never mind."

"Some not so nice." Leslie knew all too well about rich folks who just couldn't get enough. Great Southern Insurance, being one of the world's most sought-after companies for high-end artwork coverage, must deal with a good percentage of sleazy characters. That could explain why Silver befriended her. Give to get. When he needed a name run through a database, or when an art deal goes bad, she was certain her phone would ring. "I can always say no," she promised herself, resolving to never forget that vow.

The pilot, Pam's husband, announced their descent into Pittsburgh. ETA almost exactly three hours after takeoff. Except for the first forty minutes, the flight had been smooth. Pam had offered, and Leslie had accepted, a small Greek salad with the best feta cheese she had ever tasted. A marvelous dinner roll, which appeared to be freshly baked, highlighted the meal.

"Mind if I join you?" Silver asked as she finished her coffee. "We won't be on the ground for another twenty minutes. I see you had one of Pam's famous salads. I don't know what we'd do without those two. Pam and her husband are the best we've ever had."

"Please," Leslie responded. "I was hoping you'd brief me on what this is about?"

Silver sat across the aisle and swiveled his seat to face her, motioning Leslie to do the same. When they were face to face, Silver asked, "Does the name Morris Dexter Stratis mean anything to you?"

Leslie instantly searched her memory and responded, "Can't say as it does?"

"Not surprised. Family fortune in windows for high-rise buildings. One of the wealthiest people in the world. Into art. Supports many galleries and museums around the world. Short version, he also maintains several private collections, some of which are open to invited friends. Some are for his eyes only."

"All originals?" Leslie asked, not knowing where to begin.

"With Stratis, nothing is straight forward. He has more than his share of originals. Along with it he collects copies, albeit perfect copies, of masters."

"Why would he invest in forgeries?"

"That's a discussion for another day. In June every year, in conjunction with the Three Rivers Arts Festival held in downtown Pittsburgh, he has an invitation-only viewing of his most recent acquisitions. This year, of course, the arts festival was canceled because of the virus and is being held on-line. Stratis, good-citizen that he is, canceled his private showing."

Leslie was confused as to where this was all leading. "What's all this talk about originals and forgeries have to do with the phonograph? I'm not following."

"The reason we were in Fort Myers last week is because of the break-in at the museum. The reason I stopped to get you is that Stratis has been in a bidding war with a woman named Riya Kumar who, with her husband, also collects Firsts. They were bidding on a phonograph. The bidding has ended, and I am led to believe Stratis was the winner. Great Southern is being asked to quote insurance for something called the Edison One. As I've told you, we already insure the Edison Two, which I am assured remains locked in a case at the Edison Museum so we are the natural company to insure the One."

"So, where did..."

"The phonograph in question, I believe was last in the possession of Docent Sarah McDermitt."

"Are you suggesting the phonograph this guy Stratis has was stolen from McDermitt's home?"

"First of all, I am not saying Stratis has anything. However, if he now has the original Edison One phonograph it most likely came from her home, yes. In my business I have found things are not always what they seem to be."

"What's the phonograph worth?"

"What it's worth and what it's selling price are two different questions. Let us assume for a moment they are the same. I believe Stratis will ask fifty million in coverage. The bidding was in the neighborhood of eighteen million."

"What makes it worth that much?"

"The simple answer. Rich folks want it and to them money is not the issue."

"What's the full answer?"

"I'm sorry we don't really have the time now. I'll say this though. There's a group of billionaires who are hell bent to own Firsts from what they call the Seminal Society."

"Is that who you meant the other day when you referred to seminal collectors? I looked it up and found nothing."

"Billionaires hide their tracks. Every day they scrub the Internet of anything they don't want out there. The Collectors, as they call themselves, believe two things. First, that beginning in 1376 with a guy by the name of Oswald Von Wolkenstein, and including Leonardo da Vinci, Galileo Galilei, Isaac Newton, Ernst Chladni, and Thomas Edison, all shared the same spirit. When one physical body dies the spirit would, perhaps after resting a while, come back to inhabit the next body. They believe the spirit that made Thomas Edison the genius that he was is the same spirit that made Chladni, Newton, Galileo, da Vinci, and Wolkenstein the geniuses they were. The Seminal Society is how they refer to the deceased principals."

"That's...that's preposterous!"

"Think what you might. To them, and frankly to many before them, this is their belief. To own a First from any one of the Seminal Society is of paramount importance in their life. As I said, we don't have time now, but look up what kind of Firsts we are talking about. Here, I'll write out that list for you."

"Just say it again and I'll record it."

Silver waited for Leslie to turn on her phone, then repeated the names. He then added, "Don't misunderstand me. There are any number of very valuable Firsts. Such as the first clock, the first battery, the first gun, the first steam engine, the Wright brother's airplane, Magna Carta. The list is endless, so long as it is the very first of something."

"So, where do inventions, Firsts, from the Seminal Society fit in?"

"They are valued far above other Firsts. That's why the Edison phonograph brings such a high amount."

"And what is the second belief I think you called it of the Society?"

"He who dies with the most Seminal Society Firsts in his collection wins."

"Wins what?"

"Dies happy, I suppose. Maybe it helps..." Before Silver could finish his sentence, Pam appeared in the cabin. "Five minutes to touch down." She then walked to the back and disappeared.

"I again caution you, the numbers I gave you are all confidential, so please don't repeat them. And remember our deal, nothing you learn on this trip goes into official — or unofficial — notes. It is for your personal use only."

"Why am I here if I can't do anything about what I find?"

"Stratis may be a lot of things, but he has always refused to buy artwork — or in this case, a First — if life was lost in obtaining the piece."

Hodges thought about that a while and then realized no one outside of law enforcement knows of the homicide investigation. "Why would this Stratis character even think McDermitt had been killed?"

"You obtained a search warrant. Edison's lawyers have seen the autopsy report. High CO levels suggest carbon monoxide poisoning. Asphyxiation may not be the official cause, but it's a good take away. Why else would a warrant be granted without requiring the museum be noticed and heard?"

"I can't tell him anything about the investigation."

"He knows that full well. Just listen to him."

"You brought me all the way up here to Pittsburgh to listen?"

"He was planning on visiting you, but weather prevented that. Precious and I were on our way here anyway so think of this as taxi service if you will."

TWELVE

MORRIS STRATIS ENTERED THE PLANE and took the recently vacated seat opposite Leslie. He was not the cigar chomping bully of a man Hodges had visualized. Stratis was more in the nature of Bill Gates than of Al Capone. Yet she saw the toughness about him; in his face, what little wasn't hidden by his mask; in his shoulders; and most of all in eyes that held no hint of humor. As she would come to learn, the only time those eyes varied from dead cold was when he spoke about his collections. Then and only then did they become mostly human.

Stratis opened the conversation with a repeat of what Silver had said about everything they were about to discuss being off the record. The two of them sparred back and forth over what that really meant, with Leslie agreeing to put nothing in the record but insisting she had to brief her boss. Stratis finally said, "Listen, Detective, I didn't haul your ass all the way up here for a philosophical discussion. I have no intention of compromising you in any manner. Just the opposite. I believe you are investigating a homicide of one, Scotty McDermitt. If I had purchased the phonograph, which I am not admitting I have, then I would have done so without knowledge the old lady had died in a car accident. If I am proven wrong in my assessment, steps will be taken to correct the situation. You should know it is my intention to assist in your investigation."

"What's in it for you? I mean, why help me? What do you get out of it? And, at what cost to me?"

"Good questions. You get right to the heart of the matter. I like that. I ask you, why need there be a cost to you?"

"Famous quid pro quo. Always was, always will be."

"Sometimes the quo comes in another form. This is one of those situations. I make it a policy to avoid purchasing an art piece if a homicide made its procurement possible. Believe me, not all collectors feel as I do. You must admit, do you not, McDermitt's death initially appeared as an accident."

Corruption takes on many forms as Hodges well knew. Sensing her career about to take a bad turn, she resolved not to allow that to happen. Without answering his question, she asked one of her own. "So, how's this all work? What exactly do you want from me?"

"There's more to the phonograph story than you know. I think Silver may have told you, I collect Firsts. One of those Firsts is Edison's notebooks leading up to the invention of the phonograph. I happen to own the ones pertaining to the phonograph. They contain detailed drawings and calculations, all in his handwriting as would be expected. There are also some things I didn't expect."

"Such as?"

"For one, he wrote with a pen in black ink. Someone else overwrote a few of his calculations, using blue ink and a much finer point. Experts tell me it's a woman's hand." Stratis pulled out his cell, found what he was looking for, and turned the screen to face Leslie.

"Calculations," she said. "There appears to be two strings of them."

"One for the recorder point and one for the playback needle."

"I didn't realize there was a difference," Hodges said, curious as to where this was going and struggling to visualize the operation of the phonograph. "How did it work?"

"Simple in operational concept once Edison realized that sound, particularly voice sound, could be recreated by vibrating a membrane. That's where his immediate predecessor, Ernst Chladni,comes in. His brilliance was in acoustics and the speed of sound. Edison elaborated on Chladni and on Newton and da Vinci before them."

"I thought Bell created sound?" Leslie responded, not fully comprehending what Stratis meant by predecessor, but guessing it had something to do with the Seminal Society and the shared souls mumbo jumbo Silver had spoken about.

"Bell didn't pioneer sound, but yes, a year before Edison, Bell patented the telephone which allows sound to travel over wires from a transmitter to a receiver. The transmitter captures sound waves from a speaker's mouth, converts the sound waves into electrical signals which are then put on a wire and connected to a receiver, which, in turn, converts the electrical signals back into sound waves by vibrating a membrane."

"If Bell did all that, what did Edison do?"

"He went one giant step further. He captured sound from a human voice by using a large cone-like device. When the sound concentrated at the bottom of the cone it created enough energy to move a diaphragm which moved something Edison called an 'indenting point'. The indenting point rises and falls as the sound energy presses on it. The rise and fall of the point presses indentions into a metallic foil rotating on a cylinder under the point. Helical grooves are cut into the cylinder causing the cylinder and the foil to move sideways under the pen so that the foil indentions stretch along the length of the cylinder."

Leslie, struggling to visualize the recording operation, said, "I suppose it plays like an old gramophone plays, using a needle riding up and down in those indentations."

"Exactly!" Stratis' eyes were now alive, "but with the difference being that a record is flat. Edison's recordings were made on thin foil wrapped around cylinders."

"That's harder to visualize. Is the same indenting point used to play back a recorded cylinder?"

"Heavens no. A very light weight point, hence the word needle, is required to prevent the recorded indentions from being disturbed Remember, Edison used metallic foil, which is easily dented and ripped, so the playback point is much more delicate than the recording point."

"You said someone other than Edison made those calculations. Does that mean whoever that other person was actually invented the phonograph?"

"Certainly not. The inventor of the phonograph was Thomas Alva Edison. There is no question about that. If the overwriting is genuine, then whoever made those revised calculations should get credit for making it work properly. At least on the recording side."

"Is there a doubt about the overwrite?"

"There is always doubt. People are always up to mischief. Truth is, at least for me, that's what makes Firsts so valuable. The mystery and stories that surround them."

Stratis' story corroborated what Scotty's daughter had told Leslie. "If there was someone who made those additional calculations, I assume you know who it would have been?"

"A lab assistant by the name of Sarah Johnson. Her maiden name was Sarah Davis in 1877. Mrs. Sarah Davis Johnson was Scotty McDermitt's great-grandmother. I suppose you already knew that."

"I also know she had been a mathematician for Edison. I didn't know she actually calculated the recording point sizes."

"That's the rumor making the rounds. So why are you here, you ask? I'm interested in the original disk. It might prove or disprove the rumor."

"I assume you have the phonograph that's missing from Scotty's house. Why not just listen to the cylinder and hear for yourself? End the speculation."

"I don't deal in speculations. If I had listened to the Edison One recently, then I most likely would report that the sound coming from the phonograph is the Semper Fidelis March music, maybe recorded by Edison at a parade or some such thing. I certainly would not be reporting that the sound was 'Mary Had a Little Lamb,' which is what should have been heard." Stratis smiled and added, "Mind you, what I just told you is…shall we say…educated whimsical speculation."

Realizing she was up against a man who had evaded the FBI for years, Leslie abandoned any attempt to trick him into an admission of being in possession of stolen property, concentrating instead on gathering information. "Why the focus on the foil cylinder," she asked, "when I thought you were interested in the phonograph? Edison One, I believe you said."

"I'm interested in Firsts. They are both Firsts in their own right. The phonograph as well as the cylinder. Here's what's fascinating. There's a rumor that years after Edison invented the phonograph, he recorded, or was tricked into recording, depending upon which version of the rumor you believe, a statement acknowledging that it was Sarah Davis' calculations that worked and not his. In that recording Edison personally credited the original phonograph, Edison One, to Sarah."

"What is it you want from me? Where do we — you and I — go from here?" Leslie still didn't know why she was there. A phone call could have accomplished everything she had heard so far. "I'm a police officer. I'm the last person in the world you want to confide in."

Ignoring her comment, Stratis, his eyes again as cold as steel, leaned across the aisle and said, "I now know for a certainty where Edison Two resides; in a display case at the Edison Museum in Fort Myers. That location won't be changing any time soon. I also know for a certainty that Edison One has been authenticated as the very first phonograph ever built, although its sound quality leaves a lot to be desired. I know of no Three."

"Why does the museum have the Two and not the One if, indeed, the One was the first to actually work?"

"Great question. And the answer goes back to what I said about calculations for the recording point. Edison One, at the time, was considered a failed experiment. Its recording was scratchy and barely audible. To Edison, it proved he was on the right path, but not yet at his goal. It wasn't until Cylinder Two was recorded on Phonograph Two with its recording point modified by Davis' calculations, did Edison celebrate. Edison Two, the one on display at the museum, had near perfect play back sound. So strange as it might appear, the Edison museum has Edison Two on display. And rightly so."

"Where is Cylinder One?"

"The man who first presented the opportunity to buy Edison One is someone who has served me well in the past. I was assured Cylinder One, the scratchy cylinder with Edison later reciting his dedication to Davis, was physically on Edison One. As I have indicated, if I were to listen to Edison One today, I would hear lovely marching music, but not Edison's voice. That man has failed me." Stratis leaned even closer, his eyes again alive. "Cylinder One has apparently gone missing! I must have that recording! I must hear Thomas Edison acknowledge Sarah Davis' contribution in his own voice!"

Leslie was unprepared for the intensity with which Stratis expressed his desire — his need — for the missing Edison cylinder. She took her time before responding, sensing herself at a crossroads, her future in balance. "It's certainly not mine to give you. Or to find for you, Mr. Stratis. And please may I remind you, I'm a detective, a cop, not an art agent. Please understand that if I managed to find the missing cylinder it would be returned to its rightful owner."

"I'm not asking you to do anything other than your job. I suspect if there's been a homicide, you'll eventually solve it. In so doing you may very well locate missing Cylinder One. I'll buy it for five million US dollars."

"As I said, I'm not a dealer. And certainly not a seller."

"Just locate it. I'll do the rest. You want a handsome finder's fee, give the owner my name. I pay ten percent."

"I have no interest in your money."

"Everybody has interest in money. Everybody."

"What makes the recording cylinder so valuable to you?"

"It's a true First from a seminal inventor."

There's that word again. Seminal. "What's that mean to you? Seminal inventor?"

"We believe, as have many seminal collectors before us, that the genius of Edison was embedded in the soul that attached to him at birth. That soul, some call it the Seminal Soul, can be traced back to a songwriter, a man named Wolkenstein, born in 1376. He died in 1445. Almost seven years later that same soul passed to DaVinci. Then on to Galileo, Newton, Chladni, and Edison. As I said, First's from each of these Seminals are extremely valuable to me — as they are too many others I might add."

"I never heard of Wolkenstein. Or Chlad..."

"Chladni. Ernst Chladni. Early 1800's. Father of sound. We believe Edison's fascination with electronic sound reproduction stemmed from Chladni's work on the nature of sound waves and their propagation."

Leslie was fascinated, but physics not being one of her strong suits, didn't know the questions to ask so she reverted to what she did best. Gathering information. "Any chance you have anything I can use in my investigation?"

"You can begin by easing up on the museum. They are honorable people."

"Yet you're willing to privately collect items they would love to have on display."

"Don't confuse business with pleasure. I am one of the world's largest contributors to the arts. I have donated hundreds of millions to museums all over the world. Many of my private artifacts are on display at galleries or museums. There are, I must admit, certain items I alone must have."

Leslie studied Stratis a moment before saying, "I doubt very much if I can help with your quest to acquire more art. Certainly, if it's legal for me to do so, I'll be happy to be of service to you."

"Thanks for visiting me. Hope to see you again." He shook her hand and made for the door.

The meeting was clearly over and Hodges still wasn't sure why, as Stratis had put it, her ass had been hauled a thousand miles north.

Stratis turned in the doorway. "Two more things. All communications go through Silver. My name is never to find its way into any official or private notes. That understood?"

"Not a problem," she said. "Until it is," she told herself.

"I understand the tropical depression played itself out. Airports down there will be open in a few hours. I have a plane here at the airport available for your flight home. I very much appreciate you saving me the trip south."

Leslie stood and looked him straight in the eye. "Thank you, Mr. Stratis, but I prefer to arrange my own transportation home."

"Have it your way, Detective. I'll be in touch."

When Stratis disappeared through the door, Pam walked over, her voice low, "Not my business, but you handled yourself well. I've seen him in action many times. He likes you. That's good. There's an American flight leaving at 4:10. Want me to book it for you?"

"Only if it goes on my card."

"You got it."

"How'd your meeting with Stratis go?" Silver said a moment later, appearing from the front of the plane. "Obtain anything of value for your investigation?"

"Nothing that couldn't have been accomplished over the phone."

"Not the same. You want a long-term relationship with anyone, need to break bread, so to speak."

Leslie was unsure why a long-term relationship with a man who buys stolen and forged art was in her best interest, but she held her tongue. "It seems he wants me to broker a deal for him. Not going to happen." She then went on to fill Silver in on the tin foil recording medium and the missing cylinder.

"I happen to know about that foil medium. Been discussions going on for years about it. Originally, it was thought to be at the Menlo Park museum. It's not. The one in the museum is Cylinder Two. The so-called perfect cylinder. The scratchy original is believed to be on the Edison One. The phonograph Scotty has — or had. He doesn't need you to broker the original cylinder. What he's looking for is the foil where Edison acknowledges Davis' contribution."

"That's not truly a First. So, what's he..."

"To him, it's a First. What I'm about to tell you is even more private than everything else you've been told. Stratis has for years been collecting art and artifacts pertaining to women. He's thinking of donating a major collection celebrating contributions of women. What could be better than a recording in Edison's own voice acknowledging Sarah Davis' calculations for the original Edison phonograph? He's just letting you know the value of the item and that people could get hurt if they're not careful. How much he say he'd pay?"

"Five million."

"Double that. Actually, double, quadruple, it again. He wants the original recording cylinder. In truth, the sky's the limit. Money's no object."

"Truth is, I'm investigating a crime, not chasing missing objects, unless of course, they're part of a crime committed in Florida. Stratis said he's dealt before with the person who brought him Edison One. Have any idea who that might be?"

"I honestly do not. Nor would I tell you if I did. I doubt very much if he confessed to owning the missing phonograph."

"Not in so many words, he didn't. He's apparently too good for that. My takeaway — he has it. If you won't tell me who he's dealing with can you at least tell me what art piece he's talking about?"

"Stratis buys so many pieces it's hard to know." Silver allowed that piece of information to sink in a moment before continuing, "I understand you turned down his offer of a ride home."

"I did."

"Your stock went up in his eyes. He likes principled people."

Hodges' eyes set hard and her shoulders went back. "I have no intention of being bought off. Not by you. Not by him. Not by anyone!"

"Relax, Detective. Nobody's trying to buy you off. Just the opposite. Keep in mind almost every art heist in the world is run past him in one way or another. He smells something bad in your neck of the woods, he drops you a clue. You roll the perp up. Your star shines."

"At what cost to me? Why the hell would I go along with that?"

"Because that's what you do. You catch perps and put them away."

"And what does Stratis get for it?"

"One less perp to deal with."

"What the hell's he care about perps in jail. He's their…their fence for God sakes!"

"You might say it helps keep the prices under control."

THIRTEEN

"DIDN'T EXPECT YOU BACK SO soon," Sergeant Oakmore said the first thing Thursday morning, his wide frame throwing a shadow over Leslie's computer screen. "Cap wants you in her office ASAP." He crushed a yellow paste-it note in his large hand and threw it toward the waste basket, missing by several inches. "Told her it might be late today, so you have a reprieve if you got something you need to do, I'll come back later."

The Jewish grandmother of a childhood friend, the only Jew Leslie had ever known, often used an expression when talking about authorities. "May the Czar stay healthy...and far, far away from me." In Leslie's mind, a summons from Captain Karen Stetson, was an appropriate time for that expression. Leslie also knew a problem never got better with time, so she sucked it up and said, "No time like the present, Sarge. Let's get the bad news over with."

"What makes you believe it's bad news?"

"Junior always said that in our business good news comes to you. You're summoned to the bad."

"Never heard that. Could be right. Truth is, I doubt if Boots even knows where the hell your desk's located."

"Boots" was Captain Stetson's nickname. Apparently, as a young officer Stetson had mentioned to a partner that she liked wearing Stetson boots. He started calling her Boots and the moniker stuck. When Leslie first heard the story of the name's origin, she believed the name sexist and refused to use it because the Stetson brand is best known for its men's shoes and boots. After considerable thought, however, Leslie decided that if it didn't bother the boss, it shouldn't bother her. "That works both ways," she replied, "I've never been to the brass side of the building and don't know where her office is either."

"Probably not a bad thing. At least according to your theory."

———●———

They were instructed to take a seat in the plush waiting room, the secretary assuring them it would only be a few minutes. Two of the four chairs bore taped Xs and a sanitizer dispenser had been bolted to the wall, in haste judging from its less than vertical orientation. The few minutes stretched into a half-hour before they were ushered into the large corner office.

Leslie didn't know whether to stand at attention or not, so she followed Oakmore's lead and maintained her normal posture, expecting at any moment to be chastised. But it didn't come. She studied her captain, assessing for herself how true the rumors were of Stetson's toughness.

"Please be seated, both of you. Leslie, you and I met only briefly at your graduation. This is, shall we say, a get-to-know-you-better meeting. Before we get to that let me first congratulate you on that nice piece of work on the construction site theft ring. I was beginning to take political heat and frankly was about to, well to be blunt, reassign it to one of our more seasoned folks."

"Thank you, Captain," Leslie managed, not knowing what else to say.

"What made you suspect the storage units? That's almost never where they stash the merchandise, at least not while we're in hot pursuit."

"Frankly, Captain, I was out of options. Eight thefts, from eight locations. Even when the response was within minutes the Silverado was gone. Two weeks ago, we managed to get a drone on site within five minutes, but still no luck. I asked myself how could a truck disappear? At first, I thought of garages. Gas stations with bays came to mind. Only two of the locations had gas stations in close enough proximity. Then I thought about storage locations and sure enough, within a two-block radius of each of the theft sites I found at least one storage place. You know the rest."

"Great piece of work. I understand you've been assigned to a homicide. How's that going?"

"Slow, at best."

"What's with the trip north? I approved it, but I saw nothing in the file to warrant the trip."

"Not sure it was worth the time." Leslie then went on to provide the basic who, what, where's.

"Hud, you have anything to add?" Stetson asked her boss when Leslie finished.

"She's covered it all. Nothing to add."

"Okay, then. Give us a few minutes, please." When Oakmore left, Stetson said, "I had a call from Lieutenant Keystone up in Tampa. Bill and I go back a long way. He has only good things to say about your time up there."

"That was nice of him. I really didn't know him. I was too far down the line."

"But he knew your husband. Wanted to know how you're doing. So, how are you doing?"

"In all honesty, I have good days and not so good days."

"That's to be expected. Now, tell me about yourself. Why you became a cop? Why you're remaining a cop after your tragic loss? Everything I need to know about you. I'm a good listener. Go."

"I know this is all in my file, but if you don't mind, let me start with the basics."

Stetson waved her hand as if to say the floor's yours, take it away.

"I was born and raised in Gulfport, Mississippi and went on the force over there in 2009, one week after my twenty-second birthday. I married Junior in 2012 and moved to Tampa."

"How'd you meet Junior? He was a Tampa detective at the time."

Stetson had reviewed her file. That was good to know. "He was working a multi-jurisdictional organized crime case with the FBI. I was assigned as his local guide and," she blushed slightly, "things went beyond purely professional. Got married when the assignment was over and … and here I am."

"Not exactly. You received several commendations in Tampa. Why not remain up there? Judging from that phone call, Bill would have promoted you to detective without question. He says every supervisor you ever had rated you on top." She fished around her desk a moment, found what she was looking for, then read, 'Hodges was born to be a cop. It's in her blood. Her attention to detail and almost total recall, bordering on OCD, makes her perfect for detective. Tough, but fair.' Now that was a direct quote. So, why'd you come down here, start over?"

Grief counseling notwithstanding, this was a hard topic for Leslie to think about, let alone discuss with top brass. "Just…just that I needed separation. I saw Junior everywhere I went. It'd never work if I remained in Tampa. Had to get out from under his shadow so to speak."

"Glad you did. Listen, Leslie, the subject will never come up again from my part. You need counseling, or anything, just let me know and I'll arrange it. No questions asked. I'm happy to hear Oakmore's not giving you a hard time. He's good at bringing babies along. Well, truth is, you're not exactly a baby when it comes to being a cop. But you are a rookie detective and it's easy to get over your head. Happens faster than you can imagine. Perps run free when that occurs. After listening to how you solved the Silverado case I have to agree with Keystone's assessment, you're a natural. My advice to you: follow your instinct and don't get beyond your headlights. Giving you a homicide is a real feather for you — and him. Now it's up to you."

Leslie stood, thinking the interview was over.

"Oh, before I let you go, what the hell's Keystone mean about your strange color choices?"

Leslie had no idea what her boss was talking about. "I don't know. What color choices is he referring to?"

"He said he knew what day it was by what color blouse you were wearing. I note you've got on gray today. Is that Thursday's color?"

"It is," Leslie replied. "But I wore blue every day in Tampa. In uniform. How did he…"

"You must have changed in the locker room, because somebody was paying attention."

"Is that a problem?" Leslie had heard talk about her habit of assigning colors to the days of the week and wearing a blouse each day that matched the color. "Makes it easy to decide what to wear on any given day. Been doing it since I was a kid."

"If it works for you, it works for me." The phone on Stetson's desk rang. Glancing down, she reached for the receiver. "Sorry, gotta take this. Close the door on your way out."

——•——

That had gone better than expected and proved the point that there are exceptions to every rule. Even though she now felt good about herself and the job she was doing, she also knew she was going in circles with the homicide.

"Dead ends can be good," Junior would often say as he paced the apartment trying to piece together a puzzle missing most of its parts. "Saves you from running all over creation chasing invisible threads."

When Leslie pressed him, his answer was always the same. "Start from the beginning. Work the file, the evidence you have. When it fails. Start over. Just as you do when you work those jigsaw puzzles you love so much. Turn it upside down and look at each piece with a new eye."

Work the file. From the beginning. Accident Scene Incident Report now supplemented with follow up from Sam and Dotty Feinman. Car at the accident scene and at the museum was a gray Audi.

Satisfied that she had again thoroughly reviewed the Report, Leslie brought the interior surveillance tape up on her computer. Second by second, she slowly advanced the image, studying every movement. From the perp's nervous ear tug tick to his careful lifting of Edison Two, as she now referred to the phonograph at the museum, to his even more gentle replacement back in the display case. She watched as he meticulously locked the case using the alarm key. That was something new she learned and hadn't thought about before. The same key that controlled the alarm unlocked the display.

Leslie replayed the sequence from the point where the perp lifted Edison Two from the stand, examined it, then carefully replaced it. Something caught her eye. She replayed it again, this time going frame by painstaking frame as the perp, holding the Two in his left hand over his head, looks at its bottom. His right hand out of the frame.

Replaying the sequence, she observes the perp reach for the Two with both hands, but his right disappears as he begins to lift the phonograph.

Pause

Right hand still missing in action. Strange that for such a valuable object he'd be balancing it in one hand.

The perp's right hand remains out of the next frame. And out of the next several frames.

The right hand then suddenly appears in mid-screen several frames later as the Two is lowered back into the display case.

"Shit!" she exclaimed to an empty bullpen when she realized video frames had been removed, "file's been doctored. But why?"

Another hour and the headache that had teased her earlier was now in full bloom. Time to get something to eat and head on over to the Edison. Halfway downtown, on impulse, she called Allen. "Any chance of a quick lunch?"

"Thought you'd never call. Yes, and no. Have a hearing at one and can't leave my desk. But you can do me a big favor and grab a couple dogs and cokes in the lobby and we can eat in my office. Not fancy, but better than starving."

She surprised herself by agreeing.

Leslie laid a bag on Allen's desk, fished out napkins and placed two hotdogs in front of him, reserving one for herself.

"So, what's your case about?" she asked, spreading mustard and ketchup on the bun.

"You really want to know, or you just being polite?"

"A little of both. So?"

"Guy cut a cop's arm. Cop was answering a domestic at 2:30 in the morning called in by a neighbor. Guy had been out at the corner bar tying one on. Not a particularly unusual occurrence for him I understand. Comes home, sneaks across the kitchen trying to get to the bedroom unseen. Wife's waiting for him with a frying pan, conks him on the head. He screams. Grabs a knife and the chase begins, the wife keeping a table between them. Cop enters the kitchen and yells for him to put the knife down. He tries to escape by running past the cop who reaches out to snatch the knife and misses. The perp trips and on his way to the ground the knife slices the cop's forearm. Twenty stitches to close the laceration."

"I thought you handled felonies. Sounds like a misdemeanor to me. An accident. He didn't intend to harm the cop."

"Charged with Aggravated Battery."

"Whose idea is that?"

"Not mine, I can assure you. But the elements are there."

"If the perp was white would the charge be the same?"

"Leslie! You think I of all people would..."

"Sorry. Where I cut my cop teeth these same facts would have resulted in a slap on the wrist for the white boys and jail time for the blacks. I don't see the intent to use the knife. I'm sensitive is all."

"Maybe not on the cop. Certainly, on the wife. That's the felony. Perp is white, matter of fact."

"Doesn't make it right."

"Glad you're not the judge, all's I can say."

"Good luck. As they say in the theater, break a leg. See ya."

On her way to the museum she called Nikolson to give her a courtesy heads up, cutting her off when she began to ask questions. The truth of the situation was that she herself didn't know what she was looking for. The only thing she knew was that the museum was a crime scene, at least a quasi-crime scene, and she wanted to immerse herself in it, as she had been taught in training.

Leslie didn't make it halfway across the museum floor before Nikolson was on her. "Detective. You didn't answer my question. What are you looking for?"

"Truthfully, I don't know. Just a feeling I have."

"About what?"

"Frankly, about why you — and your managing director — are both so...so jumpy. If nothing's missing, then nothing's missing and you have nothing to worry about."

"But..." Nikolson lowered her voice, "what I don't understand is this; if we haven't reported anything missing what crime are you investigating? You can't just snoop around looking for something that never happened."

Nikolson had a great point. Except there had been a homicide, but Leslie wasn't ready to share that tidbit. "Tell you what. I'm just going to go look at the phonograph as any tourist would. I'm told I should be referring to it as the Edison Two. I'd like to take a picture of its base. You can hold it for me if you'll be so kind. Then I'll get out of your hair. Deal?"

"You're taking a picture? For what purpose?"

The picture idea had just come to her as she stood across the room looking at the display case, again wondering why someone would risk holding something so awkward with one hand. Once Leslie stumbled to the idea of taking a picture of the underside of the phonograph base, the missing video footage made sense. The perp had done just that same thing using his right hand to hold the camera. Had the video not been cut, the number on the bottom would have been visible.

"I don't know. I think that's what the perp did."

"Of course, that's what he did," Nikolson responded, looking suspiciously at Hodges. "It's right there clear as can be in the video, the one you yourself watched. I had my heart in my mouth seeing him hold the phonograph up with one hand. Lucky it's in one piece."

Leslie hid her confusion. "Well, think of it as I'm just retracing his steps. I'll do it myself if you wish. Think of it as a reenactment."

"Heaven's no! One handed! You must be...well crazy to do that. Give me a moment to get my key and I'll hold it for you."

A moment later Nikolson unlocked the display, carefully lifted out the Edison Two phonograph and held it steady while Leslie snapped several photos. The phonograph was returned to the display case which was then relocked. Leslie then followed Nikolson back to the CEO's office, where she asked, "How well did you know Sarah McDermitt?"

"Scotty. Everyone called her Scotty. Wonderful woman. Loved the museum. Knew every piece of paper, display, everything. You know we are primarily a botanical museum, but she loved it all. Although I must say, she couldn't get enough of the phonograph and the technology of recording. She studied everything we have, and I swear she could design it from scratch if she had to."

"Did she ever discuss the phonograph with you?"

"Every chance she could get. Sometimes when we didn't have many guests she'd come into the office and talk her head off. About a week before...before that terrible car crash, she brought a copy of the patent in here and was talking to me about the differences between the recording needle—I think she called it a point—and the playback needle."

"What is the difference?" Leslie asked, recalling her conversation with Morris Stratis when he had explained this very question.

"The recording needle had to be heavy enough to make indentations in the foil surface in response to a person speaking into the speaking tube. The playback needle on the other hand only needed to be light enough to follow the resulting indentations. The last thing in the world you would want was for the playback needle to be heavy enough to change the indentations."

"Did Scotty understand how the two pins worked?"

"She certainly was concerned about the sizes and construction of the recording and playback needles. She told me how upset she was that we didn't have lab notebooks on the construction differences between Edison One and Edison Two. She had me phone Menlo to see if they had information. Apparently, the lab notebooks went missing a few years back."

Of course, they had, Leslie thought. Stratis bought them from the thief. "What else can you tell me about Scotty?"

"Like what?"

"Friends?"

"Everybody loved her, that much I do know. She was always the life of our year-end parties."

"Drink?"

"Not more than any other. Wine mostly."

"Dating?"

"I don't get into that."

"Does that mean you don't know? Or you won't say?"

"Won't say."

"So, can I assume she dated?"

"Assume what you wish."

FOURTEEN

"SO, LINDA," HODGES SAID, SETTLING into Murphy's plush sofa, "tell me about your mother."

"What's this about? I thought you came by to pick up the inventory list I made for you."

"That. And to be candid, I have questions about the accident."

"What kind of questions?"

"Let's just say, I'm troubled."

"About what?"

"Detectives are always troubled. That's what we do. Humor me. Here, give me a moment to read the list." Leslie scanned the sheets she had been handed. Looking up, she asked, "Was your mother a good driver?"

"She loved to drive. Yes."

"Did you worry about her being out late at night? Alone?"

"She'd been doing it for years. But, yes, I was concerned."

"Did she always drive I-75 home from the Edison? I mean, at that time of night coming down 41 would be just as fast."

"She was a creature of habit. That's how she did it every time she drove."

"Tell me about her social life?"

"What are you looking for?"

"Trying to gather a picture of your mother. I know about the docent part. I don't know about the social part. Did she have lady friends? Belong to clubs? Play cards?"

"Loved taking pictures."

"What about a camera? She have one?"

"I assume."

"Did you find it when you were at the house?"

"No. As a matter of fact, I didn't. I thought maybe it was in the car."

"Not that I know. What about clubs? Organizations?"

Leslie jotted names, and where available, phone numbers, as Linda slowly outlined her mother's life, circles surrounding several names Linda identified as being close to her mother. She'd have to interview each of these in the next few days. The good news, they all lived in or around Miromar Lakes.

"Were there any men? These are all female."

Linda blushed and looked away, reminding Leslie of the reaction she received earlier from museum CEO Nikolson.

"So, did your mother enjoy men? Hate men? What?"

"Why's it important?"

"I told you, I want to know everything there is to know about her."

"I didn't discuss her sex life with her, if that's what you're looking for?"

"Just because she had male friends doesn't mean…"

"You certainly don't know my mother if you think that!"

"Please fill me in."

"My father died in January 2001. Mother waited a year before going out. But after that, after that it was… well it got to the point where I refused to discuss her sex life with her."

"So, she was active?"

"Active! Like she was making up for lost time, active. If it wore pants, look out, active. That's why I stopped going over there. Threw her key away even. Look, I may not be a model citizen myself, failed marriage and all, but…but…that's all I'm going to say about that subject."

"Names of her male friends?"

"I honestly don't know."

"It'll be better if you gave me what you have. My alternative is to canvas her neighbors, see what they can tell me."

"Do what you need to do, Detective. I'd be surprised if they saw anything 'cause if there's one thing I know about my mother, she won't mess where she eats."

"Meaning?"

"Meaning, she's discrete. Neighbors won't know a thing, promise you."

"That's extreme, don't you think?"

"That's Scotty. Extreme to a fault. Always her own woman."

"Did she throw parties? Have people in for dinner?"

"She did all of that up until her mother died and she got that Edison phonograph. Since then house's been off limits. Extreme."

"In what way?"

"Secretive, I'd say." Linda thought a moment about what she had just said, then added, "Not so much secretive, but…but contemplative. At first when her mother gave it to her she was thrilled, kept talking about how her great grandmother helped invent it. How it had been passed down from mother to daughter. That kind of thing."

"At first? Then what happened?"

"I don't know exactly. Something changed. Back around February my brother says she wouldn't discuss the phonograph."

"In what way did he know that? What did she say?"

"Not what she said. What she didn't say. She stopped saying he or I would inherit the 'best gift ever.' I tried to talk to her about it twice and both times she changed the subject. In January, according to my brother, she was excited about recording something on the cylinder. At first, I thought it was a note or something to me. But Roland said that starting with our great-great-grandmother, Sarah Johnson, she and each daughter had recorded something on the cylinder, something to pass down."

"How interesting. You have any idea what they recorded? Let's see, that would be... how many people?"

"Four, if you include Scotty. Sarah, of course was first. She recorded the words, 'The best invention of my lifetime is the phonograph.' That is the only recording Scotty would allow me to hear. She said I'd have to wait until she died, and it became mine before I could listen to the others."

"Why, do you suppose she said that?"

"Scotty being Scotty. I told you, we had a...a strange relationship."

"What was her message?

"But that's just it, I don't think Scotty ever made her recording."

"Why, do you suppose?"

"Don't laugh. Scotty once joked that the best invention of her lifetime was Viagra. Now, thinking of my mother's activities I'm not so certain she was joking. I believe she just couldn't bring herself to record that tidbit."

"We haven't spoken about her health. How was it?"

"As I said, she cut me out of her life a while ago, so I assume no news is good news. Last time I saw her was March 3rd, her birthday. I made an apple pie and dropped by." Linda's eyes teared. "That was the last I saw her. She looked tired."

"I didn't see phonograph cylinders on your list. Did you find any?"

"Didn't find the phonograph either."

Leslie stood. "Thank you for making the time to see me. Oh, one more question. What would be your answer to the best invention of your lifetime?"

"I haven't thought about my lifetime, but certainly if I were answering for Scotty I'd have to say the microwave. Couldn't live without it."

FIFTEEN

WALKING INTO AN ONCOLOGIST'S OFFICE gives anyone reason to pause and contemplate life. It wasn't any different when Hodges noted the name Dr. Haywood Sayeth painted on the glass door panel. Only Leslie wasn't thinking so much of her own mortality as she was of the homicide victim, Sarah McDermitt and her cause of death. Doctors, Junior had often said, instinctively hid behind HIPAA laws and routinely refused to cooperate with law enforcement. To avoid having to obtain a subpoena, Hodges called ahead, told the receptionist what she wanted and instructed the woman to look up 45 CFR 164.512 (f) (3). Since Scotty wasn't the object of the investigation there was no reason for Dr. Sayeth to refuse to talk about his patient. The receptionist reluctantly set an appointment for 5:15. "We usually leave that slot open to allow Doctor to catch up. You may have to wait a while."

In fact, it was almost six when she was ushered into Sayeth's office and found a surprisingly young man sitting behind a desk littered with several open files. "I understand you're a detective with Lee County," he began before Leslie could say a word. "I don't know what all those legal-looking numbers are about, but I've been waiting to speak with someone in authority about Scotty's death."

"Did you call the Sheriff?"

"I just got the report a day or two ago. Meant to. Been busy and forgot."

"What report is that?"

"Coroner's report." He fumbled through several file folders and shoved one across the desk. It was a hard copy of what Leslie had read online. "Asked to have it sent to me. Abundance of curiosity I suppose."

"Your take?" Leslie asked, anxious to hear what Scotty's doctor had to say about her death."

"Died of carbon monoxide poisoning."

"What about the tree limb?" Leslie probed.

"To me, that's a technicality. Sure, her heart was still pumping, but her brain had closed down."

"From my perspective, it's homicide regardless, so for the moment cause of actual death isn't vital. May become so at some point, but for now we'll go with the coroner's report."

"Then what can I do to help?"

"You were her doctor, right?"

"Correct."

"And what was her diagnosis?"

"In layman's terms, pancreatic cancer."

"Her life expectancy? I mean from the last time you saw her."

Sayeth glanced toward a large painting of a snow-capped mountain in the distance with a grassy prairie spread in the foreground. A lone horse and rider were meandering across the flat land headed to the seemingly unattainable hills.

Without looking at Leslie, he said, "We had monthly visits prescheduled. Around the tenth of the month. Saw her for the August visit. Quite frankly, she appeared much better than I had expected. In good spirits. Back in June, I believed she'd not make it until the middle of July, beginning of August at the latest. She was in terrible pain."

"You prescribed Roxanol."

"Hardly took any, as far as I know. She should have had a refill but didn't. When I asked her about it she shrugged. One tough lady. I'll give her that much."

"Why wouldn't she take the medication?"

"She said she needed to drive to the museum and back. She works — worked — at the Edison in Fort Myers. I'm sure you know that. Driving with that medication in her system could be…well, dangerous. I asked her to stop working, but she said it was her life."

"What treatments did she receive?"

"Not much we could do. She presented in mid-April and had liver involvement, bile ducts closing. Palliative care was the only thing." Sayeth's eyes again went to the rider making his way across the landscape. "I don't know how that woman did what she did. She was as strong-willed as they make them."

"Is there anything more you care to tell me?" Leslie asked.

"Like what?'

"Like what's troubling you."

"You know," the doctor said, his eyes remaining on the painting, "in my line of work it's best not to become emotionally invested in your patients. With Scotty it was difficult. She was…was so full of life. Always had a story to tell. She brought cookies for the office. It was as though she felt it her job to cheer us up, not the other way around. I only knew her less than four months, but it seems a lifetime." He paused then continued. "You know, my biggest regret, failure actually. I couldn't convince her to confide in her children. You know she has a daughter living not far from her. The two of them…don't speak."

"Did you know why not?"

"She wouldn't discuss it."

"You ever meet the son or daughter?"

"No. To my regret. I suggested it several times, but she brushed it aside."

After leaving the doctor's office Leslie decided to use the South District Substation on Tamiami Trail just south of Coconut Point instead of her base HQ because of its proximity to where she now was. The short drive didn't allow much time to think about Scotty's life, but Leslie captured a picture of her last few months on this earth, which only served to add to the confusion.

According to Linda, the seventy-six-year-old woman was in good health, loved the company of men, spent time with several woman's groups, and was an active photographer. CEO Nikolson called her the life of the party. So, where were her photos? On her phone? In a camera? Uploaded? If so, where? And if Scotty was so man crazy, why didn't the daughter have at least one man's name? And speaking of camera, where was it?

Pulling into the parking lot she took several minutes to compose messages to her Criminal Investigative Assistant. One message requested the CIA to work up a forensic analysis of the video from the night of the break-in, particularly looking for any irregularities. Another message requested phone numbers for the son; and a third for the names and phone numbers of Scotty's neighbors; and a fourth, background histories of CEO Jayne Nikolson and her Managing Director William Packard Blair.

On her way inside the single-story building, Leslie had a thought, yanked out her phone and entered a request for a uniformed canvas of Scotty's neighborhood looking for surveillance cameras run by the homeowner's association or by private homes that could provide footage of people coming and going from Scotty's house within a month of her accident. She also put in a request to the RTIC unit to see what government-run video there was of cars coming into or out of the development the night Scotty died.

The Sheriff's office was mostly empty with only three administrative staff visible. She flashed her badge and was quickly shown into a bare-bones cubby with a computer sitting on a small table. The only other items in the area were a single metal chair and a waste basket.

"Shout if you need anything, Detective," the older of the two women said when she flipped the light on. "Office is yours as long as you need it. Make yourself at home."

And she did. For the next several hours she researched everything she could find on Edison phonographs and Edison's notes. There was nothing on great-great-grandmother Sarah Davis Johnson, even though she had Linda McDermitt Murphy clearly on record stating she had heard an original recording of Edison acknowledging Johnson's contributions and then of Johnson, in her own voice, claiming the phonograph as the best invention of her lifetime.

Leslie then looked up U. S. Patent No. 200,521 issued on February 19, 1878 to T. A. Edison. Her goal was to learn how the phonograph worked. More specifically, how the metallic foil worked and what it looked like. Unfortunately, the patent did not contain a drawing of the foil medium, so she had to continue imagining what it would look like if removed from the phonograph. That would depend upon whether the entire cylinder had been removed from the phonograph, or if the foil had been slipped off the cylinder, leaving the cylinder on the machine. Leslie mentally chided herself for not taking a picture of the recording cylinder when she had the chance earlier in the day.

As valuable as the foil was, and, at least in Leslie's mind, how fragile it must be, it would seem prudent to keep the foil and cylinder intact. Question: Are there any known spare cylinders?

Leslie fired off a text to Silver seeking an answer to that very question.

Her phone immediately buzzed. The message was not from Silver as she had hoped, but rather the message spelled out it was from Roland McDermitt. The 412 area code confirmed he lived in Pittsburgh. Coincidence that she had just been there on Silver's plane?

"Roland? Roland McDermitt," Leslie said into her cell a moment later. "I'm Detective Leslie Hodges, Lee County Florida. You texted me."

"My sister said you wanted to talk. Had questions, I think about Scotty's phonograph. What is it you wish to know?" His voice was friendly but reserved.

"Is this a good time?"

"No time is good to talk about death. She's gone. Ran off the road. Hit a tree. What else is there to talk about?"

"Did you attend her funeral?"

"Had her cremated. Nothing to attend. With this virus crap I'm staying close to home."

"Having her cremated, was that her idea or what?"

"Scotty's all the way. She called about a month ago and out of the blue said if anything happens to her she wanted no funeral, no casket, nothing. 'Just toss me in the fire and spread my ashes where you will,' were her exact words."

"Was that a strange request? I mean, were you surprised?"

"Nothing Scotty ever did surprised me. Never knew with that woman. One day she'd be full of life, joking, having fun. The next, well the next she'd be as ornery as they make 'em. Her mood swings in the last month were worse than ever."

"Which mood was she when she requested cremation?"

"Up, I think. Said she was tired, though. Complained of pain. Said she was getting old. In truth, she sounded high. Not on drugs kind of high, but full-of-life high."

"Any reason to believe she was sick?"

"None. I was down for New Years. She looked okay to me. Went out on a boat, did a lot of walking. She baked up a storm. Wife and I gained weight. Still haven't got it all off."

"Meet any of her friends?"

"She walked her dog several times a day and I walked with her. She knew every person we bumped into. Chatted with everyone. I lost count of how many shopping trips, lunch dates, trips to the beach she scheduled. She introduced my wife to several women from different Miromar clubs she belongs to."

"Remember which clubs?"

"A book club and something called Hearts, or some thing of that nature. She particularly liked that one. She spoke often about the great charity work they do, how much money they raise, that kind of thing. Scotty seemed really happy when we were there."

"How about male friends? Meet any?"

"I know Linda thinks she...she made the rounds, so to speak. But I saw no evidence of that."

"I assume you stayed at your mother's house?"

"Of course. Linda never invites us."

"You have a problem with your sister?"

"Not a problem, exactly. My wife says she feels uncomfortable around my sister. Linda likes her privacy and I respect that. She and mother were on again, off again. Been that way for as long as I can remember. Linda's a great kid, but marches, as they say, to her own drummer. Heart of gold. Do anything for you kind of person. Gets an idea in her head, there's no stopping her."

"Did you see the Edison phonograph your mother had?"

"Can you believe she has — had, Linda says it's missing — the original Edison phonograph! I couldn't believe it! She played it for us several times. She played three, I think she called them cylinders. Metal foil wrapped around a cylinder of some material. On the first cylinder Edison's voice was distorted, but I heard him say, Mary had a little lamb. Its fleece was white as snow. Not actually distorted but scratchy."

"My notes indicate the original phonograph is called Edison One. Did your mother...?"

"Yes. That's exactly what she called the phonograph, Edison One. And she called the recorded cylinder, Cylinder One."

"Please continue."

"The second cylinder, she called it Cylinder Two, was much clearer than the first. When the second one ended Scotty took it off and said, 'I borrowed Cylinder Two from the museum. Now for the real treat.' Not that listening to Edison's very first recording wasn't treat enough."

"What was the treat?" Roland had captured Leslie's full attention.

"She put Cylinder One back on and played it again, this time allowing it to play further. Suddenly, Edison's voice came on again, this time perfectly clear. All the scratchiness gone. He then said, and I quote, 'I wish to acknowledge the critical calculation made by my wonderful assistant Sarah Davis serving to remove the distortions from the original. Upon my death I hereby bequeath the original phonograph to her.' Can you believe that?"

"Was there anything else on that disk?"

"Cylinder, not a disk. As I said, foil wrapped around a drum is what Scotty called it."

"How big a drum?"

"I'd have to guess, but in diameter I'd say about the size of a soda can, maybe slightly narrower. And actually, about the same height. I didn't pay all that much attention to the construction."

"Did you hear anything else on the...cylinder?"

"Not on that one, but she had a third one. Scotty said the voices on the third one were of my grandparents. It was so...so weird to hear them speak."

"What did they say?"

"Three different voices. First one said, 'This is Sarah Davis Johnson in the year 1917. In my lifetime the best Invention is clearly the phonograph.' That voice was followed by a different voice, saying, 'My name is Grace Johnson Cull. It is 1937 and I vote for the electric light bulb. The Model T comes in second.' Then a third voice added, 'Hi, the year is 1992 and I'm Esther Cull Southerland. I couldn't live without frozen food.' Needless to say, I was blown away hearing them all!"

Leslie couldn't imagine what emotions she would feel hearing her own ancestors talking to her, seemingly from the grave. She had to admit it took her speech away.

"I think I have that all right," Roland said. "I've played it back in my mind so many times. It's like a real-life dream, hard to believe it happened. I was excited about the phonograph being in the family. Then in the spring Scotty called and said she was considering changing her

Will and not giving the phonograph to Linda as had become the tradition. I tried to change her mind, but she was adamant."

"Why do you suppose she did that?"

"Something happened between them is all I can figure."

"Any idea who she was giving the phonograph to?"

"Said something like it deserves to be public. Or it belongs to the public. I took it from that she had the museum in mind, but she wouldn't say."

"Do you have any idea of the value of that phonograph?"

"I'd imagine in the millions. I really don't know. No sense spending time on a value seeing as neither I nor Linda would ever sell it even if we did get it."

"You have any knowledge of where it might have gone?"

"Not a clue."

Leslie was about to hang up when something that had been nagging at the back of her mind for several minutes interrupted her. "Something's bothering me. Maybe you can clear this up. The reason Edison One is not in the museum is because it recorded scratchily. That's because its recording point, or needle, was not exactly right. Your ancestor is the one who changed the calculations for the recording needle. Are you aware of that?"

"Scotty gave me several lessons in the construction. I feel I'm a bit of an expert."

"Then can you explain why if the initial words of Edison talking on Cylinder One are scratchy why the rest on the dis...cylinder...are so clear?"

"That's easy. Scotty was so proud of that. Her great grandmother, Sarah Davis Johnson, made additional calculations and Edison changed the point in the original phonograph to reflect what he considered perfection."

"One last question. Did you hear your mother's recording? I mean what her favorite invention was in her lifetime."

"She said she wasn't in a hurry to record."

"Any idea what she was planning to put on the... cylinder?"

"No need to guess. She told me. The microwave was her favorite invention."

SIXTEEN

THE PHONE RANG WITHOUT ANSWER. Leslie counted seven…eight and was about to give up when she heard a click, a sleep-heavy voice saying, "Who's there?"

"Hello, my name's Leslie Hodges with the Lee County Sheriff's office. I'm calling a Mr. Chris Wang who witnessed a fatal car crash on…"

"This is he. What did you say your name was?"

"Detective Hodges. If I woke you, I'm sorry." It was after 10 a.m. on Friday and Leslie had been working since 7, making it feel like mid-day. "I have a few questions about the accident. I can call back later if you wish."

"Fire away. I'm up now."

"What did you see that night?"

"I was coming south from my sister's in Punta Gorda. Not much traffic. All of a sudden, this car, a Mazda, swerves to the left into the center lane. I was behind another car, also in the center lane, and the driver hit his brakes. It was all I could do to avoid slamming into him. Then the Mazda turned back to the right and drove full speed off the side of the road. Me and the car in front of me pulled off the road and we both backed up to where the accident happened. There was already another car parked there. I think I told the officer a green Audi. Two people from that car had already gone down the hill to where the wreck was. The man from the car in front of me got out and ran down the hill. I got my cell out and videoed the accident scene. Didn't think anyone would come out alive. Unfortunately, I was right."

"Anything more you remember?"

"Nothing. That's it."

"Tell you what," Leslie said, thankful for a cooperative witness, "I'll give you my number, text me the video. If I have any more questions I'll call you. That okay with you?"

"Anything to help. I feel bad for that poor woman. Can't get that scene out of my head."

———————

The video file was twenty-two minutes long, but everything beyond the first five minutes was unimportant, at least for now. At the 03:52 mark of the video, one of the two men from the already parked car walked up the hill, passing Feinman who was walking down. Words seemed to pass between them. At 04:07 the second person came up the hill carrying a canvas bag. The camera remained focused on the smoking Mazda and Feinman again came into view. He looked into the smashed window but didn't attempt to open the door. Leslie recalled Feinman saying Scotty was clearly dead when he arrived at the car.

Several minutes later Feinman turned and started back up the hill toward the camera. At that same time blue and red lights began bouncing off the Mazda. Deputy James came into view running down the hill toward the car. He immediately reached inside and then spoke into his radio.

The next seventeen minutes and twenty seconds showed the fireman working methodically to free Scotty's body from the wreckage in anticipation of the coroner's team.

Leslie replayed the pertinent five minutes several times, carefully looking for anything that would identify either of the two mystery people, or the car they were driving. The very first seconds of the video held promise of capturing the car, but even in slow motion she gleaned nothing. Of even greater disappointment was the fact that Wang's video did not capture the faces of either of the two people seen leaving the scene. The only thing of real value was their clothes; mechanics overalls with a circular logo of some sort on the right chest. It was difficult for Leslie to judge the actual height of either person mainly due to the slope of the hill. The person who was at the front of the car was clearly taller, Leslie believed about a foot taller, than the person at the trunk. The actual heights would be something forensics would have to piece together.

Leslie's phone chirped alerting her to a text message.

It was from Silver in answer to her text message late the day before.

OFFICIAL RECORDS SHOW FIVE ORIGINAL CYLINDERS OVER WHICH FOIL COULD BE WRAPPED. THERE ARE TWO PHONOGRAPHS, ONE AND TWO. THE CYLINDERS ARE INTERCHANGEABLE BETWEEN THEM, ALL HAVING HELICAL SPIRALS TEN GROOVES TO THE INCH. BOTH PHONOGRAPHS HAVE TEN THREADS TO THE INCH, ALLOWING CYLINDERS TO BE PLAYED BACK ON EITHER PHONOGRAPH.

———◼———

"What the hell does that mean?" Leslie asked Managing Director William Packard Blair two hours later over lunch. She had read him Silver's confusing reply to her spare cylinder question.

Blair, not one to impart information freely, fell silent. Leslie, having already sized him up, decided to sip her coffee and give him all the time he required. This question was more of a diversion and wasn't intended to be the centerpiece of her meeting request, which was to determine Blair's part in the doctored video surveillance tape.

Leslie continued sitting quietly waiting for Blair to decide how he was going to answer. Finally, he leaned forward, as if to impart a state secret. "Your question raises all manner of issues. Some practical, some legal, and some, well some that will affect the value of the items in our museum."

"I don't see how anything you tell me can change the value of something the museum owns and has no intention to sell."

"Oh, don't misunderstand me. The museum isn't selling anything. It's just that insurance values follow market values. We need be aware of the market at all times."

Leslie was prepared to give him that based on her conversations with Silver — and to some degree with Stratis, a potential buyer of stolen property. "Okay, I understand. What's the value have to do with interchangeability of cylinders?"

"Edison constructed two original phonographs. We call them One and Two. Two is on display here in the museum. One is…and this is conjecture on my part…in possession of the family of Edison's associate, a woman by the name of Sarah Davis Johnson."

"By conjecture," Leslie pressed, "you mean you don't know for certain."

"Not many people know. To be perfectly honest, I did find that out, recently."

"What did you find out?"

"That Scotty McDermitt was the great-granddaughter of Davis and she had in her possession Edison One, as well as the original recording made by Edison himself."

"How did you come to learn that?"

"Scotty told me. She also told me she was about to record something on a cylinder. I asked her not to do that."

"Why didn't you want her to record?"

"Didn't want to ruin the original."

Hodges wasn't buying what Blair was selling, so she decided to lay out some of the facts she already knew. "You know, don't you, that the recording point, some think of it as a needle, is different from the point that does the playback? And the recording points on One and Two are different. Is that why you didn't want her recording anything?"

Blair studied Leslie a long moment apparently surprised she had taken the time to learn the inner workings of the phonograph. "Yes, of course I knew that. As you most obviously know, the reason there are two phonographs, One and Two, is because Edison made calculations of the point sizes he wanted for the recording side and for the playback side. His assistant, Davis, made her own calculations. The original recording was made on Edison One using Edison's own calculations. It worked, but his voice was slightly distorted. The recording point on Edison Two was cut to Davis's calculations and worked perfectly. I've heard them both and there is quite a difference."

"Which one does the museum have?"

Again, hesitation, followed by, "Museum has Edison Two, because that was the one Edison based the industry on. We also have the original foil that was on that device."

"Is that original foil — cylinder — still on display?"

"Of course," Blair snapped; his hands tightly clasped together. "Where else would it be?"

"Just asking."

"Are you aware that Edison recorded a message to Scotty's ancestor on the original scratchy cylinder using Edison One?"

Blair tried to cover his surprise that Leslie knew this fact by turning sideways and signaling to the waitress to come over to their table. There not being a waitress in sight exposed the gesture for what it was. When he turned back to face Leslie she repeated her question.

"I have been told. So, yes."

"By Scotty?"

"Yes, by Scotty."

"Are you aware that the recording point on the Edison One was modified so that it now records perfectly?"

"I'm not certain I knew that. No." Now it was Blair's turn to hide behind his coffee cup, sipping slowly.

Leslie sat quietly, her idea of giving him plenty of rope.

The silence becoming uncomfortable, Blair finally asked, "What the hell are you investigating anyway? There is nothing missing from the museum. Scotty's tragic death was an accident."

"As you just confirmed, Edison One was in Scotty's possession earlier in the year. It's gone missing."

"So, you're investigating a theft?"

"You might say that."

"What else might I say?"

"You could start with explaining why the surveillance video's been doctored?"

"What the hell are you talking about?"

"You didn't know that?"

"Of course not."

To avoid giving out information she wasn't yet prepared to share with Blair, Leslie quickly asked, "Do you know Linda Murphy? Scotty's…"

"Of course, I do. Scotty was a docent here for years. Met Linda many times."

"How long have you been involved with the Edison Museum?"

"Going on seven years."

"All as Managing Director?"

"Yes."

"Is there a special degree for that, or is it on the job training?"

"Bit of each. Worked my way up in the art world. A stint at the Louvre and other places. I was assistant curator at the National Gallery of Art in Washington. The Edison hired me away from the Gallery to manage the museum."

"And that, you say, was in…"

"Thirteen. Twenty-thirteen. In those seven years I've grown to love Fort Myers and the folks down here."

"My notes indicate you're a distant relative of Henry Ford. That accurate?"

"Third cousin twice removed or some such thing. I've always thought my middle name, Packard, was my mother thumbing her nose at her cousins."

"Married?"

"Not at the moment." Blair jumped to his feet. "Hey, have to run. I'll get the check. Don't know where the time went, but…"

"I understand. Thanks for the time. And thanks for offering to buy lunch. State rules. Can't accept it. Go, I'll finish my coffee. Have a few calls to make."

One of those calls was to County Digital Forensics, returning their call-back request. The lab technician, a man she knew to be near retirement but with the voice of a person in his early thirties, gave her a brief overview of the surveillance video, saying that indeed a segment, perhaps as much as two minutes, had been removed.

"My take," Leslie said, "is that the perp in that video is left-handed. Do you concur?"

"Inconclusive. There did appear to be some awkwardness, some jerky motion if you will, but I'm not prepared to say the perp's left-handed. There's a segment missing right near the beginning as well. Almost as soon as the perp arrives at the display case you can see him reaching up and the next thing you see is the phonograph lifted. At that point it is my belief about thirty to forty-five seconds is missing."

Next call to CEO Nikolson. "Quick question for you on the surveillance video the night of the accident."

"Please make this fast. I have a VIP tour starting in a few."

"Near the beginning of the surveillance video a man goes to the alarm panel and then over to the phonograph display. What happens next?"

"He unlocks the case and picks the phonograph up."

"Before that, does he stall? Get distracted? What?"

"Let me think." The line was silent for a short while, then Nikolson said, "Now that you ask, I believe he turns it on and listens for several seconds before removing it from the case and picking it up."

"Do you know what's on that cylinder now?"

"Haven't listened to it for over a year."

"Mind if I come by and give a listen?"

"Tied up all day. Have a private party tonight from seven to nine. Got things to do then."

"Why do I feel you're stalling?"

"Don't mean to. Just overwhelmed right now. My mother's sick. Tell you what, how about you come by tonight at nine. We'll listen together. Be interesting."

"See you at nine. Thank you."

Leslie played back the surveillance tape again in her mind, all the while trying to understand what the perp was listening for. Something was nagging her, something she had seen the first time through and meant to mention to Fischer, the detective who had executed the warrant with her. She brought the video up on her cell and watched it yet again.

Timing was wrong. Scotty's car had run off the road shortly before midnight. The perp had taken the keys and left the scene before the deputy arrived at two minutes after midnight. Why would it take over four hours to get from the accident scene to the museum if the idea of killing her had been to break into the museum? Possible answers: Dropping off the person who stuffed the hose into the canvas bag? Going for a drink? Not likely, but certainly couldn't be ruled out. Maybe the lurching about in the museum was not a poor recording but alcohol induced? What about the house key and getting the phonograph?

Leslie thought of Stratis and his passion for Firsts. She replayed the scene on Silver's jet of the billionaire leaning close, his eyes alive with excitement, telling her how much he wanted the cylinder on which Edison recorded Sarah Davis' contribution.

That's what the accident was about! Getting Scotty's house keys and taking Edison One! That now seemed clear. What about the museum break-in?

The cylinder! Assuming Stratis had the phonograph and assuming his story about the Semper Fidelis March music was true, which she had no reason to doubt, then the valuable cylinder with Edison's words inscribed on them, was missing. Voilà! The museum break-in was about finding that cylinder! The thief—murderer Leslie reminded herself—must have gone to Scotty's house, gathered up Edison One, and gone off somewhere to listen

to it. Realizing the valuable cylinder was missing he —
she?—thought about where it could be. Since Scotty had
access to the museum there was a possibility she could
have stored it in the display case, or in the Edison Two
itself. Hence, the late-night visit to the museum using
Scotty's own key.

No break-in at Scotty's house meant someone had to
have both the key and the security combination. Scotty's daughter Linda didn't have the key, but she had the
combination. Scotty's killer, as of midnight on the 23rd,
had the key. Drive from the accident scene on Interstate
75 to Scotty's home at that time of night, say, twenty
minutes. Ten minutes in the house would be generous.
Time: 12:30 a.m., give or take. Drive back to the museum,
call it forty minutes. Time 1:15 – 1:30 a.m. max. Yet the
break-in wasn't until 4:15 a.m.

The timeline seemed to support Leslie's theory about
the perp trying to find the location of the missing original
cylinder. The museum was one place to look. Are there
others? Her car? Her house? The house was searched,
recordings not found. And there was nothing much in
her car. A storage unit?

If Stratis was to be believed, and Leslie definitely
leaned in that direction, then the perp hasn't yet found
the valuable first recorded cylinder — a cylinder perhaps
having a street value approaching fifty million dollars.

SEVENTEEN

AFTER LUNCH WITH WILLIAM BLAIR, Leslie was on her way to her office when a message appeared on her screen requesting her presence at the courthouse. The ASA wanted her close by in the event she was required to testify in the arraignment hearing for one Weslo Custer, the mastermind behind the string of construction project thefts she had solved. Leslie had appeared in court several hundred times as a street cop having arrested any number of thieves, hit and runners, disorderlies, public urinators, looters, the whole gambit. This, however, would be her first appearance as a detective. She was both nervous and excited.

In the past, the actions she testified about had occurred primarily in her presence. She had been a witness to the crime and her testimony consisted of what she herself saw the perp do and what she herself did to arrest the perp. Detectives rarely witness a crime occurring in real time, coming to the scene as they do after the perp is long gone. They then use evidence, witness statements, deductions, tips and sometimes dumb luck, to track down the perp.

As she sat spaced-apart in the sparsely populated hallway outside the closed courtroom doors, she played out what she should — and should not — say, if and when she took the stand. She knew the first line of attack any decent defense lawyer would raise in this case would be illegal search and seizure. She had obtained a warrant and that usually carried the day. But that wouldn't prevent defense counsel from badgering her as to how she knew which unit the Silverado was hidden in.

She had been told the hearing was set for 2:15. At 2:10 she was instructed by the court clerk to return at 3:00. It was now 3:15 and still nothing. At one point her hopes soared when she spotted Allen rushing toward her. At least she'd have a prosecutor she could relate to. She stood to greet him and realized too late that he hadn't seen her. His eyes were focused on the court just beyond where she was waiting.

"Oh, Leslie," he exclaimed, almost bumping into her, "what're you doing down here?"

"The Silverado matter. Remember the warrant you helped me with?"

"Oh, is that today? Hey, I'd love to sit in, but I'm due in Harrison's court right now. He'll ream me a new one if I don't get a move on. Good luck." He took several steps, then turned back. "Sorry, my mind's elsewhere. Heard about the McDermitt investigation. Sorry. Call, you wanna talk." He turned and race walked to the next courtroom, disappearing inside.

She had no idea what his reference to the McDermitt matter meant. His comment piqued her curiosity, but she had no time to dwell on it.

"Detective Hodges," the bailiff called, "please follow me."

Leslie noted that the court room was smaller than she had expected as she was led to the front and shown into the witness chair. No jury was present. A middle-aged woman wearing thick-lensed glasses sat at a small table hunched over a machine spewing out a paper ribbon that curled its way to the floor. The sign in front of the judge read: Hon. Jenkins Smyth. A bailiff waddled over, had Leslie raise her right hand and proceeded to swear her in, his voice a blur of words he must have memorized fifty years earlier and been reciting by rote ever since.

That formality out of the way, the prosecutor, a woman Leslie had seen once before but did not know her name, stood and faced her.

"Please tell the court your name and where you work."

"Detective Leslie Hodges. I'm a deputy with the Lee County Sheriff's office."

"I've placed several papers on the table next to you, Detective. Please read them and tell me if you're the same person who completed that report."

Leslie read the report as instructed. "I am," she answered a moment later.

"Is everything in that report true and accurate?"

"It is true and accurate," Leslie said without reading it again.

"Did you personally witness a blue Silverado truck go into The Storage Company?"

"I did not."

"But you did walk into the front office of The Storage Company and ask if a blue Silverado had come in. Did you not?"

"I did."

"If you hadn't seen the Silverado drive in then what made you ask about it?"

Leslie, in as few words as she could manage, explained her thought process as to possible explanations for the quick disappearances of what she characterized as the get-away vehicles from several crime scenes. "I then stopped by all the storage locations along the route the Silverado was known to have traveled. I asked the attendant at each location if they had seen a blue Silverado pull in within the last hour. When one of them said yes, I requested a warrant."

"No more questions for this witness."

"Defense counsel," Judge Smyth said, "the witness is all yours."

"Thank you, your honor. Detective Hodges how long have you been a detective?"

"A few months."

"Were you working this case alone or with a partner?"

"Alone."

"Isn't that unusual?"

"I'm new. I don't know what is customary."

"Surely you know you should have been assigned a partner."

"I don't know that."

"So exactly who is your supervisor?"

"Sergeant Hudson Oakmore."

"Is he here in this courtroom today?"

"No."

"Then there is no way to corroborate your testimony, is there?"

"Objection!" The prosecutor was on her feet. "This question is…"

"Overruled," the judge announced. "We have no jury. I am perfectly capable of determining who's lying and who's not. Continue Mr. Defense Attorney. I'm curious to learn where you are going with this line of questioning."

"Detective Hodges, you're a rookie. A raw rookie. Green as they come. You work unsupervised on what you want this court to believe is a major criminal investigation and you just happen to drive into the one storage location where a blue Silverado is parked and the clerk just happens to tell you he saw a blue Silverado park in a unit."

"Objection. Not a question."

"Sustained. Ask a question counselor."

"Did you have occasion to listen to my client on his cell phone?"

"No."

"Did you in any way obtain GPS information from the blue Silverado before the warrant was issued?"

"I did not."

"Can anyone corroborate those last two answers?"

"No."

"Did you tell anyone at all before you canvassed the storage units about your plan?"

"Yes."

"Who."

"My supervisor."

Defense counsel consulted his notes. "That would be Sergeant Oakmore if I'm not mistaken."

"Yes."

"But he's not here to corroborate your story, is he?"

"No."

"Your honor," defense counsel said, turning to face the judge, "I move to have the search warrant suppressed."

"Motion denied. Any more from this witness?"

"Nothing today, Your Honor."

"Detective Hodges, you're excused. Thank you for your time."

"Welcome to my world," Smith said, following Leslie out of the courtroom. "I caught just the end of that. Defense has no case. His client's going away for ten years minimum. His only hope is to suppress that warrant. It's solid. Don't worry."

"Thanks. I felt like...like crap up there. What the hell's all this corroboration shit about?"

"Cops are known to lie. He was testing the judge more than you. Some judges have anti-cop bias. Most don't. He was probing."

"What the hell did you mean when you said sorry 'bout the McDermitt case?"

Smith's dark face grew even darker. "I'm sorry. I didn't..."

"Out with it, Allen! What do you know I don't?"

"Rumors. You'd think busy as we are we'd have no time for office gossip. Truth is, nothing happens in Lee County that someone in the prosecutor's office doesn't immediately know. Just how it is."

"You're stalling. What happened?"

"Don't shoot the messenger. Daryl Fischer now runs the McDermitt case."

"Why haven't I been told?"

"One possible guess. You're following the court's rule and your phone's off."

Leslie dug her cell out of her bag and turned it back on. Sure enough, there was a message from Fischer.

5:30 MY OFFICE — PROMPT.

Leslie's call to Fischer went straight to voice mail. It was 4:36. Getting to Fish's office on time was tight — at best. So much for a rookie heading up a homicide investigation.

After the grilling she just received over a straight-forward search warrant, she didn't relish getting back on the horse and taking the heat over a homicide indictment. And not to be overlooked, she was going in concentric circles and not getting any closer to meaningful answers. She tried to convince herself Fischer taking over was for the best. In that endeavor, she failed miserably.

EIGHTEEN

BY THE TIME LESLIE MADE her way back to headquarters and to Senior Detective Daryl Fischer's office, in reality a double wide cubicle with higher glass partitions, she was five minutes late and beyond boiling. A pressure cooker with its relief valve blocked kind of steaming.

To the outside world it appeared as if her wheels were spinning. Perhaps they were. She still had leads to chase, facts to dig out, timelines to put together. She could feel the circles were narrowing. The last thing in the world she needed was to trail behind Fischer, who, according to academy scuttlebutt, was a known poacher of almost solved cases. He was credited with clearing more homicides than anyone.

"Let's get something straight right off, rookie," Fischer barked the instant she appeared at his desk. "I say five-thirty, I mean five-thirty. You gonna be late, you let me know."

"Traffic was..."

"That's why God gave you a siren! Use it or lose it! Good thing your files are so complete. I'll hand you that much. Never seen such detail before an arrest. Tell me about your conversation with Blair."

Leslie swallowed hard. All the things she had planned to say, to put him in his place, to establish herself as her own woman were better left unsaid — at least for now. Probably forever. She told Fischer about her lunch conversation as well as her conversation the previous day with Jayne Nikolson. Then she suddenly remembered her 9 p.m. meeting with Nikolson at the museum to hear what was recorded on the display cylinder and added that to her oral report.

"Busy day, I'll hand that to you. Let's be clear about one thing, Detective. You go nowhere without me from this point on. Got it?"

"Got it."

"And talk to no one without first clearing with me."

"Mind telling me what the hell happened. Hud asked me to work the homicide. Didn't assign me to you, except to serve the warrant. I screw up or something?"

"Something," he answered checking his watch. "Ask him yourself. We're due in the old man's office in five."

Oakmore pointed in the direction of a round table in the corner of his office piled with papers and files. "Close the door, would you." He pulled out a chair, removed several files, set them on the floor in the corner and sat. "Those two seats should be empty. If not, just toss the files on the table. Stale matters. Now that we have young blood it's given me motivation to sort them."

Leslie was certain the stale files were about to leave his office under her arm. Leave the murder investigation to the pros like Fish and go solve ten-year-old missing person cases. Not exactly what she had hoped to be doing.

"What the hell you tramp in, Hodges?" Oakmore began when the three of them were sitting. "Smell's made it all the way up to Boot's office. Captain's involved. That means I'm involved."

Instinctively, Leslie looked down at her feet.

"Mayor shit a brick. Claims you're harassing the Edison Museum over something that never happened. I know about the surveillance tape of the break-in. I thought it showed nothing went missing. No insurance claims been filed, no police report was filed. Nothing. Yet, you keep asking questions."

"Is that why I'm off the case?"

"Who the hell said anything about you being off any case?"

"I thought because…"

"Because I asked Fish to provide cover for a rookie doesn't mean you're off the case. Look, someone murdered the old woman. We know that much. We also know someone took her keys, and a few hours later those keys were used in an unauthorized entry to the museum — and to her house I now note. Mayor can scream all he wants, but we have a homicide to investigate. Captain doesn't want you run over by City Hall first time out of the box. Won't be a pretty sight. And it's not just the politicians that'll eat you up. You're working a death penalty felony. Lawyers who handle capital trials are a special breed of cat. They'll slice through you faster than the proverbial hot knife through butter. Trust me on this."

If there was one thing Leslie had learned from her many years in law enforcement, it was that when someone higher up in command said, "trust me", that was the last thing you should do. In Oakmore's defense, Leslie had already had a bitter taste of how lawyers treated novices. And that was over something as simple as a search warrant. She could only imagine the scrutiny she'd receive at a capital trial. Maybe they were doing her a favor. Just maybe.

"Unless you have questions, you two are free to go. The sooner you get to the bottom of this the better as far as I'm concerned."

On the way back to Fish's office Leslie's cell signaled an incoming text message from Jayne Nikolson.

"What do you make of this? You know I told you about meeting Nikolson tonight to listen to the cylinder on the museum exhibit and to see if I can locate the one missing from Scotty's house. Well, here it is six-forty-five and she has a family emergency and can't make it."

"Call her and reschedule."

A moment later, Leslie said, "No answer. Tried texting and it says not delivered."

"It'll wait till morning."

"Who the hell knows what they'll do with that exhibit between now and then."

"It's all on surveillance video?"

"They've doctored them in the past, what's to stop the same from happening?"

"Able Security is a good firm. We served a warrant on them in this matter. They've got procedures in place to be certain nothing further happens to those museum records. In fact, that's a good place to begin in the morning. Let's expand the warrant to cover from tomorrow morning back to say the first of the year. That'll get us familiar with the comings and goings of the museum. Make it easier to spot something out of the ordinary. You seem to know your way around the courthouse, so handle that. I'll visit Nikolson first thing, see what I can dig out. I want them to know we're not backing off. Call me when you have the warrant, and we'll serve it together."

———

Allen Smith called when Leslie was halfway home. "Catch some dinner? Would have called earlier but got tied up in last minute trial stuff. Just something quick, still have hours ahead of me."

What Leslie wanted was to be left alone to think through everything swirling around her. But instead of blowing him off, she said, "What do you have in mind?"

"Thinking burgers and a beer."

"Where?"

"Fat Katz. Daniels near Treeline."

"Know the place. I'm only a few, five maybe eight, minutes away."

"Take me about ten. Save a seat. Any of the craft beers'll do. See ya."

"Before you go, any thoughts on what I tell the judge so I can get a warrant extension? The video's been doctored."

"Homicide, same as before. Add in the fact about the video being doctored. That makes Able an accessory to a crime. Let the judge know you've asked to see an exhibit at the museum and been given the run-around. That museum is a public space, so to speak. As warrants go, this should be a no brainer."

"Hey, there," Allen called, noticing Leslie's half empty glass as he came through the door. "I wasn't all that late, was I?" Business was brisk, considering only fifty percent of the tables could be used.

"More to do with the day I've had than your time estimation skills."

"Okay, so it was closer to fifteen than ten. You still stewing over that punk lawyer?"

"That was the best part of my day."

Smith lifted his glass. "Here's to a miserable day — for the both of us. Tomorrow'll be better."

"I'll gladly drink to that," Leslie said, taking another healthy swallow. "It'll only be better 'cause it's Saturday."

Allen took a long swig. "Let's order, get ourselves another round, then you can tell me about your day."

"Only if you tell me about yours."

"We'll be closing this joint we do that. But short version'll work."

"You first."

"Guy faked his death so his wife could collect insurance. Went out on a boat and never came back. The boat was found floating in the Gulf, no one aboard."

"So, who're you prosecuting? The guy?"

"Wife. Took a while, but insurance paid off. Two million deposited into her account."

"I take it the husband's not dead."

"Not by a long shot."

"Why's the wife on trial? Shouldn't the husband be?"

"Can't find the guy. Turns out, they were in it together. When she finally got the money, she refused to share. Told him to file suit. She was thinking civil. He went criminal on her. Apparently, he taped her planning the thing. Even took video of himself leaving the rental boat out in the Gulf and getting into a blowup dingy."

"Sounds like a fun case."

"It is. But the defense attorney's a bear. Won't concede an inch. Tell me about your day."

"Who handled it from our office?"

"Guy named Jackson."

"Don't know him."

"He's been reassigned. Fischer's taken over his cases."

Hearing Fischer's name sent her stomach into knots for reasons she didn't understand. She was still on the case and after her miserable experience earlier that day, she should have welcomed someone running interference. Yet...yet she somehow felt diminished. As if she had failed.

"I know part of your day. Good news. Judge wasn't buying any of the BS that lawyer threw at you in court. You held your own. Seen a lot worse. I've asked to have the case assigned to me. We'll see how that goes."

Leslie, uncharacteristically, told Allen about the runaround she'd been getting from the museum for what she considered simple questions. She then detailed her lunch meeting with William Blair and while doing so she realized the source of her agitation was misplaced. She confessed to Allen that it wasn't the injection of Fish into the investigation that had her agitated. It was Blair, or Nikolson, running to the mayor a second time, apparently trying to derail the investigation. "Perhaps," she mused, thinking aloud as she went, "it wasn't Blair at all? Could the mayor himself have involvement with the museum? Or with the missing phonograph?"

"Hold up a moment, Leslie," Allen instructed, his hand in the air, palm open. "I wouldn't be adding the mayor's name to any investigative list until you have good and sufficient reason. Once a political name goes in the file the ramifications can be enormous. I wouldn't share your thoughts along that vein, even with your new partner. I can promise you one thing. Mayor catches wind of an investigation into him and you're toast. Burnt toast at that.

NINETEEN

LESLIE HAD THE WEEKEND OFF and puttered around her house, cleaning, doing laundry, food shopping, all in a funk she couldn't exactly identify. On Sunday she called Allen to see if he would join her in a picnic and a stroll on the beach.

No answer. She left a message asking him to call back. While waiting, she retrieved a 1000-piece puzzle, dumped the jumbled pieces onto the dining room table, and began sorting the edges, tossing the center pieces back into its bag. Working puzzles, hour after hour, was how Leslie had managed her grief over losing Junior. This was a new puzzle and one she had not worked before. The picture was of straight, crisscrossing, black and white lines rated as having a high degree of difficulty. Just what she needed to focus her mind away from the job.

Hours passed. An entire corner was filled in when she realized Allen had not returned her call. And no response to her text message.

She pushed back from the table, grabbed her keys and drove over to Sanibel Island and spent three hours, her shoes off, the water rolling over her feet as she walked. The funk was long gone when she climbed back in her car. 'Water magic' her mother called it. The magic still worked.

Leslie was ready for a new week.

———■———

"All rise," the deep-voiced bailiff called as the door at the side of the courtroom flew open and a tall, slender, silver-haired, black-robed man strode through, pulling up his mask as he approached his chair. "The Honorable

Harold Stymington presiding. Court is now in session. All those having business, draw near."

Punctual, Leslie noted for future reference. The next hour was set aside for warrants and emergency motions with warrants going first, presumably because they were faster. Leslie knew that to obtain a search warrant she had to show probable cause to believe that elements of a crime or evidence of criminal activity are likely to be found at the location specified in the warrant. She had once asked Junior what constituted probable cause. His answer still rang in her head. "It's akin to pornography, Leslie. The judge knows it when he sees it!"

The procedure for hearing and granting search warrants had changed years ago, now almost all being done digitally. Communication with the detective, if required, was by phone or video. But Stymington steadfastly refused to, in his words "lose contact with reality. That will come soon enough!" He even refused to hear the sensitive motions in his chambers, preferring a closed courtroom. He did, however, allow in lawyers whose matters were scheduled in the next hour. For sensitive matters where leaks could be devastating, he reluctantly adjourned to chambers, otherwise the courtroom. God help anyone caught leaking warrant information. His wrath was legendary.

Sitting behind a stack of files at a table directly in front of the judge's podium was the woman who had started in the prosecutor's office the same day as Allen. ASA Julie, if Leslie remembered correctly. She represented the state and was, in essence, Leslie's lawyer. If this went sideways, it was Julie's neck on the line. Leslie had filed the paperwork on-line at eight that morning and if Julie hadn't agreed the matter would not have been listed. All the same, Leslie could only hope, in Allen's words, Stymington "knew it when he saw it."

The matter of Sarah McDermitt, Leslie's case, was third on the docket.

The court clerk announced, "In the matter of Crayson. Is the state ready to proceed?"

"The state is," Julie said, jumping to her feet. "ASA Julie Heverson for the State of Florida. Your Honor, if it pleases the Court, we are asking for a two-week extension of the existing warrant. As you can see, the subject did make contact with..."

"Counselor. I've read the paperwork. Here's my problem. This warrant includes an existing wiretap that has been on for over a month. You know I have no jurisdiction over that. It belongs in State court. But I will say this. All you have is one contact with the target, nothing of importance said. You'll need a better reason to extend."

"May I answer?" A voice from the audience asked.

"Please come forward and give your name to the stenographer."

"I'm Detective Byner. Spelled B-Y-N-E-R, of Fort Myers."

"Okay, detective, I won't have you sworn in but be mindful of your obligation to the court. What is it I should know?"

"Only that we have other evidence the heist is scheduled in two days. The subject is the transfer point. Now that we know they've made contact it's only a matter of time."

"Two days you say. Okay. You have a week for the warrant. As I said, the wiretap's not my concern. Frankly, I think you're fishing. Prove me wrong. Next matter."

"In the matter of Welsley v. Welsley. State ready?"

Julie again stood, only not as quickly as before. "We are, Your Honor." This time instead of Julie presenting the matter she motioned to a middle-aged man whom Leslie recognized from her prior life. "If the Court pleases, I wish to introduce Detective Wilber Craighton. He's with the Sarasota County Sheriff's office."

Leslie hadn't yet learned all the protocols, but she was pretty certain courtesy would dictate Craighton informing Lee County he was working a case down here.

Her bosses knew she was in court today and could have asked her to lend a hand. Either they didn't want her involved or — or he was poaching without notice.

Craighton, not a slender man when she had met him in Tampa, had gained at least fifteen pounds and perhaps even more in the four intervening years. His checkered sport jacket gapped open in front a good three inches. His tie lay on top of his ample belly as he slowly made his way forward. "Your Honor," he puffed, "I'm Detective Craighton, Sarasota County."

"And what brings you to our fair neighborhood, Detective?"

"We've been working a drug case up and down the coast and there's reason to believe drugs are being unloaded right here on your gorgeous river." Craighton lowered his voice and stepped even closer. "We need a warrant to search the Last Tap House and Grill."

"What's your basis for believing you will find illegal drugs at the Tap House, Detective. This is most unusual. No local representation."

"Wiretap information, Your Honor."

"Tap of what? When? What was said? Do you have a copy of the wiretap order?"

"All confidential, Your Honor. Sorry."

"Let me understand this. You think you can just waltz in here and pick up a warrant and roust a law-abiding local restaurant owner without providing me access to your sources. You call that probable cause? That might work up there in Sarasota, but down here it won't fly." The sound of his gavel hitting the desk reverberated off the back wall. "Next case."

Leslie's case being next, she didn't know if she should remain seated or approach the bench. Her dilemma was solved when Julie nodded for her to come forward. Craighton looked her up and down as they passed, his eyes not revealing whether or not he remembered her. His jaw moved under his mask, but nothing was said.

"In the matter of Sarah McDermitt," the clerk called, not looking away from her computer screen.

"Your Honor," Julie began and stopped when the judge's hand went up.

"I remember this. Edison Museum surveillance video. I had reservations about granting the original warrant, but I now see there's been footage removed. Or shall I say, allegedly removed. My only question is why need we go back to January? A month should be enough I should think."

Julie looked toward Leslie. "Your Honor, I'm Detective Hodges and…"

"Yes, Detective, I remember you. Go ahead."

"Your Honor. We're frankly confused about what Able Security provided us. Someone clearly doctored the video. A woman is dead. Property of hers worth considerable money is missing. The suspected killer used her key to enter the museum shortly after her death. We now have reason to believe the killer, or killers, used a key from her key ring to enter her house and remove that property. As I said, surveillance footage has been doctored. We need to see the whole time frame in question to learn what has been going on in the museum, perhaps even without their knowledge."

"You still haven't told me anything that would convince me to extend back so far."

"I don't know what to say, except, we are trying to find a pattern at the museum. Who comes? Who goes? What do they do there? We believe someone was listening to a phonograph and cut that footage out? Someone may have been taking a photo and cut that out as well? Clearly, the surveillance footage was doctored and it is our hope to go back further than they did to see what was really going on. And one further matter. It would be good if we can find out just who at Able Security did the doctoring. That's why we're asking to review any records pertaining to people who had access to the museum accounts."

"The doctoring convinces me. After all, it's a public space with a low expectation of privacy. Search warrant back to January first for Able Security is approved. Next case."

"Your Honor," Leslie tentatively said, "What about the warrant for allowing us to listen to the phonographs at the museum?"

"Denied. That is a public location. They can't prevent you from being there and looking around. Ask them to play for you whatever you need to hear. They're there to help. Come back if they refuse. Okay, let's move it. Next case."

No gavel, but Stymington looked up, saw Craighton at the back of the courtroom and raising his voice, said, "Detective Craighton, if you would have prepared the way Hodges just did, you'd be on your way to raiding the Tap House. Suggest the two of you team up. She works Lee County, have her show you how we do things down here. You're welcome back when you can demonstrate probable cause for a search warrant."

——●——

"Hey, Hodges," Craighton said when they were both in the hall, "I thought I recognized you up there. Couldn't immediately place you, not with that mask half covering your face. Didn't expect to see you down here."

Leslie slowed her pace, allowing the wheezing detective to catch up. "Sorry to be in such a hurry but my partner's waiting to serve this."

"There's always time to say hello. Last I saw you, you were with the Tampa department."

"Moved down here about a year ago."

"Oh, hell, yes! Oh, shit, that's right. Sorry about your husband. Now I recall. I'm sorry."

"Appreciate that. Now I…"

"How 'bout I take the judge's advice? Work with you on this? He always that ornery?"

"Need to call my boss. Sergeant Oakmore. Got to run now." Leslie increased her pace, leaving the laboring detective in her wake.

———◆———

Jack Silver called while Leslie was driving over to Able Security. "You sent me a photo of the underside of Edison Two. Your note said it was taken inside the museum. That's correct. It matches our file. The recording cylinder that goes with it should be the second one, Cylinder Two. The recording on it is Edison reciting Mary Had a Little Lamb without distortion. Is that what you found?"

"Haven't yet listened to it. Going to do that soon."

"Let me know what you find, but I can tell you for a certainty that since Great Southern has that piece insured, Stratis will not touch it."

"Thank you, Mr. Silver," Leslie said as upbeat as she could. "I'll call back when I can talk further. I have an appointment to keep and I have just enough time to stop at the museum and check the cylinder."

———◆———

Leslie entered the building flashing her shield at the first docent she saw, a well-dressed woman Leslie pegged as being in her late seventies. The woman's badge proclaimed her name as Marge. She wore a small gray mask that barely covered the end of her nose. Marge balked and looked to the office for help when Leslie inquired if she had a key to the phonograph display. When no help came to her rescue Marge reluctantly walked Leslie back to the display stand where Edison Two proudly stood inside its custom-made acrylic housing.

"Now just what is it you want me to do here?" the docent asked, stalling in the hope she'd be rescued by someone in authority. But the main office remained empty, the light out, the door closed.

"Play it. I would like to hear what's recorded on the cylinder."

"Suppose there's no harm in that. We sometimes do it for VIPs for fund raising." She produced her alarm key, inserted it in the lock, opened the display case and gently slid a lever to the side.

Edison's tinny voice began reciting Mary Had a Little Lamb just as Silver had predicted. The sound not as full as Leslie had imagined, but perfectly clear with no trace of scratchiness. Without a doubt the museum was still in possession of Cylinder Two — or a replica of Cylinder Two.

"Thank you very much, Marge. That's all for now."

———◆———

Leslie pulled up behind Fish who was parked directly in front of Able Security, his police business sign prominently displayed on the dashboard. That wasn't Leslie's style, but she didn't recall a line on the expense voucher form denoted as Parking Fees, so paying for parking didn't appear to be encouraged.

"How'd your conversation with Nikolson go?" Leslie asked Fischer as he stepped from his car. "I was just there, and the office was dark."

"Apparently, she had some sort of an emergency. Something to do with her mother. I think she's in the hospital."

Leslie hadn't been around the senior detective all that much, so his nuances were not yet second nature to her. But his skepticism came through loud and clear. "You're not buying it."

"I'm not."

"Because?"

"Because of the way you were told. A text message from her cell. Not a phone call. That's the same way the secretary had been informed. She showed me the text message. Identical to yours. Doesn't feel right. Checked the airlines. No one named Jayne Nikolson flew anywhere last night, or this morning for that matter."

"Could have driven."

"Possible. But unless it's close by, I'd think flying would be the way to go in an emergency? But, hey, in this business, strange things occur all the time. The real trick is to sort the naturally strange from the criminally strange."

"Your take on the museum? Natural or criminal?"

"Too early to tell. We'll keep poking." Then he added, "I'd say closer to criminal than natural."

"I'm with you. I'm calling it criminal," Hodges said.

"Be careful with conclusions and opinions. Colors your thinking in ways you don't realize. You can get yourself so far down a rabbit hole you can't claw your way back. Happens. Let's serve this warrant, spend the rest of the day studying video."

They entered Able Security, found the same receptionist as before and went through the same drill, only this time they essentially had two warrants. One for the surveillance video back to New Year's Day and the other for company records pertaining to employees who could have accessed the files. The surveillance video warrant, as before, was processed smoothly. When it was time for the woman to call for a tech to come help, Leslie said, "How about Alice Tyson. She helped us the last time."

"I'm sorry. Alice is no longer employed by us."

"Since when?"

"Two days ago. She quit."

Fischer leaned forward and placed his hand over her keyboard. "Move your chair over there away from the computer."

"But..."

"Do it now!"

The frightened woman pushed her chair to the back wall. "We have procedures for this. This is not..."

"See this warrant? It's for company records. Where are those records?"

"Depends upon...depends what records."

"Who had access to what files when?"

"Second floor."

"Where on the second floor? Who has control of those records?"

"Comptroller."

"Name?"

"Gina."

"Gina what?"

"Gina Napoli."

"And she's on the second floor? She in today?"

"Yes."

"Leslie, wait here. I'll let you know when I secure the files. Then go ahead with the techie and get the video. Meet me on two."

Fischer dug in his pocket. "Here's a couple of thumb drives, you'll need them."

"Thanks. I brought my own drives this time. See you on two."

Before Fischer left, he leaned close to Hodges and whispered, "Keep her away from her phone. We have the warrant, but that won't stop their lawyers from mixing it up with us and who knows what happens from then on? First Nikolson goes walkabout, now Fireplug. Could still be nothing, but hackles are up. Be alert."

While Leslie waited for the okay from Fischer, a guy wearing thick lensed glasses and sporting a ragged haircut came through the door from the tech side of the building, adjusting his mask as he walked

"Hi, my name's Kurt Watkins," he announced. "I understand you need help with copying certain surveillance video." He glanced over at the receptionist, her chair against the wall, eyes frozen in fright. "Keren, you alright? What's going…"

"I'm…I'm okay. But…but…"

"I've asked her to not use her computer for now." Leslie said. "We'll wait here a few more minutes."

"And who are…"

Leslie flashed her badge. "Detective Hodges. Lee County Sheriff's Office. Have a search warrant for a few videos."

"I can't…can't do it until Keren gets an authorization for me," Kurt said, his face turning red, his eyes focusing on the corridor he just come from. It was obvious he was contemplating his chances of escaping from whatever mess he had managed to get into.

"Don't even think about it, Kurt," Leslie calmly said. "In a moment Keren here will get you the authorization and then you and I will go back and copy the files. By the way, have you any idea why Alice left?"

"Fired."

"She tell you that?"

"Boss did. It's no big secret. Called her. No answer."

"Boss's name?"

"Russo."

"That Alice's boss also?"

"Yeah."

"Russo. Is that a first or last name?"

"Millie Russo. We both work for her."

A text from Fischer popped up. RECORDS SECURE.

"Okay, Keren. How about you come back to your desk and sign whatever it is you have to sign so Kurt here can get us the video files we came for?"

Reluctantly, Keren did as she was instructed. Within a half-hour Leslie was at the door of Comptroller Napoli's spacious office. The well-tailored woman was sitting ramrod straight in a side-chair, her eyes on fire. Detective Fischer sat at her desk snapping photos of page after page of what appeared to be time logs.

"Detective Hodges," Fischer called when Leslie hesitated, "please do join us. I want you to meet Gina Napoli, she's controller of Able Security Systems. Ms. Napoli, this is my partner, Leslie Hodges. With the cooperation of your surveillance technicians we have just downloaded a copy of the museum footage back to the first of the year."

"Pleased to meet you," Leslie said to the rigid woman opposite her.

"Wish I could say the same," came the curt reply. "Now please finish your business and get off the premises."

"Doing my best, ma'am," Fischer replied, taking his time with the files. "I note from the pictures over there on your credenza you are, or were, involved with the Edison Museum."

"You have a warrant to search our records, not to ask questions. Now finish up and get out of my life. I have a luncheon today in less than an hour."

"You're free to go anytime you wish. We'll close the door behind us."

"Not on your life! I don't trust you any further than I can throw you."

"Now, now," Fischer said, his eyes again focused on the open pages in front of him. "You're taking this way too personal. I'm asking myself if there's a reason for that?"

"How about I come to your house and go through your things? See how personal that feels."

"You're certainly welcome whenever you feel the need," Fischer responded, refusing to be pressured by the controller.

Leslie reluctantly admired her partner for his low-key baiting of Madam Stiffback. Junior often repeated stories of people under stress making incriminating statements they later regretted.

Leslie studied the pictures Fischer had referenced and there Napoli was holding a glass of wine as if giving a toast. A magnificent diamond pendant perched atop her amply exposed cleavage. Standing next to her was William Packard Blair looking very much at home in his expensive tuxedo with red and green tie and matching cummerbund. Off to the side stood Jayne Nikolson, also holding a topped-up wine glass. Sarah "Scotty" McDermitt was next to Jayne, her wine glass mostly empty.

TWENTY

THE VOLUME OF INFORMATION OBTAINED from the security company was so large that the tech guy Watkins had burned several DVDs which had all been uploaded into the Lee County digital forensics database. Fischer spent the next several hours analyzing the data obtained from Comptroller Napoli's files. Leslie busied herself watching hour after boring hour of surveillance video, running the footage backward in time on a day-by-day basis. She would begin each day at midnight and view forward twenty-four hours.

Following that convention, she dialed in midnight last night and settled in front of her computer screen. No movement for seven minutes. Then William Blair appeared from the office, walked to the alarm panel, inserted his key and turned it. He then proceeded out through the front door. Working late Leslie noted.

Nothing further moved on the video, allowing Leslie to fast forward until she saw movement. The front door opened at 08:58. Blair reentered the museum, walked to the security panel, inserted and turned his key all in one smooth motion. He then turned the lights on and disappeared into his office. At 09:15 two women, one of whom she identified as Marge, arrived and went directly to the office, quickly coming back out. At 10:00, the other docent opened the doors to the outside and several people, including two families with young children, came in. Blair came out of the office at 10:12, closed and locked the door and then left the building through the front door. Leslie watched as the docents mingled with the visitors, but mostly remained to themselves except for answering what Leslie believed were questions from guests. At

10:43 Fischer walked through the front door, headed to the secretarial station, had a brief conversation and then retraced his steps. Then at 11:10 she saw herself enter, speak to docent Marge, and then both were standing in front of Edison Two while the docent unlocked the display case. The surveillance camera angle was such that she could see exactly what lever Marge manipulated. Leslie watched herself leave the museum at 11:27. The video ended at 12:45, which was the time she and Fischer left Able Security. Other than a note to herself to watch her posture and to pick up some new work shirts, she noted nothing unusual.

One day down and about two hundred forty more to go, she told herself.

Leslie settled back in her chair, made a few notes in the file and brought up the previous midnight. Same drill all night. Fast forward until movement at the front door at 08:35. This time it was CEO Nikolson coming in and walking straight to the security box, then into her office. At 09:15 the same docents Leslie saw previously arrived and proceeded to the office. A few minutes later the three women came out, each holding a Styrofoam cup of what probably was coffee.

People began coming in at 10:01 and the day repeated as before with people coming and going. Tour groups formed, some lead by Nikolson, some by one or the other of the docents. At 17:30 the last of the visitors was gone, but the docents remained. They and Nikolson left by the front door but did not set the alarm.

A man Leslie did not recognize came in at 18:05 trailed by several people carrying covered trays. They all went to work setting up a serving area, complete with a bar.

Blair appeared at 18:40, going directly to his office without speaking to anyone. A few moments later the two docents returned, followed almost immediately by a group of men and women dressed as if they had just come from nearby offices. Leslie guessed them to be professionals, perhaps bankers, lawyers, accountants. Some wore masks, Others did not. The only person she recognized was Comptroller Gina Napoli wearing a charcoal gray skirt, a white blouse with crisscrossing panels and a darker gray vest. Several people immediately surrounded her causing her to retrieve a paper mask from her handbag and secure it over her ears.

Leslie paused the video to check her notes and to think a moment. This would have been the time, around seven, when Nikolson said she had a private party to attend. That was also when she had sent the text about a sick mother. Blair must have been covering for her. Restarting the video, Leslie watched as the docents divided the folks into tour groups and answered what appeared to be endless questions, the subjects of which Leslie could only guess.

Hors d'oeuvres were passed around and wine glasses continuously filled. Just before nine, Blair came out of the office and walked up onto a small platform at the side of the room. Folks turned to him as he began to speak. When he finished, people clapped politely and accepted envelopes from the docents. Blair disappeared back into his office while the patrons mingled around a table where the envelopes were being collected. Fifteen minutes later the last guest was gone.

The next three hours showed the caterer packing up and leaving, the cleanup crew dusting the exhibits, sweeping the floor, emptying the trash, moving tables back into their proper position. The last of the crew went out through the front door at 11:44. At midnight the video ended.

No one had yet armed the alarm. That made sense because Blair had performed that task seven minutes later according to Leslie's notes from the first video she had watched.

The remainder of Leslie's day was consumed watching the repetitive video surveillance footage going back day by day in twenty-four-hour chunks. The only good news was that the museum was essentially closed from mid-July back to March 15th allowing her to speed through this period, pausing only for sporadic movement associated with maintenance and cleaning. She was about to bring up February 1st when Fischer appeared beside her.

"Anything exciting?" he asked, pulling up a chair.

"Only that Nikolson didn't show up for the private party. I think it was some sort of a fundraiser. Blair covered for her."

"Oh, it was a fundraiser all right."

"How do you know that?"

Fischer produced his cell phone, pulled up his photo file and scrolled through several images. He turned the screen to face her.

"That's the ledger you were examining back at Able Security," Leslie exclaimed. "Ten thousand to Edison M. dated the night before. Am I reading that right?"

"Most definitely."

"But that's outside the scope of the warrant."

"Guess my camera took too broad a view," he said with a straight face. "Guess also that's why it won't be in evidence."

That's not what Leslie wanted to hear. Small steps close to the line, she knew, easily led to much larger steps over the line. "Napoli was at the museum, but only for a few minutes. A patron I suppose. Nothing inherently wrong with that, is there?"

"Not on the surface, no. We'll see what develops. Seems Alice Tyson earned a five-thousand-dollar bonus. Records show her still employed, but on leave. How about following that up. Address is in the file. Have you seen McDermitt on the tape?"

"Not yet. No."

"Something's going on over there and I'd be surprised if it didn't pertain to McDermitt. Watch for her. She should be there almost every day. Would be easy to miss her doing something as she moves around. Pay particular attention to distractions. She knows about the camera so she could take advantage of some kid falling down, crying, you name it. The security folks wouldn't notice her doing something. Same for Nikolson and Blair for that matter."

"I'm on it."

"Fresh eyes, Leslie. Knock off for the day. There's only so much video you can look at without missing critical stuff."

"I agree with that. Any more on Nikolson?"

"That's my first to do in the morning. I'm taking my own advice. Have a good one."

Leslie sat for several minutes after Fischer left contemplating what he had said about McDermitt and how to watch for her. Then she took his advice and knocked off early.

Forty minutes later she turned into her driveway and a car pulled in behind her. Realizing it was the same vehicle she had noticed several miles back, a white Ford Escort, she placed her weapon on her lap.

The driver in the Escort sat still making no move toward her. Leslie had been a cop long enough to know it was better to confront a stalker on your timing, not his. On three, she told herself.

One.

Two.

She flew out of the car, her Beretta level in her hand.

Halfway to the Escort, the driver door popped open and a large man unfolded himself from behind the wheel and slowly made his way onto the driveway, his hands in the air where she could see them. His face was in shadow, but from his size and profile Leslie knew immediately who it was. What she had no way of knowing was why he was following her. Or what he wanted.

TWENTY-ONE

DETECTIVE CRAIGHTON! WHY THE HELL'RE you following me?"

"I come in peace," he said, his hands remaining in the air. "Let's get inside. Don't need this called in."

Leslie knew it was bad form to invite a stalker into her home. But in this case Craighton was a sworn police officer and if he had intentions of harming her those intentions would already have been carried out. Holstering her weapon, she stepped backward, motioning Craighton to pass in front of her. He waited to the side while she unlocked the front door and then preceded her inside.

"This better be good," Leslie snapped the instant the door closed. "Been a long day and I've work to do."

"All work and no..."

"I'm in no frickin mood to play games! Get to the point of this stalking or get the hell out of here!"

"Why such hostility?" the big man asked, sweat dripping from his forehead and around his eyes. "I told you, I come in peace."

"I checked and you're not welcome around here. I can do a pretty good job of it myself without help.

"Can we sit? I need to get a load off my feet."

"How long's this gonna take? You're infringing on my time as it is."

"Trust me on this. It's business all the way. Business just might prove beneficial to you — as well as me."

Reluctantly, Leslie pointed across the room to a side chair. She flopped on the sofa, thought about offering a drink and declined. "Go for it. And this better be good."

"The reason I came into Lee without notice is, as you rightly found out, I'm not welcome here. Truth be told, I brought this on myself. I promise if you work with me, you'll earn brownie points, but you'll have to finesse a bit. I'll lay out for you what happened, warts and all, and what I need from you. Mind getting me some water?"

"Be right back." Leslie went off to the kitchen, filled two glasses from the refrigerator tap, and handed one to Craighton. "Better be good, all's I can say."

Craighton drank half a glass, placed it on a thin coaster, then went on to explain how his problem went back over ten years when a then young Detective Oakmore, now Leslie's boss, was working a serial homicide investigation up in Sarasota. "To tell the truth" Craighton confessed, "the man was a hotshot even back then. He went by the book and properly checked in. His investigation had already uncovered two, possibly three, bodies in Lee County, but Oakmore had tracked the perp to Sarasota. I was assigned to work with him. The take-down was set for five in the morning."

"Sounds okay so far. Need more water?"

"I'm okay. Here's the thing. I realized that this same perp was good for several homicides in Sarasota as well. My commanding officer wanted credit for a solved homicide, so he and I went in early."

"Oh, shit!" Leslie exclaimed, "I recall Junior telling me about that."

"Bet it wasn't none too nice. Well, the end result was we shot the perp in the head. DOA." Craighton downed what remained of the water.

"That's what I recall. Oakmore must've been pissed."

"Pissed is the nicest word for it. With that hair-trigger temper of his I thought he'd shoot my head off. I'll say this for Oakmore," Craighton added, "he's one fine detective. Up until I screwed it up he played it by the book, piece by piece. We had the perp dead to rights. Would have made a great murder trial."

"Why you telling me all this? Need to confess, go find a priest. Better yet, man up and tell Oakmore directly."

"You think I haven't tried? When the shit hit the fan, my captain hung me out. Oakmore got reamed a new one by his management and needless to say he still won't take my calls."

"Still don't know why you're here. If for one minute you think I can intercede, then..."

"I've tried all that. Man's deaf to it."

"Look..."

"I told you, this'll be good for your career. All I'm asking is for you to put eyes on the Last Tap House. Fifty keys of fentanyl's being dropped off between three and five a.m. Street value; in excess of fifty million."

"The court today asked you how you knew. You said wiretap, but couldn't, or wouldn't, provide details. You know as well as I that I'll have to divulge my reason for being there. If that tap's illegal, I'll go down in flames. Can't afford to go that route. Sorry."

"First off, you have my word the tap's legit. Second..."

"Didn't you just explain how your word down here's not worth a shit?"

"And second, forget the tap. The captain of the trawler tipped me off. The drugs are in four frozen shrimp boxes, green check mark on the side. Part of a larger shipment."

"Why'd he tell you?"

"Owes me a big one. Look, it's all above board. No pun intended."

"I should believe you when no one in Lee'll even take your calls? Can't think of a dumber ass thing I could do. I bet you have a cop buddy over in Fort Myers. Why the hell can't the two of you just happen to be on the dock when the boat comes in? He can arrest them. When Lee jumps your ass just say you tried to tell them, and they wouldn't listen."

"I can't be anywhere near the takedown. I'm a known entity and they'll tie it right back to the Sarasota operation in a heartbeat. They'll figure it came from a wiretap and that'll blow everything we've worked sixteen months on."

"You said the tap's legal. Why worry 'bout that?"

"Tap's lot larger than this. Goes way up the line. Going to bring down a lot of folks, some pretty high up in our own government. Tap's too important to blow on a couple hundred pounds of fentanyl."

"You got this all wired — at least in your mind. Lay it out for me. In terms even a rookie can understand."

"Hodges, you may be a rookie by the calendar, but you're no rookie. Junior'd be proud of you. Here's what I have in mind. You'll be on the dock fishing with your boyfriend when the shipment comes in."

"They'll buy that?"

"That's the easy part."

"And the hard part?"

"You can't go alone. You need a boyfriend. My sources tell me you're working with Fish. He's one of the good guys down here. Another guy with a temper. He explodes and it passes. We've worked a case or two on the quiet over the years."

"So why not go directly to Fish?"

"He's tight with your boss. As I said, he and I've done a bit of moonlighting. What Hud doesn't know won't hurt him. Fish'll support you if you tell him you have a good source."

"I'll have to give you up."

"Here's where the finesse comes in. Tell him to meet you somewhere close to the Tap House and you'll fill him in. That way, when you two make the arrest Fish can explain he didn't know the source until too late to run it up the pole."

"What makes you think Fish will jump out of bed in the middle of the night and join me in a witch hunt?"

"Where the hell you think I got your name from?"

"Fish!" Leslie exclaimed, confused. "I thought it was because we bumped into one another in the court room!"

"That was most fortuitous. After getting beat up by the judge, I called Fish and together we conjured up this little plan."

"What do you get out of it?"

"Based on your arrest and confiscation of the drugs two beneficial facts will emerge. First, I'll be able to obtain the search warrant for the restaurant and that'll effectively remove a major drop off point."

"And second?"

"Second, they've a big obligation to meet with those drugs. Confiscating that shipment'll force the bad guys into a major move. That means the top guy will get involved. We'll be ready for them. Win, win."

Nothing about this sounded right to Leslie. If Fish was already involved she had to call him. Perhaps that was why he had suggested knocking off early. "Okay. I'll take it from here. Get out. Let me get to work."

Craighton's taillights were still visible from Leslie's front window when Fish answered the phone on the first ring.

"I just had a visit..."

"Say nothing else," Fish instructed. "Meet me at the Edison Museum at 2:00 a.m. and we'll go from there."

"Museum?"

"Convenient to the dock's all."

Fish was waiting for Leslie when she pulled into the museum lot at 1:50, lights off. She pulled beside him, driver side to driver side, window rolled down. "Good morning," she called across the divide. "Hope you weren't waiting long."

"This promises to be a long day. Meet me at the base of the Cape Coral Bridge. I'm thinking of leaving both our cars there and walking over to the Tap House. Special Ops are already in position one minute out. Set up for channel six."

"Got it. See you in a few minutes."

Two people out fishing. That was the plan. That meant no Kevlar vests, helmets or visible weapons. They were easy targets for shoreside guards overseeing the operation.

"Be alert," Fish said when they came out from behind the bridge abutment, each of them carrying a fishing pole, "for anyone paying attention to us. Craighton says they've been surveilling this operation in this manner a while now with no problems. No reason to believe tonight will be an exception."

"There's a two-hour window," Leslie reminded him. "That's a lot of time for us to kill. If they have a lookout we're made."

"That's what fishing's designed for. Killing time. Two lovers hanging out on a dock fishing. Not so unusual." Fish produced a flask, assuring Leslie it only contained water. "In fact, we may not be the only folks out there. We'll have to clear them out."

Neither of them noticed anything troubling on the way to the pier. As luck would have it, no other fishermen were out there when they took up positions near the far end of the pier shortly after three.

The Last Tap House and Grill was on their right as they looked back at the parking lot, lights out, wooden shutters closed over the windows. The wooden structure hadn't experienced a coat of paint in many years. If Leslie didn't know better, no one would blame her for assuming the place had been abandoned by its owner.

"What the hell I do if a fish bites?" Leslie asked, shortly after lowering her line into the water. "Father never took me fishing. Wasn't Junior's thing either."

"That's obvious from the way you're holding the rod." Fischer readjusted the pole in her hand. "Try it this way. We're not tying on hooks, so unless a fish jumps on the dock you have nothing to worry about. Here, take a swig. Pretend its strong, so go light."

Leslie took a short drink, confirmed it was water, then another. Fish meanwhile reeled in his line, expertly recasting it far out into the dark river.

Time seemed to stop. A few fishing boats made their way slowly down the river, the ripples from their wake fanning out gracefully.

"What do you know about something called the Seminal Society?" Leslie asked her partner, uncomfortable with not entering into the file what Stratis had told her.

"Can't say as I know much. Heard something about a society. Billionaires if I recall right. Something to do with science, new stuff. Firsts, I believe they call them. These guys spend their lives chasing after these Firsts. Money doesn't seem to be an object. Why?"

"A source I'm working, a guy named Silver, he was..."

"Great Southern. That's in the file. Took you up to Pittsburgh."

"Same one. Introduced me to another guy. One of the billionaire collectors. This so-called Society believes Edison shares the same soul with several brilliant scientists, like Isaac Newton and da Vinci. When one of them dies his soul takes up residence in a new body."

"I heard something along those lines. Give you all the names to go with those...those soulmates?

"Edison. Then before him a guy I never heard of, name of Ernst Chladni then..."

"Chladni?" Confusion appeared on Fischer's face.

"German physicist. Said to be the father of acoustics. Before Chladni there was Isaac Newton. Before that Galileo. Then da Vinci and back to a guy who wrote songs for the king. Guy by the name of Wolkenstein."

"What's all that got to do with McDermitt? You thinking there's some kind of connection between the stolen phonograph and...and Leonardo da Vinci?"

"That missing phonograph is a First from Edison and extremely valuable. I believe it's now in the hands of a Society member. I also believe the original recorded cylinder from that phonograph has gone missing."

"You think the Society is after that cylinder as well?"

"Don't know who's after it. But here's the thing. According to Silver, the important contributions, the Firsts if you will, of the soulmates, as you called them, are worth premiums to the seminal collectors. Billionaires as you correctly point out. And when big money is involved, we both know life has a way of going sideways."

Before they could explore the topic further their attention was diverted by the sound of a diesel engine slowly making its way from the Gulf of Mexico up the Caloosahatchee River. "Show time," Fischer said. "If there's ever going to be surveillance on us now would be the time." He again handed Leslie the flask from which she took a quick swig. "Cast your line out and concentrate on reeling something in. Keep your head down, think about the great fish you're about to haul up."

Five minutes later a fishing trawler broke out of the mist in mid river and began a slow arc toward the far side of the dock on which they were standing. Leslie, keeping her eyes focused on her line, keyed her mic with her forearm and said, "Trawler four minutes out."

In her ear she heard the acknowledgment. She also heard a door open behind her. The only door she had seen was one leading into the restaurant. So far, so good.

Then voices, three of them, were heard coming from the vicinity of the now open door. Leslie snuck a peek and confirmed three men lined up on the pier apparently waiting for the trawler to dock.

Slowly, the vessel crept forward, several gulls trailing behind. Leslie was busy winding line onto her reel when the bow of the trawler quietly slid by the end of the dock, no more than ten feet from where she stood. The big boat came to a stop leaving the stern jutting out into the river a good twenty feet, screeching birds circling overhead.

A line from the trawler landed with a thud not far from her feet and she looked up in time to see a man on deck motion for her to wrap it around a piling. She laid down her fishing rod and took a step toward the filthy nylon rope. Before she reached it one of the men standing on the dock picked it up and quickly made it fast.

A man wearing a white shirt appeared on deck, as did five others, all wearing blue. Within minutes wooden crates were being lined up near the side of the boat and being passed from the crew to the men on the dock. In almost no time, a neat pile of shrimp crates were neatly stacked across from the restaurant door.

Leslie reclaimed her fishing rod and again cast her line into the river. She began to slowly reel it in. Fischer did the same. Neither in a hurry.

Leslie became aware of one of the men approaching. He was still ten feet away when she nudged Fischer with her elbow, keeping her head facing the river.

At five feet Fischer nudged her back. It was time to take action.

The man was less than three feet from them when the ship's captain called, "That's the load. Get it into the freezer and call it a night. Hey, you over there, release that stern line."

The man stopped, looked up, realized he was being summoned by the captain and took a step sideways to untie the docking line.

His task finished; the man turned back to the fishing couple. "Catch anything?" he asked.

"Been here a couple hours and nothing," Fish yelled back. "Going to knock off in a few minutes and call it a night." Turning to Leslie, he said, "Had enough fun for the night, honey?"

"You promised we'd catch something. Let's stay."

"Whatever you want, dear."

"Good luck," the man said, turning his attention back to the shrimp crates piled on the dock.

Leslie leaned closer to Fish. "That pile of four over there have green checks as advertised."

"Go for it."

Leslie then said into her radio, "Ready. Crates are about to be moved inside. Three men. The four crates closest to us are marked with green checks. Those are the ones we want. One minute. Then Go."

Leslie noted the time as 04:42.

"What do we do with the fishing gear?" she asked Fish.

"Leave it. I'll buy the kids new stuff." He pulled two pairs of protective eye shields from his pocket, handing one to her.

"Oh, shit! Forgot mine!"

"Stop talking and follow the countdown. Here's some ear plugs. Push them way in. On one, drop to your knees the way you were trained."

Leslie studied her phone. At precisely 04:43 she began, "Five…four…three…two…one…" Down they both went. The glasses protected their eyes from the brilliant flash, but nothing protected either of them from the violent air turbulence caused by the stun grenade the tactical team employed. Had they been standing, one or both of them would have been launched into the Caloosahatchee.

Leslie ripped her glasses off with her left hand, her Berretta now in her right. Glancing to her left she confirmed Fish was up and with her. In truth, there was no real need to hurry.

The only people moving on the dock were the black clad tactical team. Everyone else was lying flat, their arms stretched over their heads.

TWENTY-TWO

LESLIE STOOD AT THE BACK of the crowd when Boots, whom Sheriff Jamison Radcliff would soon introduce to the press as Captain Karen Stetson, walked into to the County Office Building. Her dress uniform was nicely pressed, her hat under her arm, her back perfectly straight. "Nice work, Hodges," she whispered, "made national TV. How you managed it I don't know. Perhaps it's best that way." She then continued toward the podium where the Sheriff stood in full dress uniform.

The presser had been set for eleven and it was already 11:15. Sound checks were complete, cameras ready, the reporters clamoring among themselves trying to ferret out what their competitors had. Rumors had been circulating for hours of a major drug bust on the river involving the Last Tap House and Grill, but nothing had been confirmed. Reports of an explosion were making the rounds. One TV station went live with a reporter, microphone in hand, standing in front of a pier, breathlessly reporting a major explosion and fire. Great scoop except for the fact the young man was several miles north of the Tap House at a long-abandoned dock.

Leslie was startled when a voice on her right said, "Exactly forty-five kilos. Nice work."

It was Craighton wearing the same rumpled sport jacket and slacks as the previous night. "No arrests. That's good. Would'a been a dead end anyway. Those guys know nothing. Bet I get my warrant now."

"That's where Fish is now. Up in Smyth's court."

"He's doing the honors with the judge but agreed to allow me to tag along for the execution. Just wanted to watch the show down here. Love it how these politicians run toward a microphone. You did the heavy lifting; they get all the credit. Just love it."

"Hope they don't ask me to say anything," Leslie confessed. "That's not my thing."

"Don't go worrying your sweet little head over that. Not a chance in hell they'll share the spotlight with a worker bee. Just be happy if Boots acknowledges your part. Doesn't always happen that way."

"She has. At least to me. Woman's been great to work for."

"So far. What's it been, three, four months."

"Four."

"And you're working a homicide?"

"How in the hell do you..."

"That's what detectives do. Got my sources all over the state. As you will in due course. Got me thinking when you mentioned in court you wanted a warrant for the Edison. A few months back we had an incident with the Ringling Circus Museum. I suppose you know about the Firsts Club. Collectors pay big bucks for artifacts first in their class."

"I've heard that, yes. What was taken?"

"Substituted. The replacement was so good the experts were fooled. Museum dropped the complaint, said nothing was taken."

"What was purported missing?"

"Not purported, you ask me. Actually gone. I can't prove it cause the insurance adjuster says nothing's missing. Original stilts."

"Stilts?" Leslie questioned, thinking back to her pleasant day with Allen visiting the circus museum. "They can't be new with Ringling."

"Learned more than I ever wanted to know. Sixth century goat herders used them to watch over their flocks. These had springs. Maybe pogo stick is a better term. Neat the way..."

"If I can have your attention, please," A booming female voice called out from the podium. "If you'll all please settle, I'd like to introduce Mayor...."

"Come on," Craighton said into Leslie's ear. "Let's get out of here. We can do more good getting that warrant." He hurried out of the briefing room with Leslie at his heels. On the elevator, Craighton said, "I was thinking about the Ringling heist — or non-heist as the case may be — and I agree it's a case of the Firsts. Just as the McDermitt robbery. Wouldn't be a bit surprised if those objects were sold to the same buyer. Values are not even close though. Your phonograph is an Edison First. That puts it in the sights of the seminal collectors, and makes it..."

"You know about the Seminal Society!"

"Sure as hell do. Single soul back to the fourteenth century. Some say back to Moses himself. Don't think I buy all that, but there may be something to this single soul theory. I've been giving it a lot of thought. There may actually be dual paths."

"Like more than one chain."

"Something like that. When I was investigating the missing stilts, before the insurance company had me stand down, I made a list of what I called Firsts. They may not have been the actual first pieces, but they were from the Seminal chain."

"And?" Craighton had captured Leslie's full attention.

"Have you heard the story of Edison's last breath?"

"What are you talking about?"

"It's reported that when Thomas Edison was on his death bed, his good friend, Henry Ford, requested his last breath be collected in a test tube. The idea being that Ford, who had curious beliefs, thought the soul passed with the last breath. A test tube believed to contain Edison's last breath is on display at the Ford Museum up in Dearborn, Michigan."

"Why in the hell would someone like Ford collect Edison's last breath. And how would you know it was going to be his last breath anyway?"

"Take off your detective hat and accept the story for what it is. A story."

"Go ahead. I'll be quiet."

"One theory holds that Ford wanted Edison's last breath because that's where he thought the soul resides. If he had the soul, he could resurrect the genius. Another theory is that Ford was a Seminal Society believer and to him Edison's soul was the very essence of everything Ford held dear. Perhaps he was hoping to direct the sacred soul to the next recipient. Perhaps he was trying to keep it for himself."

"I'll suspend judgment on those theories — for now."

"Here's one based in fact. A da Vinci is housed at the National Gallery of Art in Washington, D.C. It's an oil-on-wood portrait of Ginevra de' Benci, a 15ᵗʰ-century Florentine aristocrat teenager and is the only painting by Leonardo on public view in the Americas."

"And you're telling me this because?"

"Because several years ago a bidding war took place among the seminal collectors over the de' Benci. Bids were up over five hundred million."

"Was it stolen?"

"Not officially. Still hangs there. Score yourself a ride east and you can see it in all its glory. National Gallery insists to this day the original hasn't been touched."

"Unofficially?"

"Reason to believe a forgery was substituted about seven years back."

"You know that how?"

"'Cause that's when the bidding war suddenly stopped."

"Not conclusive of anything."

"As these things go, as conclusive as you'll ever hear."

TWENTY-THREE

THE NEXT DAY AND A half quickly passed with Leslie running point on the forty-five-kilo fentanyl seizure. Or, as the sheriff's press releases called it, the forty-million-dollar drug bust. No mention was made of the twenty-five kilos found in the Tap House freezer and another twenty or so million lost to the cartels and drug traffickers. This last was by design, as Craighton had laid out for her, to force the big bosses from the supply side to meet personally with the folks who controlled distribution. That's how Craighton and his team planned to roll them up. Keeping it all legal was a logistical challenge, all centering around Leslie. It wasn't likely anyone from the Tap House would go public demanding the return of illegal fentanyl. Not making arrests meant there was no need for arraignments, bail hearings, posturing lawyers, or damage control press releases.

Craighton's parting words to her had been, "Remember, Hodges, how fast the brass was to climb up on the podium? That's what brass does. When the shit hits the fan, you'll get your time in the sun, 'cause there won't be a single one of those folks up there with you. You can take that to the bank."

On Friday, Leslie and Fischer, along with their boss, Sergeant Oakmore, and his boss, Captain Karen Stetson, had been invited to lunch with Sheriff Radcliff. Everyone but Oakmore was animated. Oakmore still obviously harboring resentment over Craighton.

The sheriff asked Leslie how she was liking her assignment and inquired as to what she was working on. Leslie outlined the homicide of Scotty McDermitt. "That's the Edison Museum case! Didn't know that was you. Shit!

Mayor got all the hell over me about a search warrant. A warrant for craps sake! What's that about?"

Leslie explained the connection, all the time watching Radcliff's eyes which revealed nothing of value. Not exactly cold, but not encouraging either. When she finished, the Sheriff turned to Stetson. "This young lady might be good for drug busts, but I want a senior detective assigned to the homicide."

"Yes, sir," Stetson immediately responded. "Got that covered. Daryl Fischer's been assigned to the matter. He has case management."

"See to it. Those Edison folks are well connected up in Tallahassee. AG's called wanting to know why the Governor's supporters are being harassed. I get another call like that there'll be hell to pay." Turning his attention to Oakmore, he said, "Son, it's time to move on. Let bygones be bygones. Craighton's made a peace offering, leave it be. In these times, good press is hard to come by. Enjoy it while we can."

"Yes, Sir," Oakmore responded, not appearing to change his attitude.

———————

A while later Leslie was back at her desk, her head down, working. Fish came by and asked, "Don't let the boss get you down. He's a good guy beneath it all. I wouldn't want to be the top guy in a climate like this. Just put your head down and keep at it."

"Been doing it for what seems all my life. They're all the same. You come by for a reason?"

"Where are we on McDermitt?" Fischer sat on the corner of her desk listening while she brought him current.

When Leslie fell silent, he asked, "You satisfied you've extracted everything you can from the video?"

Leslie started to say yes but caught herself. "Something's been nagging me," she confessed. "Don't know exactly what, but I saw something that now seems wrong."

"You have any idea what? What day?"

"Been trying to visualize it. Can't."

"Then we'll do it together. Sometimes it's not what you saw, but what you didn't. Key it up."

The video from midnight until shortly after noon again came up and together they watched as Blair came out of the office, set the alarm and left. Leslie fast-forwarded to the next morning when Blair reentered, disarmed security and walked directly into the office.

The morning repeated itself just as Leslie recalled with Blair leaving the building shortly before Fischer arrived. They watched as she and Docent Marge stood in front of the phonograph display while the docent opened the display case and operated the phonograph. The tape ended a few minutes later.

"What's that sound about? See something?" Fish asked. "I certainly didn't."

Leslie sucked in air when she realized what had been nagging her. "As you said, it's what you don't see that counts. Well, in this case it's just the opposite. It's what I did see!"

"Explain."

"I saw the docent's every move as she operated the phonograph. And you could see above the display case almost to the ceiling."

Fischer was puzzled. "That's what I would have expected. The camera's positioned to capture the most valuable object in the museum."

"That's just it. The surveillance video of the night McDermitt died had a different focus. Sure, it caught the phonograph, but missed anything much above the case."

"Pull it up."

Leslie went back through her notes, found the index numbers, typed several strings into her computer. Within seconds they were back on the early morning of August 23rd watching a tall man come into the museum, proceed to the security panel, then walk over to the phonograph display case. As Leslie had remembered, the upper portion of his body was above the view angle of the camera, unlike the image when the docent had approached that same case.

They watched the display case being opened, the phonograph being lifted, a picture being taken, the lever being pushed, ostensibly so the perp could listen to the recording. Only a portion of the lever was visible and at no time did the perp's face or even the back of his head appear in the video. Totally unlike when the docent had been recorded and her whole body, including her face, was clearly visible.

"Someone's fooled with the camera," Fischer remarked, stating the obvious. "Good news, we have the footage going back to January. A little patience — and a lot of coffee — and we'll know exactly who did it. A step closer to a clearance."

Leslie wanted to correct her partner — and mentor — but thought better of it. Even assuming they ferreted out who changed the camera angle, it was still a far leap to McDermitt's murderer. But it was certainly more than she had two hours ago. Instead she said, "I watched the footage back to the beginning of February and didn't see anything."

Fischer took a long drink of coffee from the Styrofoam cup he had brought from the break room. "We'll watch January and then redo the rest. You've been working backward. How about starting at the beginning and watching it continuously forward. We know the camera was adjusted. Now that we have something to go on, we'll find it."

"Actually, this can be easier than when I did it the first time. I spoke with the lab and they showed me a feature of the review application I didn't know existed. We can set the video on what's called AutoFF. In that mode, the app itself monitors the video for activity of any kind and shows us only the portions that have motion, anomalies as they call them. Ready?"

"Go for it," Fischer said, draining his cup.

Leslie tapped the n key and almost instantly the screen showed 01-02-2020 09:00 when Nikolson arrived. "I can set this on slow fast-forward, and we can do the whole day in fifteen minutes. Let me know if you want me to stop at any point."

Neither of them saw anything unusual and at 18:00 Nikolson left. A few minutes later the screen went blank. Leslie pushed the n key again and the screen displayed 20:40 as the cleaning crew came through the door. Nothing unusual happened while they cleaned and a minute after the door closed behind them the screen again went blank.

Another tap of the n key and the time stamp showed 1-3-2020 08:55. The day repeated, with the only differences being that Blair opened the museum and Scotty arrived at 14:42 and took up her docent duties. The last visitor departed shortly before five, the maintenance folks arrived at 20:10 and finished up exactly at 22:00. The video, however, continued, even though nothing appeared to be moving.

"Whoa," Fischer suddenly said. "What the hell's Scotty doing?"

"Opening the phonograph case. Looks as if she's about to clean it. She's got a dust rag in her hand."

Only Scotty didn't dust the phonograph. Instead, she carefully removed the cylinder and replaced it with one she produced from somewhere out of camera view.

Fischer leaned closer to the screen, as if being close allowed him to see better. "Where the hell'd the new one come from? I didn't see a bag or anything."

"Behind her from the table." Leslie replied, her eyes glued to the screen. "Let's see where she puts the one she took."

Scotty turned; her face now centered in the camera lens. She took a step forward and immediately disappeared from the screen. A moment later she was back in view and closing the display case. The second camera picked her up at the security panel where she switched her water canister from her right hand into her left so that she could retrieve her keys from a jacket pocket and set the alarm. She then unlocked the main door, went out, closing the door behind her.

A moment later the screen went blank.

"I didn't see her take anything with her," Leslie said. "Could she have left the cylinder somewhere in the museum. Perhaps hidden away in an exhibit?"

"Possible, I suppose. But one of the cameras should have caught it. Let's get some lunch. I forgot how tedious this is."

After lunch the two detectives spent the remainder of the day with their eyes glued to the computer screen as February merged into March. When the museum closed because of the COVID-19 lockdown the time frames available for review became shorter and were spaced farther apart. On July 15th, the museum resumed almost normal operations switching over to summer hours. Visitors appeared to be limited and family groups kept together. Nothing unusual was seen by either viewer until finally the application displayed: FINISHED. REVIEW FILE AGAIN?

"We now know Scotty changed the recording cylinder on January 3rd and we didn't see her change it back. We also know the cylinder in there now is correct. Puzzling."

"Should we assume Scotty was replacing the original. Maybe before the first of the year she borrowed the original."

"Could be. That would explain how her son listened to the original with her over New Years. What we just saw was her returning it." Leslie then had a thought. "The software detects motion and captures only those portions where things change."

"That's what we just did. Am I missing something here?"

"This is pretty sophisticated software. I wonder if it could automatically identify missing footage. Like if stuff was erased from the original. Should be easy to do based on time stamps you'd think."

Fischer stood and stretched. "Can't imagine that's not fundamental to the forensics folks."

A moment later they had their answer. It was a simple matter of asking the application to run an integrity check. "Command I, on your Mac," the forensics lab tech said. "Piece of cake. First thing we run."

Leslie pushed Command and I and the screen displayed: DISCONTINUITIES: SUNDAY, 08-16-2020, 19:30 TO 19:40; MONDAY 08-24-2020, 21:10 TO 21:22.

"Two chunks gone from the originals," Leslie commented to Fischer. "Someone over at Able Security is up to their eyeballs in trouble here. We saw the logs. Nothing was noted as missing."

Fischer paced the area, whether thinking or simply stretching wasn't clear. Coming back to Leslie's desk he said, "If there was any doubt before about museum involvement it's gone now. The relationship between them and Able is also now a question. Tell you what. We have two missing persons and possibly a person of interest. In the morning you track down Nikolson and I'll see what I can do with the missing techie, what's her name?"

"Tyson," Leslie responded. "Alice Tyson. Who you have in mind for the person of interest?"

"Comptroller Gina Napoli. She's a museum donor and controls the security video."

"How about adding William Packard Blair to your list."

"Managing Director? What the hell's he got to do with missing time stamps? Nothing's missing from the museum."

Leslie reminded her partner of the video showing him, or someone built like him, photographing and listening to the original Edison recording. She also reminded him the original surveillance disk had been destroyed at his suggestion.

"Or so Nikolson says. Okay, make that two persons of interest. But be careful with Blair's name. He's more the face of the museum than you might think. He's the one in tight with the mayor and the big donors."

"How do you know that?"

"Run him through the social pages, see what you get. Man's well-heeled and very well connected. That's a tiger with teeth. See you tomorrow."

"You working tomorrow? I didn't see your name on the weekend list."

"Between the drug bust, McDermitt and a thousand other things I need to move my bed over here."

Leslie's cell sounded, effectively ending her time for dwelling on Fischer's last comment. Caller ID displayed NIKOLSON.

"This is Detective Hodges."

"Hello, Detective. Jayne Nikolson. Sorry that I had to leave so suddenly. My mother had a bad fall. I need to talk to you. How about my office at eight tomorrow morning?"

"How about now?"

"Not on the phone."

"Where are you? I'll come to you."

"The Villages. Busy with Mom until late. Then I'll be driving home. Eight would work best."

Being a former Tampa cop, The Villages, centrally located between Tampa, Orlando and Gainesville, was well-known to Leslie. She also knew it was a solid three-hour drive and the idea of driving up there tonight didn't sit well. Reluctantly, she replied, "Eight it'll have to be. Drive safe."

TWENTY-FOUR

THE NEXT MORNING, EIGHT O'CLOCK came and went. So did 8:15…as well as 8:30. Leslie continued to check her phone for messages only to find nothing. She accessed the state database for indications of accidents along the Interstate and saw the southbound lanes were closed three miles south of Tampa. Single vehicle fatality at 06:12. Leslie knew the area well and knew that it would be hours before the accident was cleared and the lanes reopened. Entering Jayne Nikolson's name in the Florida vehicle registration database yielded a green 2019 Acura sedan. Leslie cross-checked the Acura with the preliminary accident report, but no vehicle make had been entered. Several calls to Nikolson went directly to voice mail.

At 8:40 she received a message from Fischer.

PLS FOLLOW UP WITH TYSON. CAUGHT A SHOOTING IN LEHIGH ACRES. MORE LATER.

Leslie entered Tyson's name in her computer and retrieved the techie's phone number and address. She transferred the information to her GPS. Before heading out she brought the file up again and noted a new entry from the forensics tech pertaining to the video of the accident scene taken by good Samaritan Chris Wang and the surveillance video from the museum break-in. In the accident scene video, the two unknown people walking up from the wrecked car were labeled Person1 (front) and Person2 (rear). The perp at the museum was known in the report as Person3 (museum).

PERSON1: HEIGHT 6′7″; WEIGHT ~260 LBS; MALE

PERSON2: HEIGHT 5'4"; WEIGHT ~135 LBS; GENDER INCONCLUSIVE

PERSON3: HEIGHT 6'7"; WEIGHT ~260 LBS; MALE

Leslie's take-away: Person1 and Person3 are the same. Not a lot of folks are six foot seven. Should make identification relatively straightforward. So far it hadn't.

At nine, she slipped her car into gear intending to pursue the missing techie. She drove across the parking lot to the entrance and turned south onto McGregor Boulevard. A car suddenly appeared from the north and turned into the driveway as Leslie was turning left, almost clipping her rear bumper. It was a green Acura. Realizing it could be Nickolson, Leslie turned back.

"Oh, I'm glad you're still here," Nikolson said, smiling apologetically then pulling up her mask when Hodges walked into her office a few minutes later. "Thought I missed you. Big accident up by Tampa."

"Have to admit you had me worried there for a while," Leslie replied, trying to calm the agitated woman, "when I didn't hear from you. I saw the accident report. Nasty one. Surprised you got here so soon given the traffic backup."

"I was near the front. Didn't see it, but heard it. They let the close cars through I think to clear out working space for the wrecker. Fatality from what I could see. I tried to call, but my phone's dead. Forgot my charger. Sorry for that—and for skipping out on you. Mom took a nasty fall."

"Sorry to hear that. Is she okay?"

"As well as can be expected. It wasn't as bad as they first thought. Nothing broken. Bad sprain. She tripped over her walker and caught herself. Some therapy. Should be back to herself soon."

"That's always good to hear. You called me."

Nikolson got up, closed the door and took one of the two chairs in front of her desk, motioning Leslie into the other. They were sitting face to face when Nikolson leaned as close as protocol would allow and said, "I don't want anyone getting into trouble, but I have some concerns."

"I can't make promises, but I can listen. Things will fall out as they will. If you didn't do anything wrong, then you'll be fine."

"Oh, it's not me I'm worried about. It's the museum. I love this place. It's…well…it's my life."

"As I said, no promises. I can't see as how anything you do or say will affect the museum. Unless something's been taken you haven't reported."

"Oh, no! Nothing's been taken — that I know of."

"Then what's troubling you?"

"Scotty. To tell the truth."

"What about Scotty."

"I don't know…maybe there's nothing. Anyway, she worked here for many years, perhaps the best we ever had. At least in the time I've been here. Oh, it's hard to think of her as gone now. I relied on her for so very much. Most nights she was the one who remained late and closed up after the janitors. That was especially true for party nights when things went much later. Donor parties are always the worst. Liquor does funny things to folks who otherwise are well behaved. They go around touching exhibits that are off limits. Things like that. She was always so good with those folks. Kept them in line with no complaints."

"What changed?"

"Don't exactly know. But sometime late last year, I'd say early November, she took a fancy to the phonograph. Had Bill teach her how to change cylinders. Then, at the annual large donors Christmas party she went and opened the display case and played the phonograph."

"Do you remember what was played?"

"Of course. The only cylinder we have. The original one with Edison reciting Mary Had a Little Lamb."

"That it?"

"Wish that were all. In late January, I got a call from Able Security informing me Scotty was observed changing the cylinder on the phonograph. Twice, in fact."

"When exactly was that?"

"They notified me, let's see I have it written down." Nikolson went around to the far side of the desk and rummaged through a drawer, gave up and started on a second drawer. "Here it is. December 27th and then again on January 3rd."

"What did you do with that information?"

"Discussed it with Bill Blair and he said he'd take care of it."

"And what did he do?"

"I asked him several weeks later and he seemed like it was no big deal. Said it was taken care of."

"What does that mean?"

"Other than to suggest I not mention it any further, I don't know."

"Did either of you report the exchanged cylinders to the insurance company?"

"Bill said he'd do it."

"Did he?"

"If he did, I have no record of it."

Leslie leaned back as if to end the conversation. But instead of standing she remained seated studying Jayne who seemed to have something more to say. "You've been exceedingly helpful, Ms. Nikolson." Leslie said, her voice encouraging. "Anything further you'd like to add?"

Nikolson took a deep breath, exhaled slowly, then replied, "I have reason to believe one of the technicians from the security company recently serviced our equipment without my knowledge."

"Could Blair have ordered it?"

"Could have, but it's not on the books that I can find."

"Routine maintenance perhaps. Part of a yearly contract?"

"Bill usually schedules their visits. I'm always in the loop. We do it early morning or after visiting hours. I always know ahead of time."

"Not this time?"

"Twice, as a matter of fact. On a Sunday, late, about seven-thirty on the 16th, and then again about three weeks later, Monday, 7th Labor Day, around 9 p.m.

"How do you know this? I assume you weren't working Labor Day."

"The Sunday visit. Our premises patrol made an entry about a service truck in the lot. I saw the truck myself on the seventh. That's the Labor Day night service call. I had an early morning donor meeting Tuesday morning and I forgot to bring the handouts. I stopped by to pick them up."

"Did you see the technician?"

"If you mean, did I recognize the person? The answer is no, I did not."

"But you saw him?"

"A her. Short stubby-looking woman. Shoved a ladder in the back of her van and off she went."

"Did she see you?"

"I waved and she waved back."

"What was she doing here?"

"I have no idea. I was waiting for the invoice to sort this all out."

"Do you know the names of any of the technicians who service your account, or work on your files?"

"Never had the occasion. Sorry, no."

"Anything further I should know?"

"Not that I can think of right now."

Standing, Leslie, out of habit, handed Nikolson her card. "You know how to find me. Don't hesitate. You never know what's important." Noticing the pictures on the wall and remembering the one in Comptroller Napoli's office, Leslie asked, "I suppose you take pictures of the parties you host here. The Christmas parties and such."

"We do, indeed. People love them. They make great thank-you presents."

"Mind if I look at them?"

"Do one better. I have them in albums on my computer. I'll send them to you."

"Without editing or deleting please."

"Exactly as they are on my machine, I assure you."

TWENTY-FIVE

TECHIE ALICE TYSON LIVED ON the second floor of a four-floor walk-up. As Leslie expected, her knock went unanswered as had her several phone calls over the past hour. Time to do what she had done for so much of her time in Tampa, and before that in Gulfport, knock on doors. Four floors, six units per floor. Piece of cake compared to her last canvas of a four-hundred-unit high-rise on Bayshore in Tampa. Except that knocking on strangers' doors in uniform is one thing. Doing so in plain clothes while wearing a mask is another. Leslie didn't know what to expect.

Only one of the six apartments on the second floor answered the knock, a man in his later years, hard of hearing, having trouble walking. Nothing there.

Nothing from the two third floor units who answered. Nothing concrete from the fouth floor where Leslie spoke only to a teenage girl, Abby Washington, home sick from her job at Publix. "Alice is a nice lady, "the kid wheezed. "Great with the computer. Been giving me lessons, teaching me cool stuff."

"Lessons in what?"

"Computer stuff's all. Zoomin' and that."

Leslie wondered about hacking, but that was a problem for another day. "When did you see her or talk to her last?"

"She in trouble?"

"Just want to talk with her. When did you see her last?"

"Don't know. 'bout a week, maybe less."

"Talk to her on the phone?"

"No."

"She give anybody else lessons?"

"Dangle down on one," she said, waving her hand toward the steps. "He's always hanging around her place, playing games and stuff."

"This Dangle. He have a last name? Or is that his last name?"

"Don't know."

"Alice have any friends other than this Dangle?"

"Me. Don't rightly know anyone else."

"She married? Divorced?"

"Never says. I think married a while back. Not sure."

Leslie handed her a card. "Call me if you see her. Tell her to call me. What apartment does this Dangle live in?"

"In the front. 101."

"Remember, call me when you see her."

"She in trouble?"

"Just want to talk. You'll be in trouble if you don't call when you see her."

Unit 101 was the last door Leslie tried on the first floor. Of the five other doors, four were home but three knew nothing. The fourth, a woman in her thirties in the apartment directly below Tyson with a two-year old hanging on her leg, claimed she had heard noise, "maybe a wheeled suitcase a few nights ago." When pressed, the woman, Elizabeth Hayden, didn't recall exactly which night it had been and wasn't certain it had been a suitcase. "Could'a been a chair. I don't know. Just thankful it didn't wake Chris here."

"It was at night, then?" Leslie pressed.

"Yeah. About eight."

"You said you haven't seen her for a week or so. Anyone else might have seen her?"

"Guy in front there," Hayden said, nodding in the direction of apartment 101. "Spent time up with her. Doing what I could only guess."

"By chance was he up there when you heard the… the noise?"

"Could'a been. I might'a heard heavy footsteps."

"Guy in front got a name?"

"Jamaican man. Higgins. Dinkle or something like that. Dinkle Higgins."

"This Higgins. He heavy or what?"

"Not heavy, but he walks solid."

"He work?"

"Keep my nose outta people's business. Better off that way."

"Is he home most of the time?"

"Home more than most, he is."

Leslie handed Hayden a card, asking for a call if she remembered anything further, or if she saw Alice.

It took several hard knocks before the door to apartment 101 opened a crack. Through the small opening Leslie, herself standing five feet seven inches, found herself looking up into the dark eyes of a light-skinned black man with dreadlocks down to his shoulders, who she guessed to be in the six-foot six, six-foot seven, range. "My name's Leslie Hodges," she began, watching the eyes across from her go even darker, "I'm a detective with the Lee..."

"Go away! I've done nothing wrong!"

"I'm not here about you, Mr. Higgins. I have a question about your friend Alice Tyson."

The door, which was already closing, paused. "I don't know..."

"That's not what my notes say." Leslie took a chance, and said, "We have reason to believe Alice is in...in difficulty. This is a wellness check. Making certain she's okay."

"What difficulty?" The door opened wide enough for Dangle's tall thin body to be fully outlined. The opening was also wide enough for him to grab Leslie by the throat if that was his intent.

Instead of stepping back as her training suggested, she held her ground. "Mind if I come in? I assure you this has nothing to do with you personally. It's for Alice's safety."

Dangle didn't move while he thought over his options. Then he slowly began stepping backward.

"Are you alone," Leslie asked, carefully pushing the door fully open.

"See anybody else?"

"Are you alone?"

"Yah, I'm alone."

The apartment was surprisingly clean, orderly and bright. A large flat-screen TV was mounted on one wall with recliner chairs facing it." A desk sat against the far wall, two computers positioned on top, their screens blank. A joy-stick console and a pair of headphones with an attached microphone lay in a black swivel chair off to the side.

"I have extra masks, you want one?"

"Don't believe in them. Take my chances."

"Your choice," Leslie replied, happy to observe his full face as she quizzed him. "You a gamer?"

"Pretty much."

"Good at it?"

"Hold my own. Hey, said this wasn't about me. So, hey, what's goin' down?"

"How about giving me your full name. I have it down here as Dangle Higgins."

"Got it right."

"Dangle. That your given name? Show me your driver license?"

Higgins' body stiffened. "Thought this wasn't about me." His eyes were again dark, his fingers active.

"It's not. Listen to me. This is not about you. I promised you that. I'm thinking now you're undocumented. Look, unless you've done something wrong while in this country, I couldn't care less. Just want your full name for my records. Forget the license, just be straight with me. I know where to find you."

"Dangelo. Called Dangle most my life."

"Okay, Dangle. When'd you last see Alice?"

"Night before last."

"Where?"

"In her apartment."

"Was she still there when you left?"

Dangle's smile disappeared while he contemplated how honest he was going to be with the cop sitting in his living room. The smile returned. "She was leaving on vacation. Helped her down the steps with her bag."

"Know where she was going?"

"Didn't say."

"How long?"

"Didn't say."

"How long you know Alice?"

"Year or so."

"She married?"

"Divorced."

"Any children?"

"Not that she talks about."

"Any pictures?"

"Not that I saw."

"You spend time in her apartment?"

"Some."

"Doing what?"

"This and that."

"May I assume, 'this and that', includes having sex with her."

"Assume what you wish."

"I'm taking your response as a yes."

"Take it for what you want. No law against it."

"Has Alice called or texted you since she…she went on vacation?"

"No."

"Have you called or texted her?"

"No."

"Do you know when she'll be back?"

"No."

"Have a guess?"

"A while."

"Why do you say that?"

"Took almost all her stuff."

"Any thoughts of where I could find her?"

"No."

"She take a taxi? An Uber or what?"

"Her car."

"Make?"

"Honda, Accord."

"Color?"

"Blue."

"When she was packing, did she seem concerned? Or was she happy to be going on vacation?"

"I assume happy for the vacation."

"Why do you say that?"

"Got a large bonus. Said there was more where that come from."

"And that made her happy?"

"I guess."

"What aren't you telling me, Dangle."

"Nothing."

"Listen to me. You have sex with Alice. I assume you care about her. If she's in trouble I can help her. But I need your help. If you care about her now's the time to say something. It might be too late later."

"I have nothing to say."

Leslie stood, pulled out her card and handed it to Dangle, repeating the ritual that went with it knowing full well that most crimes are solved by tips and unexpected calls. She wasn't naïve enough to think it would happen in this case, but there was procedure and one never knew.

Leslie sat in her car pondering what she had learned and debating next steps. She punched in Fischer's number. Answering on the first ring, he said, "Your timing's perfect. Lefty's taken over here and I'm back with you on McDermitt. How're you coming with the techie?"

Fischer listened quietly while Leslie filled him in. When she finished, he said, "Sounds like a runner. Declare Alice Tyson a POI and file a BOLO on her. Then meet me over at Able Security. We'll talk to Comptroller Napoli together. Could be a while before I get there."

"It's Saturday. Napoli might not..."

"I called. She'll be there."

Leslie planned to use the time for lunch but instead received a message from Nikolson indicating the albums had been sent. Thinking about what she might see in the file, Leslie thought back over the many office parties she and Junior had attended over the years. Some were fun. Some got out of hand. Alcohol tended to do that, and it was always the same people who spent the month of January hiding or apologizing, some doing both. For the most part they had been great years for her and Junior, with talk of starting a family always on the horizon. For one reason or another it had always been pushed down the road. Looking back, she was ambivalent about not having a child by Junior.

She found herself parked by the river lost in thought when her phone brought her back to reality.

TEN MINUTES OUT — FISCHER

Leslie arrived at Able Security two minutes ahead of her partner and the two of them walked in together. As promised, the comptroller was waiting.

"What brings you two back? I thought you received all you came for the last time.

Leslie, by pre-agreement, took the lead. "Just a few follow up questions if you don't mind," Leslie began. "Is it..."

"For the record, I do mind. But go ahead, seeing as how you're already camped out in my office."

"Is it a fair assumption on our part that you are a contributor to the Edison Museum?"

"It is."

"Is that for yourself, privately or for the company?"

"I don't see as there's a distinction. For the record, the donations are from the business."

"Who owns Able Security?" Leslie had checked the business records and knew that the company was owned by an LLC named Sling. Who owned Sling was yet a mystery.

"Sling LLC owns Able. Why is that important?"

"Dotting the i's, crossing the t's. Who owns Sling LLC?"

"That's private information."

"I'm certain it's on your business permit. Why's it so secret?"

"I didn't say it was secret. Just private."

"Do you know?"

"Partially."

"Then tell us the part you do know."

"Do I have to answer your questions?"

"No, you don't. But we'll get a warrant for the documents."

"Perhaps that's what you should do then." She stood signaling the meeting was over.

"Not so fast," Leslie said. "Unless you throw us out, which you have every right to do, we have more questions."

"Fire away. You're on a short leash here."

"Why was Alice Tyson given a $5000 bonus?"

"A what?"

"A five K bonus."

"She was given no such thing!"

"You signed the check."

"I did not!"

"She was told to take a vacation."

"She was not! She'll be out there working."

Leslie looked to her partner. Fischer said, "Then call her in here, please. We have a few questions for her as well."

Napoli picked up the desk phone and issued instructions. While they waited questions and answers were exchanged, mostly pertaining to Napoli's support of the museum.

A woman Leslie recognized as the secretary entered the office, handed Napoli a note and briskly retraced her steps.

"Seems as if you are correct. Ms. Tyson appears to be on vacation."

"And you didn't set that up?"

"I most certainly did not."

"Any idea who could have?"

"Not in the least. But I will find out."

"And when you do please let us know," Leslie said, laying her card firmly on the wooden desk. "The sooner the better."

TWENTY-SIX

DARYL FISCHER FOLLOWED LESLIE OUT of Able Security into the high-humidity, about-to-thundershower, afternoon, the kind of day Fort Myers is known for in late August. Pausing before entering his car, he said, "Suppose it's time for me to meet the daughter, Linda Murphy. And didn't I see a note indicating the son was due in town tonight or in the morning. Why don't you get something set up with him as well? How about our offices this time?"

On the way back to headquarters, Leslie arranged a four p.m. meeting with Murphy and then called Jack Silver. She left a message telling him about the changes in camera angles as well as the cylinder substitutions by Scotty. Checking her watch, she realized she had time to get lunch before her meeting with Murphy. On impulse she dialed Allen on the chance he was working the weekend.

Dispensing with customary greetings when he came on the line, she instead asked, "Any chance you breaking away for lunch? I'm in your neighborhood."

"Actually, yes. I can get away for a while. Have a big hearing first thing Monday, but I got things pretty much in order. You have something in mind?"

"Thinking Chinese?" Which was always her favorite.

"I know you like Ginger Bistro. But the rain should hold out a few more hours. How about you pick me up, we go up the river just past the place you made famous — or infamous depending on how you look at it — for lobster rolls? Have ourselves a picnic. Up for it?"

"Feels like rain?"

"That's why they made car roofs."

"I'm game if you are. Don't be thinking in terms of hours, plural. I'm still on the clock."

"McDermitt matter?"

"Eating my lunch! No pun intended. Turning into your parking lot now."

"See you in three."

———◆———

They were within sight of the Tap House sitting along the wharf eating their lobster rolls, wave after wave of ominous dark moisture-laden clouds rolling over them in a seemingly unending parade. Allen finished his lunch, washed it down with water, and without taking his eyes from a small sailboat, its sail almost flat against the water, coming across the river, asked, "Where are you with McDermitt? Making progress or going in circles?"

"By definition we're learning things, so I'd say progress. But it sure feels like circles. Something as simple as interviewing a young woman who serviced the security camera is proving to be a missing persons case of its own."

"Missing?"

"Officially said to be on vacation. Employer says she's on vacation. Neighbor says the same. Nobody knows where she went, or when she's expected back. Cell phone off-line."

"Why's she important?"

"Unscheduled service calls at the museum. Adjusted the camera angle facing the original phonograph so faces would not appear on surveillance audits."

"Could it have been a random accident, the camera wiggling loose?"

"Not likely. Her visits bracket the break-in. Both unscheduled and by a person not authorized to make service calls. Could be a coincidence, but not likely. Now she's gone on vacation. How likely is that?"

"Need a warrant? That one shouldn't be hard. I remind you, coincidences do happen."

"Thanks, I'll let you know." Now it was Leslie's turn to study the sailboat as its bow turned north and its sails came up off the water. "That looks like fun. Ever sail?"

"Never. But I'd love to learn."

Leslie fell silent, wanting to question Allen on why he hadn't answered his phone or returned her texts the previous Sunday, but thought better of it. Some things are better not being known.

"Thinking of the case?" Allen gently asked after several minutes passed in silence.

"Nothing but."

"Want to bounce your thoughts off me? Go for it."

"Certain you want to do this?"

"Try me."

"I don't know if I'm going in circles or what, frankly. Sorting through this has me doubting myself, seeing criminals at every turn. An old lady is asphyxiated in her car and I'm spending my time chasing Edison's original phonographs."

"There's more than one?"

"There were two; not surprisingly called Edison One and Edison Two. Edison One is the machine that produced the very first recording in human history. Some consider that a First. Recorded directly from Edison's mouth onto a foil covered cylinder. It was a scratchy recording, but a recording, nonetheless. A woman assistant by the name of Davis, Sarah Davis, suggested using different calculations for the recording needle. Edison tried the new sizes with a second machine, Edison Two, and the sound was near perfect. Long story short, there are two phonographs and two recorded cylinders. Following so far?"

"Two phonographs and two recordings. Following."

"Edison Two, because it was the first to work so well, and because it's the phonograph Edison himself considered as the first phonograph, is what's on display at the museum."

"And it's still there I assume?"

"So everyone says. Scotty McDermitt has, or I should say, had, the Edison One in her possession before her death. It went missing and I believe sold to a collector around the time of the accident."

"Missing before or after her death?"

"Million-dollar question! I believe after, but I could be wrong. Hence the circles. Compounding the problem, her son claims he listened to three cylinders being played at New Years. The original scratchy cylinder; the near perfect cylinder; and a third cylinder recorded later than the other two."

"I suppose you're about to tell me one or more of these cylinders are missing?"

"You suppose correctly. Cylinder One hasn't been located. And if there really is a third cylinder, it's missing as well. Cylinder Two seems to be in the museum where it belongs. If that's so, which I'm positive it is, why all the break-ins and camera angle changes? And why's the techie gone missing?"

"I'd think Cylinder One was in the stolen phonograph. Could that be the answer?"

"I wish it were that easy. Not there. In fact, the collector offered me five million for it. I'm told forty million would be low. Edison's Firsts are coveted by the seminal collectors I told you about."

"As I recall, they believe there's a link, you may have called it a human spirit, linking Edison back to the fourteenth century. The Seminal Society."

"That's correct. The link goes from Wolkenstein through da Vinci, Galileo, Newton, and Chladni to Edison."

"Sounds like if you find the missing cylinder, you'll find the killer. I can see why your head's spinning. I gotta check out that Seminal Society thing. What did you say, a spirit connecting Edison back generations?"

"Not spirits. Souls. A common soul, to boot. Knock yourself out. Sounds like whack jobs to me, tell the truth."

"Whack jobs with lots of money."

"Billionaires. All with tentacles into everything and everybody." Leslie glanced at her phone, jumped up and said, "Hey, this has been nice, but I gotta go. McDermitt's daughter's due at the office and I have a lot to do before then. Thanks for lunch. Best lobster. This place is a keeper."

"Dinner soon?"

"Soon. But no promises when."

Leslie dropped Allen back at the courthouse and headed directly for her office. On her way she received a message from Silver thanking her for the heads-up about the switched recording cylinders and asking her to confirm that Cylinder Two had been returned.

At 3:30 Leslie pulled into the parking lot in front of her office and recognized Linda Murphy's car. Not that she had a lot of experience in this, but it seemed odd that someone would arrive over a half hour early for a police interview. She hurried to her desk and found a hand-written note.

In interview room 5. Fish

The room log showed the start time to have been less than five minutes earlier. Not a bad plan, Leslie thought. I've had my time with her, now it's Fish's turn. Instead of going directly in, she brought up the conference room on her computer watching as her partner built a relationship putting Linda at ease with his broad smile and easy manner. Leslie noted that empathy seemed to be Fish's trademark with potential suspects. She sent a message indicating she was watching and asking him to signal when he wanted her to join.

Fischer glanced down at his phone, saw her message, nodded. "I see from the file," he continued without interruption, smoothly moving away from generalities, "you spoke to your mother about the original phonograph your mother had in her possession."

"I knew about it. Only vaguely. She said it came from Thomas Edison. Only, I wasn't sure about that. Then she refused to discuss it with me. When my brother and his wife were down here for New Years she played some disks, I think cylinders is the word my brother used, for them."

"And she didn't play them for you?"

"Only the one as I told you. The one my grand-mothers recorded."

"Why was that?"

"Let's just say we had our differences."

"Over what?"

"This and that."

"Specifically?"

"Well, if you must know, she was...shall we say... man crazy."

"I would think liking men is a good thing."

"Not so much at her age."

"She was what? Seventy-six? For some folks, that's not so old."

"Not the way she flaunted it. Not very becoming. It just...well, it just wasn't right."

"Is that the reason you weren't speaking?"

"You'd have to ask her that question. It was she who wouldn't speak to me."

"Unfortunately, I can't do that. I have to ask you. What caused her not to speak to you?"

"Don't know."

"Guess?"

"I called her out for...for her behavior."

"About men?"

"Yes."

"What about her health? She have any problems?"

Leslie studied the daughter's eyes for signs of deception, but the answer came too fast. "Nothing she told me about."

"Was there something you suspected?"

Linda took a long moment answering. "Let's just say I had my suspicions. She seemed to be getting tired fast and she...she just looked to be in pain. I didn't see her often, but she was losing weight."

"I understand she had a dog."

"A lab. I have it now."

"How did you get it?"

"Went over to her house and picked it up."

"When was that?"

"After the police notified me of her death."

"Was that the next morning?"

"I suppose so."

Fischer made a big show of going through his notes, but Leslie knew better. He had a memory similar to hers and if he had to review a file, he could just about do it in his head. Seemingly finding what he was looking for, he said, "I see you were notified at seven in the morning. You recall that?"

"In the morning, yes. Don't know the actual time."

"Deputy log shows she came by your home at 2:12 a.m. with no answer. Then again at 6:58 a.m. Does that seem right to you? Could it have been earlier than seven?"

"Don't think so."

"Says here when you didn't answer the doorbell the first time, the deputy called you."

"My phone was off. I didn't hear the bell."

"Had you been home all night?"

"Yes."

"Alone?"

Linda glared at him across the table, apparently angry at the question.

Realizing the possible sensitivity a single woman would have with this question, Fischer said, "Sorry, but I do need you to answer the question."

"Of course, I was alone," Linda snapped.

"What time did you fall asleep?"

"Why's that important?"

"Just guess. Before midnight? After midnight?"

"Around midnight I suppose."

"Were you sleeping at seven when the doorbell rang?"

"I was. It woke me."

"How long after that was it before you went to get the dog?"

"Later that morning."

"Around when?"

"I'd say eleven. Why's all that important?"

"Just checking the boxes." He again pretended to search through the files, finally looked up and said, "When Detective Hodges went with you to your mother's house, you didn't have a key. Says here she had to call a locksmith. If you didn't have a key, I'm confused as to how you retrieved the dog."

Now it was Linda's turn to take her time, to contemplate her answer. Finally, she replied, "To tell the truth I used the garage door code. I took a chance that the door from the garage into the laundry room was unlocked, which it was. Scotty almost never locks that door and my plan was to force it open if need be to get the dog. I locked it when I left."

Fischer changed the subject. "I understand your brother's coming down. Is it today or tomorrow?"

"In the morning. He's getting her place ready to go on the market. This Miromar Lakes house will sell fast. The community is hot, what with all their lakes, beaches, golfing, tennis, great club house and restaurants. I understand he's had two offers already."

Fischer stood. "Sorry Detective Hodges didn't make it back in time, but thanks for coming in to see us. It's much appreciated. Will you be seeing your brother when he's here?"

"I plan to. Yes."

"Please ask him to call one of us. We'd like to speak with him."

"He's already talked to the other detective on the phone. I don't know what else he can tell you I haven't."

"He spent time with your mother in January. Listened to the phonographs. Her phonograph went missing. I'd like to hear more on that."

"Is that what this's about. The missing phonograph?"

"It's a valuable object. I'd think you'd be very much concerned."

"My mother had every intention of passing it to Roland, her favorite. Why should I be upset as to its whereabouts? Scotty probably squirreled it away somewhere. It'll show up. What I don't get is my mother ran off the road and killed herself and you're concerned about an old phonograph gone missing. What's one thing to do with the other?"

"I'm not certain it does. Are you?"

"Of course not."

Fischer opened the conference room door causing Leslie to flip her computer closed and hurry in the direction of Interview Room Five.

"Oh, Ms. Murphy," she exclaimed in mock surprise, sorry I'm late."

"Oh, you're not late. I was just passing by and thought I'd drop in early."

"Well, I apologize for not being here. Looks like you two are finished. I won't hold you up. Detective Fischer will fill me in. Just stay safe."

"You also, Detective."

"What do you make of the key inconsistency?" Fischer asked when Murphy was out of hearing.

"She told me she didn't have a key to her mother's house. Technically accurate, but she did know how to get in. She didn't mention the garage keypad at all. She certainly never told me about the dog." Leslie was agitated with herself for not realizing Scotty had a dog. She played the scene over in her mind and couldn't remember any signs of a dog. She promised herself to review the house video.

Fischer also was replaying portions of the previous conversation. "Says she locked the inner door. Can't prove it one way or another now."

"And I forgot to cover that door," Leslie apologized, her self-doubts boiling over. "That's on me. Sorry."

"Would'a been a nice piece to have," Fischer respond-ed without much passion in his voice, "but I'm more troubled by her lack of concern for the missing original Edison. She must know it's worth a lot of money. People just don't shrug off fifteen, twenty million that easily. Hell, drop a two-dollar ice cream cone on the floor and see how upset you become. She should be in orbit, yet she's not."

"Hiding something?"

"My sense says yes, but I'll be darned if I know what it is. With the brother arriving in the morning we won't be able to keep the coroner's report private much longer. Things are about to heat up when that happens. Be ready.

"For what?"

"Wish I knew."

"You saying the clock's ticking?"

"Clock's always ticking, Leslie. Sometimes we hear it louder than at other times."

"Next steps?"

"Go find the techie. We need to get to the bottom of the security system and who's behind all that. Doubt if I can lay that at Murphy's doorstep, but you never know. Someone killed the old lady, we know that."

As timing would have it, before Leslie made it back to her desk, her phone rang.

"Dangle, here. Worried something's wrong with Alice. Called, no answer."

"Any idea where she might be?"

"She has a cousin, or an aunt, or something, out on Sanibel. I have a key to her apartment upstairs if that helps."

"See you at your place in twenty minutes," Leslie said, already halfway to her car.

All the lectures on illegal searches flooded her mind as she raced across town to meet Dangle. On the one hand, Alice wasn't exactly a suspect, so would a court exclude anything found pertaining to McDermitt? On the other hand, Alice's good friend was worried and willing to let her in with a key. That made the search borderline legal. Leslie knew these are the problems Allen loved working on. Well, better him than her.

"Hey, Allen," she said a few minutes later when her friend answered, "remember what I told you earlier about that techie? Name's Alice Tyson. Here's the facts. Do I need a warrant?"

After Leslie laid it out, Allen said, "Most likely not. Better to err on the side of being safe. Look, I'm here in the courthouse. Weekend Judge's in her chambers a few feet down the hall. Give me Tyson's address and I'll put the request on her desk. Looking for a missing person always plays well. Just don't toss the place. Remember, you're looking for a person, not stuff. I'll text when I have it."

"Within fifteen?"

"Hopefully within five."

Nine minutes later Leslie's phone screen read:

GOOD TO GO. GOOD LUCK.

Alice Tyson's apartment was non-descript, except that instead of one computer she had four, one with a screen measuring at least twenty-seven inches. Padded earphones were lying on every horizontal surface, along with joysticks, keypads of every size and various pieces of equipment Leslie could not identify. Dangle preferred to remain in the doorway seemingly frightened by what he might find inside, even after Leslie called 'all clear'.

"Anything look odd or missing to you?" She asked after determining for herself she saw nothing.

"This the way it always looks. I thought I heard something, but I suppose I didn't. One thing though...she never goes anywhere without her portable game computer. That's the smaller one over there."

"She only have the one?" Leslie asked, leaving nothing to chance.

"Can only use one at a time. Those puppies are expensive. Only the one."

"You have the address or name of her cousin, or whatever, over on Sanibel?"

"Alice kept an old-fashioned address book. Said it was the best backup ever."

"Look if you will."

Dangle pulled the drawer open. "It's here," he called out.

"Cousin in there?"

Dangle thumbed quickly through the book, found what he was looking for, and held it out.

Marcy Tyson, with an address on Sanibel Island. Leslie took photos of all the pages and had Dangle return the book to the drawer.

Her phone rang. It was Allen.

"Any luck?" Allen asked. "Find what you went looking for?"

"Didn't find Alice, if that's what you're asking. But have a lead. Hey, you interested in going with me to Sanibel. Kill two birds."

"Which two birds might that be?"

"Find Alice. You and I have dinner."

"Mixing business with pleasure. What could possibly go wrong?"

"Is that a no?"

"That's a yes," Smith answered, "a most definite yes."

TWENTY-SEVEN

THE CAUSEWAY TO SANIBEL ISLAND was surprisingly empty considering it was late afternoon on a weekend. "You know," Allen said from the passenger seat, "a guy could easily become accustomed to a good-looking woman driving him around. First lunch, now dinner. What more can a man ask for?"

"Keep talking that way and they'll be dredging your body out of the bay."

"Just stating a fact."

Smiling, Leslie quipped, "Some facts are better left unstated. Didn't they teach you that in law school?"

"Really, now? Can't a guy ever tell a gal what he thinks about her? How would you ever know I find you attractive if I didn't tell you?"

"You accepted lunch, didn't you? And dinner?"

"Maybe I'm a freeloader type."

"I'd be a hell of a stupid detective if I didn't know the difference. Cut me slack. You a water person?"

"If you mean by that do I enjoy being on or near the water? Then the answer is definitely yes. I don't know about you, but my spirits lift every time I cross this causeway. Water all around."

"Why do you suppose that is?" Leslie asked, realizing she also felt better when surrounded by water.

"For me, it's the mental vision of faraway places accessible by boat. Just cut the lines and you're free to go anywhere in the world. North to the Arctic, south around Cape Horn, perhaps a short cut through the Panama Canal."

"Those are big adventures. I'm more focused on close-by hidden and isolated places. Private beaches and coves where the world leaves you alone."

"For a person who wants to be left to herself you sure chose the wrong profession. The way I see it, you go out of your way to stick yourself in the middle of people's messes. You see people at their worst."

"That should explain why I dream of being away from it all. I look at what I do as making life better, cleaning up our human surroundings, making the world a better place."

"How's that working out?"

"Ask me that in five years. Right now, it's all new and exciting—and truthfully, frustrating."

"Talk about frustrating. Think about spending months preparing a case against a drug dealer caught with his kitchen oven filled with fentanyl pills having a street value in the millions."

"You can thank some detective for wrapping it up so neat for you."

"Until this afternoon when it turns out the search warrant was obtained based on wiretap info for which no warrant had been issued. Judge tossed the oven evidence and the defendant is already back selling. Says he has to make up for lost time."

"One of ours?"

"Not Lee County if that's what you mean. It's public record, you can find it. By the way, did you find anything useful in Alice's apartment?"

"Thanks for the warrant. A few names and addresses on Sanibel. Cousin, or aunt. But her friend, a guy by the name of Dangle Higgins, is worried about her. Said she was nervous for several days. He knew that because she's either playing interactive computer games or reading. She's an avid sci fi fan as well as a world class gamer. He claims she can't sit for long without doing one or the other. Says she didn't take her gaming computer."

"I take it we're heading to the cousin's place."

"Or aunt. Dangle wasn't certain. It's on Casa Ybel Road, to the left off Periwinkle."

"Isn't everything?"

"Okay," Leslie said a few minutes later when her GPS instructed to turn left at the next street. "About a quarter mile ahead."

Neither of them saw anything other than trees and vegetation on either side of the road. Leslie slowed as much as the light traffic would allow and continued until the GPS announced their destination as being on the right. She pulled off the roadway and proceeded slowly until a driveway appeared framed on either side by trees. Whatever house sat on this lot was positioned a distance from the roadway. A moment later a three-story set of attached row houses came into view. Six individual homes in all, each with a garage underneath. From Leslie's experience she guessed the living rooms and kitchens would be on the second floor with bedrooms up on the third. A laundry, and possibly a bedroom or office on the ground level.

Leslie turned to Allen. "Probably best if you remain in the car. Or take a walk around if you like. Shouldn't be but a few minutes."

He nodded his consent. "I'll poke around over there," he said, pointing to a small patch of sand. Won't be far."

Leslie was back at the car within minutes, her face indicating failure.

"So?" Allen asked, joining her. "Why the frown?"

"Woman I'm looking for, name's Marcy Tyson, I'm guessing its Alice's aunt, moved out months ago. The couple that lives here now thinks she moved to Key West, but they're not sure. I'll have the office search the records, see if anything comes up. But, that's Monday's problem."

"Plan now?"

"Dinner. I'm thinking Traders Cafe."

"Love that place," Allen replied. "Perfect."

On the drive over to Traders Leslie exclaimed, "Just had an idea. Mind if we stop at Gene's Books? Alice is a gamer and a reader. She didn't take her gaming computer, so the bookstore is a good place to begin. Shouldn't take but a few minutes."

"Famous last words. Okay, go for it."

Leslie was correct about one thing. It took less than a minute for the manager to study Alice's photo on Leslie's phone. "I know her," the woman said, helpfully, "comes in when she's on the island. Into Sci Fi. I'm right now holding a book for her. Called last week, said she'll come by."

"Know where she stays?"

"With her aunt. Marcy, I believe her name is."

"Know anything about Marcy moving?"

"Haven't heard."

"Call me please if either of them come in." Leslie handed the woman her card. "It's important I speak with Alice. Please call."

"I take it you didn't have any luck." Smith said when Leslie was again behind the wheel.

"I'm that transparent?"

"You are when you'd rather telegraph your thoughts than express them. I sure as hell wouldn't want to play poker with you. That's for darn sure."

"Okay, so what's your favorite Traders dinner?"

"Love their Pompano."

"Had lobster for lunch."

"Get it while the gettin's good. Can't eat too much of a good thing, the way I see it."

"So, Pompano it'll be," Leslie said, concentrating more on her case than on her dinner.

"They have great oysters," Allen said, trying to break through.

"Sounds good."

"If you'd rather go get a drive-through chicken sandwich over at Wendy's and call it a night, I'm game for that as well."

"What brought that on?"

"You're still working. What's troubling you?"

"Sorry. Promise to drop it for the night."

"Easier to say than do. I know. Get that way myself far too often. 'You're livin' in the future,' my Momma always said. 'Come join us folks in the present. Be great to have you.' And you know what? She was right, of course."

Leslie studied the man across the seat from her, seeing him, really seeing him, perhaps for the first time. "Allen," she said, "you're absolutely right. I promise to join you in the present. Sorry."

The restaurant was properly social distanced and because of that seemed mostly empty. They sat away from the few other diners in a back corner enjoying their oysters. Leslie had, as promised, pushed McDermitt to the back of her mind. Allen told her funny — and some not so funny — law school stories. She found herself laughing, deeply laughing, for the first time since Junior's death.

Walking out to the car she felt lighter than she had since leaving Tampa. And happy for the first time. They were walking hand in hand when her cell buzzed. It was an effort to unclasp her hand to answer it. In fact, had it not been for Fischer's name popping up she would have allowed it to go to voice mail.

"I see you're over on Sanibel," Fischer began. "Business or pleasure?"

Leslie was tempted to ask what business that was of his. But it was his business. She was driving a Lee County vehicle and her every movement was logged. "A little of each, frankly."

"Tyson's aunt moved. Records folks were gone when that came in. We'll trace her in the morning. The photos you took of her address book showed an entry, MR on Turtle Road. On a hunch I ran a property search and found a Millie Russo over on Turtle."

"Name's familiar but..."

"Millie Russo is Fireplug's boss. It's not the address she has listed with Able Security, so it might be a rental."

"It's late. You want me to make contact tonight?"

"If that doesn't mess with your plans too much."

"Just a lawyer friend."

"That guy Smith? Guy who processed the Tyson search warrant?"

"One and the same."

"Thank him for me. Night."

Leslie turned to face Allen. "Sorry about that. I'll say this: Fish might be a pain in the ass, but he's good at what he does. Guy doesn't miss a thing."

"He's a prosecutor's dream. Cases all neat and tidy, wrapped tight with a bow on top. Conviction rate is highest in the State of Florida. He want you to do something?"

"I can't hide anything from you, can I? As a matter of fact, yes. Tyson's boss, woman named Millie Russo, has a rental home over here, up on Turtle Road."

"Who am I to stand in the way of a criminal investigation? Go for it."

Leslie set the GPS and six minutes later they turned left off Turtle Road onto the driveway of a small house, again partially hidden from the road by trees.

"Hopefully, this won't take long," Leslie said as she opened the car door.

"I've nowhere to go. I'll sit here and go through my email."

The woman who answered was in her late sixties. When pressed she told Leslie her name was Marcy Tyson.

"I'm looking for your niece Alice. I have reason to believe she's here with you?"

"Haven't seen her."

"I told you I'm a detective with the Lee County Sheriff's office."

The woman's feet set hard and her fists clenched. "That still don't make it your business who's visiting me. Git and leave me be."

"I have a few questions for Alice. She's not in any trouble. I just need to ask her a few questions about her job."

"You got a warrant or anything?"

"Do I need one?"

"You want to search my place you do."

"Tell you what. Have Alice step outside and we'll talk out here. I need to see that she's okay. A missing person report's been filed."

"Now who did that?"

"Her friend. A man named Dangle." Leslie lied. She cringed thinking of what Allen had said about Fischer playing it straight.

"I know Dangle. He think she missing?"

"He's worried about her."

"Stay here. I'm not saying she's here or nothing."

The woman shuffled off, pushing the door closed behind her. Leslie heard two female voices but couldn't make out what was being said.

Suddenly, the door flew open and Fireplug stepped out. "What are you doing bothering me? I'm on vacation."

Continuing the guise of a wellness check, Leslie said, "Just being certain you're okay."

"Of course, I'm okay. Why wouldn't I be?"

"Your employer didn't know you were on vacation."

"My employer? You mean Millie?"

"Who's Millie?" Leslie asked, playing it close.

"My supervisor. Millie. She gave me a large bonus and told me to take a nice vacation. Who told you I wasn't on vacation?"

"Comptroller Napoli."

"What the hell does that hag know about me?"

"Obviously, she was wrong."

"Obviously. Now you know I'm okay you can go."

"You went into the museum at least twice to adjust the camera angle. Is that correct?"

"I didn't do anything wrong."

"That's not my question. We have you on video going in on," Leslie consulted her cell phone, not because she needed to, but to make it appear more official, "Sunday, August 16th, you moved the camera angle down. And on," Leslie again glanced at her cell, "Labor Day you went back in to return the camera to its original angle. Do you recall this? Or do you need the exact times of your visits as well?"

"I did nothing wrong. They were service calls."

"Ordered by whom?"

"How would I know? Someone at the museum?"

"Did you enter it on your time logs?"

"Don't recall."

"There was no billing for the time and no service record noted to the museum."

"I'm not in charge of billing."

"Alice, stop dancing around. We have you on tape — video — going in and changing the camera angle. If you did it on your own without authority, it's trespassing. If your adjustment facilitated a criminal act you could be held for that crime. If, on the other hand, you were instructed to go in by your boss, or someone at Able — or even someone at the Edison — then you're in the clear. Which is it?"

"I need a lawyer."

"Okay," Leslie said, shoving her phone into her pocket, "have it your way. Just who do you think will be paying for this lawyer? If you were working on behalf of the company they might hire one for you. Who do you think that lawyer will be representing? You or Able?" Leslie held out her card. "Call me if you change your mind. The next time I show up it'll be with a warrant. Oh, and please don't leave the state."

Leslie was halfway back to her car when Alice called, "Millie! It was Millie who had me erase some of the video and go change the camera. You need to talk to her and leave me out of this!"

"You just made a smart decision, Alice. I'll tell Dangle you're okay."

"Have him bring my gaming computer. I'm going crazy without it." She turned and marched back into the house, the door slamming behind her.

TWENTY-EIGHT

DESPITE GETTING HOME SLIGHTLY AFTER midnight, Leslie was up early, her mind far too active to allow her to fall back to sleep. The only topic that could compete with the McDermitt homicide was Allen. But every time she focused her attention on their growing relationship, her mind quickly slid back to Scotty and the phonograph — and the missing original Edison recording cylinder worth over forty million dollars.

The sun wasn't yet over the horizon when she began a several mile jog to clear her head. Back in her dining room, she idly added puzzle pieces to the now half completed jigsaw puzzle while nibbling toast and sipping lukewarm coffee. She couldn't help noting that if the McDermitt file fit together this neatly her life would be much easier.

At 8:15 she drove to the office, again mentally reviewing the Edison Museum Christmas party photo albums obtained from Nikolson.

Around noon she called in an order of chicken and broccoli from a local Chinese restaurant. Not her favorite, but okay. Instead of taking lunch home to eat, she decided to return to the office and continue working on the file. Halfway through her meal a voice over her shoulder said, "See you have the McDermitt file open. Anything in those photos float your boat?"

Startled, Leslie looked up into Fischer's smiling face. Leslie had no idea how long he had been standing behind her. "You startled me," she said, standing to face him. "I'm guessing you saw something, so how about you answering that question for me?"

"Why not finish your lunch, or is that breakfast? We can talk in a few."

"Not all that good anyway." She flipped the cover closed and tossed the Styrofoam container in the trash can. "It's convenient to my house. What did you see?"

"A hunch. Nothing to hang our hats on, but worth discussing. It seems to me our buddy William Packard Blair likes the ladies. He hides it well, I'd say."

Leslie had heard talk about Fischer's hunches and knew not to discount what he was saying. "Hunch? Based on what?"

"Nothing overt. There seems to be a particular woman each year that he's in more snaps with. I was just about to count them up when I realized you were here."

"Same woman every year? Or different women?"

"Most certainly different."

"Could be random. Luck of the snap type of thing."

"Could be. I agree. That's what makes it a hunch and not a certainty."

"Show me what you're saying. I'll start with 2016. Let's see, Blair was close to Scotty five times and to Napoli, let's see, eight times. He appears in twelve photos with this unknown woman." Leslie scrolled through the photos once more. "Seems he's with no other woman more than twice."

Together they tallied up the years for which they had photo albums.

	2016	2017	2018	2019
Scotty	5	6	7	15
Napoli	8	10	4	3
Unknown	12	3		
Murphy			12	3

"I'll say this," Leslie said when they were finished. "I don't know about Blair being a ladies' man but last year Scotty clearly had her eyes on him. From my read, it was mutual. The other years it was less obvious that he was with a particular woman."

"Bring up 2018 and look at the sixth shot of Linda Murphy and Blair. Tell me they weren't getting it on."

Leslie studied the file a moment before commenting, "Linda one year. Her mother the next. Man makes the rounds."

"Accounts for Linda's comment about her mother's idea of the best invention being Viagra. It also accounts for the falling out between them. Mother taking daughter's man from her."

Leslie, not for the first time, marveled at Fish's seemingly total recall. "I'd say we might now have motive. The mother steals the daughter's lover. People have killed over less."

"Way too soon to go there. Even if that's true, we don't have factual support. Just thought of something. Bring up the video, the one from the phone of the witness, what's his name? Wang?"

"Wang. Right. What are we looking for?"

"The imaging software compares movements. We have the Wang video and we have video of Murphy leaving the interrogation room."

Leslie brought up the requested videos and ran them side by side on her computer screen. "I'm not seeing similarity, but let's see what the imaging software does for us."

While they were waiting, Leslie's cell displayed a text from Roland McDermitt indicating he was in town and available to meet with her at any time.

HOW ABOUT IN AN HOUR?

she replied.

LOCATION?

Came the almost immediate reply

Leslie gave the address of their offices and scheduled Interview Room Five.

"Match is back," Fischer announced. "No likelihood of Murphy being the person who went to the passenger door and reached in for the keys. Software is eighty-percent certain that person is male. The second person has a sixty-five percent match with Murphy. But—and this is important—there's a ninety percent probability the second person is a woman."

Leslie began adding up what they had on Linda. "We know she picked up the dog sometime. She wasn't exactly truthful about her ability to get into her mother's house. Most troubling, she's not in the least interested in the extremely valuable missing Edison phonograph. And I think she's not telling the full truth about her mother's last illness. I believe she knew full well her mother was terminal."

"I'll buy all that," Fischer agreed, adding, "I say we change her status to Person of Interest. But we need a hell of a lot more than we have. A thirty-five percent error possibility of her being at the scene of the accident won't cut it."

"My immediate thought would be Blair for the front door perp."

"Except Blair's six-three. That guy coming up the hill is over six-five, probably six-six. Consistent with the break-in. Forensics puts them both at six-six."

"A third person?" Leslie suggested.

"Possible. But crimes of a close relative tend to be one, possibly two, people at most. Not ruling anything out, but we need to keep digging."

"The guy in the Edison Museum footage later that night used Scotty's key. I'm willing to say the person on the hill and the person in the museum are the same person."

"Timeline appears to fit. Accident at midnight. Drive to Scotty's, get in, get out, drive to Linda's, drop her and the dog. Maybe have a drink or two. Listen to the phonograph and realize the cylinder's been replaced. Plenty of time to get to the museum by four."

"Another reason to go slow on Blair, besides being the wrong height, is he didn't have to rely on Scotty's key. He had his own."

Fischer disagreed. "Blair's key would be traced back to him. The use of Scotty's key confuses the picture. The fact the surveillance camera was adjusted around that time suggests an inside job. Leading back to him. Still, height is wrong." Fischer fell silent for several minutes lost in thought. Finally, he said, "Leslie, I'm afraid we have far too many unanswered questions. We're back to shovel time. Keep digging. If we're lucky, somebody'll say — or do — something stupid."

Waiting for someone to say or do something stupid, Leslie was learning, was the essence of being a detective. That thought was first planted by one of her instructors when she said, "I don't care how bright they are, something always goes wrong. Fact is, life's messy. Things, even well-planned out things, get overlooked, forgotten, dropped, broken. Just work the case until you find the messy part. It's there somewhere. Run every lead, no matter how trivial, to ground. There is no other way."

The only person involved in the McDermitt matter that was anywhere near six feet six was the Jamaican guy Dangle. Leslie couldn't envision him involved in any manner. If he was, he would be long gone by now, she was positive of that. For now, he had to remain on her radar screen.

While waiting for Roland McDermitt to arrive Fischer went off to work another pressing matter and Leslie began digging into Millie, Alice Tyson's supervisor. She started by running the name Millie Russo through the state licensing databases. She managed to obtain two hits almost immediately. Motor Vehicle Registration and Security Company Registration and Licensing Board. The two pictures on file matched each other. Even more important for Leslie, she was surprised to see they had found

Unknown from the museum Christmas photo album. It was Millie Russo who had been Blair's hot woman in 2016. Blair, it appears, has many connections to Able Security.

"Hi, Mr. McDermitt," Leslie said when Roland was escorted to her desk. "Let me just close this up here and we'll go over to the conference room. She flipped her computer closed, unplugged it, stood and said, "trust you had a good trip down. You planning on being here a while?"

"A week maybe. Found mother's will. Need to hire a lawyer, get all that started. Clean out her house, that sort of stuff. Surprised to find you working Sunday."

"Cleaning up paperwork, getting a jump on the week." Leslie thought about her own anguish when it came time to sell their home in Tampa. "I know what it's like to clean out when a family member passes on," she sympathized, "just went through it myself."

"Parent?"

"Husband. Up in Tampa."

"Sorry to hear that," Roland said and fell silent.

They walked to the conference room, each lost in his or her own thoughts. Almost immediately after the door closed behind them it opened and in came Leslie's partner.

Leslie said, "Detective Fischer, this is Scotty McDermitt's son Roland. He's been so kind as to come in and visit with us."

"Pleased to meet you," Fischer said, his broad smile replacing his normal handshake.

"Detective Fischer and I are working this case together," Leslie added.

"And just what case is that? My sister said you had her in here yesterday for hours grilling her. For what?"

"I assure you, it wasn't hours, Mr. McDermitt," Fischer said, "but we do need some answers."

"What kind of answers? Mother drove off the road and hit a tree. End of story."

"Let's just say there's some confusion we want to straighten out."

"Confusion?"

"Someone removed her car keys after the accident. A key of hers was used later that night to gain entry into the Edison Museum."

"Someone used her key? Was anything taken?"

"That's one of the open questions for sure."

"I know nothing about any museum break-in. I can assure you as much."

Fischer pressed him. "Did your mother leave a will? I think you said you came down to handle her estate. Found a will. Are you the executor?"

"I believe so. Yes."

Sensing hesitation, Fischer asked, "You don't seem certain. Have you seen the will?"

"Last year her lawyer sent me a copy."

"Generally, who gets her estate?"

"Me and Linda."

"Split evenly?"

"Yes."

"Even though she and your mother didn't speak?"

"That was just temporary. You know how those things go. Buds one day, fighting the next." He laughed to lighten the tension.

"Who's her lawyer?"

The question seemed to confuse Roland. He thought a moment, then said, "That's something odd. The Will she sent me a few years ago was from the firm of Hand and Harness. William Gunnsy was her lawyer. I met him once. Nice guy. "

"And?" Leslie asked, encouraging him to continue.

"And when I went through her papers last night, I found a new Will."

"People change their Wills all the time," Fischer said. "Not so strange."

"It is when they change their lawyer as well."

"Who's the new lawyer?"

"Lawyer named Susan Morehouse. Know her?"

How could either one of the detectives not know Morehouse? She was the woman on the other end of the line reaming the big boss a new one when Leslie was investigating the Edison Museum. "Law firm of Morehouse, Young and Cohen," Fischer said." I believe they represent the Edison Museum, among others."

"I assume the new Will is different from the old one. In what way?"

"For starters, the Edison phonograph is given to the Edison Museum."

"And you didn't know about that change until today?"

"Last night to be exact. I read the new Will last night."

"For the first time?" Fischer asked.

"For the first time," Roland replied.

"By any chance," Leslie asked, "do you know what company monitors your mother's home alarm system?"

"As a matter of fact, I do. Saw a bill from them. Company called Able Security. Don't have a phone number for them. I can get it if you need it."

Leslie smiled and said, "No need to bother, we know them well. But please call and request cooperation with us. I'd like to see door openings and closing from August 20th onward. If they'd email them to me at this address." She held out her card, but he shook his head saying he already had her info.

"That should be easy. There should be only one or two openings. House has been closed since her…passing."

"That's what I'm thinking. We'll see."

Fischer stood as if to leave the room. "One final question before I scoot. The night of the accident Sheriff Deputy Bobby James called you at around one and again at two in the morning. Got your name from the State License Bureau as emergency contact. You didn't answer. Why was that?"

"Didn't get the call. Maybe an old number?"

"Leslie, show Mr. McDermitt the number Deputy James called."

Leslie turned her cell phone screen in Roland's direction. "That still your number?" She already knew the answer because it had come up with his earlier text. Fish was just crossing the t's.

"It is."

"Any idea why it didn't ring that night?"

"Don't know. Might have been off."

"Where were you?'

"Sleeping."

"Where?"

"At home."

"And where would that be

"In Pittsburgh. Well, I call it Pittsburgh, but Verona exactly."

"And your phone was off?" Fischer again asked.

"I assume so. I didn't hear it ring."

"Thanks for stopping by, Mr. McDermitt. And good luck with Lawyer Morehouse."

"My sister, Linda, and I have an appointment with her tomorrow at three. You wish us luck like we're going into a lion's den. Should we be worried?"

"Don't have advice on the worry part," Fischer responded. "I can tell you, however, some folks have likened it to that — and a lot worse."

TWENTY-NINE

MONDAY MORNING WHEN LESLIE ARRIVED at her office, Fischer was agitated. Everyone in the office knew to give him room to work it out. Within an hour, two at most, he'd be back to normal, his temper again well concealed. Leslie, being relatively new, had not seen him act this way before. Thinking it was business as usual she walked over to where he was pacing and began, "I think we…"

"Leslie, frankly, I don't give a shit what you think right now! I need space alone to work through this mess!"

"Well, pardon me for interrupting," she replied, getting right back in his face. Eleven years as a cop had taught her to stand up to the best of the bullies. Junior had drilled it into her. Never ever back down, he had cautioned her. They'll walk all over you if you do. If Fischer wanted to take her on, she was ready. "You better give a shit what I have to say! I'm your partner and until I'm told to step down, we do this together. You hear me?"

The pacing stopped. Fischer turned to face her. The folks in The Pit sucked in their breath, knowing exactly what was coming. The rookie was about to get a public dressing down.

Leslie stood with her back straight, her shoulders back, all five feet seven of her tense as a lion about to pounce. She was ready for whatever came her way, knowing she was creating a legend and willing it to be one she could live with when the next bully thought about coming for her.

Perhaps it was her posture and the realization she wouldn't back down. Perhaps it was simply a mood change. Whatever it was, Fischer brought his demeanor back under control. The legend of Leslie Hodges, hard ass, was instantly cast when he, in a conciliatory tone said, "Okay, partner, you're right. Let's hear what you're thinking."

"It's time we drilled down on Blair. It appears he was having some kind of relationship with Docent Scotty McDermitt. The outcome is the museum's lawyer revised Scotty's Will so the museum would be granted her Edison One, the absolute first phonograph ever made, albeit with a recording that was a bit scratchy. That very phonograph was stolen the night Scotty died. I'm not buying coincidence. Not a lot of people are familiar enough with the workings of the phonograph to listen to it, determine it had the wrong recorded cylinder and then go look in the museum to see if it was stashed there. Not to mention preplanning to have the surveillance camera angles adjusted. Don't know about you, but to me this reeks of an inside job. There may not be open flames yet, but it's certainly smoldering."

"I can't disagree. Go with it. Only start by calling Lawyer Morehouse."

"Morehouse! Why the hell we want Blair's attorney, I suppose she's really the museum's attorney, involved? Either way. Morehouse of all people!"

"You think for one minute a guy like Blair will say anything other than 'hello' or 'goodbye' without advice of counsel? Not on your life."

"Why the hell'd Morehouse agree to see us? Woman's out for our hides the way I see it."

"'Cause she has more than one client. She needs the Sheriff's cooperation as much as we need hers. She won't compromise a client, that'll never happen. But, you wanna talk, she'll listen. Next week she'll wanna talk, we'll listen. That's the way it works."

Leslie called Morehouse's office and before she could explain what she wanted, the secretary asked her to please hold a minute. Almost immediately Morehouse herself was on the line. "I've been expecting your call, Detective Hodges. My client has briefed me on your harassment of him and the museum. Perhaps it would be good to sit down and discuss the situation. How about lunch at my office, say one o'clock. I'll have Bill here so we can get to the bottom of this."

Leslie took pause at how non-confrontational the lawyer sounded. She replied, "Sounds good. Any problem with Detective Fischer joining us?"

"The more the merrier. See you soon."

Leslie had the distinct feeling she had just been played. The meeting was set and for now she had what she wanted.

Hodges and Fischer took the elevator up to the receptionist on the twenty-third floor. After a short wait, they were escorted up a massive winding staircase two more flights to a conference center where several meals were being served in different rooms, all from what appeared to be a central kitchen. Lunch in the offices of Morehouse, Young and Cohen was not going to be a side table of cold meats, condiments, and breads.

William Packard Blair, wearing a dark blue business suit, light blue dress shirt with French cuffs and a neat paisley tie, was indistinguishable from the myriad of lawyers scurrying about. He sat alone in a small conference room with capacity for ten, but today had place settings for four.

"I don't believe we've met," Fischer said, extending his hand in the direction of Blair. "I'm Detective Daryl Fischer. I work with Detective Hodges who I believe you already know."

"I have indeed met Detective Hodges," Blair said. "Nice to see you again, Detective. Susan was here a moment ago and had to run off, some fire or another. Said for us to eat and she'd be back in time for any discussion you might want."

Two men and a woman, all wearing masks, entered the room. The men each held two salad plates which were substituted for the plates at each position. The woman carried a tray of dressings and spooned out each person's selection. Water was poured all around. One of the men said, "Lunch today is roast chicken, red potatoes and asparagus. We also have available grilled cedar plank salmon if you would prefer. That comes with butter roasted sweet potatoes and green beans. Substitutions are encouraged. Does anyone wish coffee or tea with your meal? Or perhaps anything else?"

"Do they always eat this way?" Fischer asked when the serving folks were gone.

"Judging from their hourly rate," Blair replied, "I'd say they do. The firm prides itself on their gourmet kitchen. This floor is reserved for clients and business meetings. There's a floor above this where the junior lawyers eat. A perk of the job; free lunch every day. When they work beyond eight, free dinner."

"Pays to go to law school," Leslie quipped.

"They provide free lunch because the baby lawyers are broke after paying their law school loans. How's that old song go? Owe my soul to the company store...."

"Sixteen Tons," Leslie said.

"How'd you know that?" Blair asked.

"That's what my Daddy said about his life. Owed it all to the company store. Tennessee Ernie Ford was Daddy's favorite."

"Mind telling us about yourself, Mr. Blair," Fischer asked, moving the conversation away from Leslie. "I understand if you wish to wait for your lawyer."

Surprisingly, Blair talked about where he was born. Michigan. How he was a distant relative of Henry Ford. Hence the middle name Packard. How for his tenth birthday his parents brought him to the Edison and Ford Winter Estates. It was at that time he fell in love with Edison and his inventions. "I wasn't all that good in school, but I loved science and always tried to invent things. Not very successfully I hasten to add."

"You had some success," Fischer responded. "You donated more than three million dollars to the museum. That is if the State records are correct."

"They're correct all right. I made money from investments. Took some money my mother gave me and did okay for myself."

"When was that?" Leslie asked, and almost immediately regretted the question.

Blair's fork, about to deliver a tomato slice to his mouth, stopped short. Instead of continuing the motion, the tomato was returned to the plate, and Blair sat back in his chair. "When was what?" Blair asked, his eyes focused directly on Leslie.

"I didn't mean to upset you," Fischer hastened to add. "I was just wondering when your mother passed on."

"She's still very much alive. Thank you! Gave me a gift—about eight, nine years back."

"Oh, I see. You invested that gift and did well."

"I did. Lucky, I suppose."

"We all should be that lucky," Leslie commented. "Do I understand correctly you worked for the Washington National Gallery?"

"I did. I left there for this job."

Leslie closed her eyes as if visualizing the file, then said, "About seven years ago, is that right?"

"About then. I can't believe it's been that long. Time passes quickly when you're having fun."

Fischer leaned forward. "Are you aware Scotty had one of the original Edison phonographs in her house?"

"The real original. We call it Edison One. Museum has Edison Two. The first perfect phonograph." Blair's eyes were sparkling as though he had just invented the phonograph himself. The proud father.

"We understand Scotty also had several recorded foil cylinders."

"I believe so, yes."

"Which cylinder do you believe she had?"

"Not the perfect one, that much I know. That would be Cylinder Two and that's in the museum."

"So, did Scotty have Cylinder One when she died?"

"I assume so, yes. I prefer to wait for Susan before any more talk of the museum."

"Fair enough," Fischer agreed. "I visited the National Gallery a long while back. I recall an oil I believe it was, on wood, by Leonardo da Vinci called ..."

"Ginevra de' Benci," Blair injected, his bright eyes back. Only this time a dark veil closed quickly. "What of it?"

"Just remembering is all. Nice piece."

"Only da Vinci in the U.S."

"There are rumors..." Fischer began, but was interrupted when the imposing figure of Susan Morehouse swept into the room.

Fischer had met the lawyer several times before. He immediately stood, started to thrust out his hand in greeting, but remembering the COVID-19 protocol, allowed his arm to drop. Leslie, stepping forward, said, "I'm Leslie Hodges."

"Young lady, I know exactly who you are. You're Lee County's newest detective."

Leslie noted the power behind the lawyer's eyes. There was no doubt Morehouse had taken command of the room. "Pleased to meet you. Look forward to working with you."

"Likewise, I'm certain. Always good to have a friendly ear at Lee County. I'm sorry to be late. I had to take a call. Are you enjoying our little lunch so far?"

"We are," Fischer replied. "Your client was telling us about how he came to be a Florida resident and became involved with the museum."

"Great to have him in our community. Museum is all the better for it. Washington's loss is our gain." The lawyer took a few bites of salad and pushed her plate aside. The wait staff immediately swept in, cleared the table and placed roast chicken plates in front of each of the guests. A cedar planked salmon was served to Morehouse.

"If anyone would like to switch to salmon, it's never too late." Sweeping her eyes around the table, she said, "Going once. Going twice. No takers. Okay, then. Enjoy lunch." A wave of her hand sent the staff away.

"You asked for this meeting, Detective Hodges. By way of background, I understand you and your cohorts have been harassing Jayne, Bill, and even one of the docents, over what I believe to be a non-issue. Tell me where I've gone wrong. A woman, a docent of the museum, ran off the road and died up on Interstate 75. Tragic, I must admit. Happens all too often. That's just it. It does happen all too often." Morehouse worked on her salmon before continuing. "Someone allegedly using that woman's security key entered the museum early the next morning, looked around and left. Nothing was vandalized, nothing stolen, nothing damaged. Yet you continue to question Mr. Blair and Ms. Nikolson. What am I missing?"

Hodges responded. "If you'll agree to hold what I'm about to tell you in confidence I can update you."

Morehouse, obviously having gone down this path before, countered with, "In confidence only until it's made known to the public or becomes available to the public without my help."

"We can live with that," Leslie agreed. "So, is that a yes?"

"It is."

"Okay. We're investigating the museum operations only as a part of a separate criminal investigation."

"Now you have my attention," Morehouse said, putting her fork down and wiping her lips with a cloth napkin. "Mind telling us more about the nature of the criminal activity."

"Homicide. Sarah McDermitt was intentionally asphyxiated. Fumes from the exhaust pipe were routed into her car." Leslie brought up the image of the two people walking away from the wrecked car and held it out facing across the table.

Morehouse studied the image a moment before saying, "I'm certain you're not overlooking the fact that my client stands six-two, six-three at best. One of the people in that photo is a good four, perhaps five, inches taller. The other appears to be five-four. So just how are you tying the homicide to my client?"

"We never said we were."

"Then just why is Mr. Blair here today. You said you had questions for him. If he's not a suspect in the homicide we're wasting our time."

Leslie brought up an image from the surveillance video and again held it out.

"What's this?"

"Taken from surveillance video of the museum at that early morning entry you spoke about. Remind you of anybody?"

"I instruct my client to say nothing," Morehouse said, turning to Blair.

"But, I..." Blair began, before he was silenced.

Morehouse's hand shot up and she demanded, "Nothing! Say nothing at all!" Turning her head back toward the detectives, she barked, "This interview is over!"

"How about this," Leslie suggested, struggling to keep her voice under control, "I'll ask the questions I came prepared to ask and you listen. Then you'll know what we're looking for — and why."

"How do you suppose that will help you?"

"Might not help. Can't hurt. You'd figure them out without us."

"Fire away." Turning to Blair, she repeated her warning. "Don't respond to anything they say. You understand me?"

"I understand."

"Just listen."

"I will."

"Go ahead, Detective. Let's hear what you have to say."

"Here are our open questions. Was that you in the museum surveillance video? Height is wrong, but otherwise it's identical. If not, any idea who? Why was some of the footage removed from the master? Where were you from midnight that evening to six the next day? Any alibi witnesses? Do you now or did you ever have a relationship, other than a business relationship, with anyone currently working at Able Security? If so, when? Did you ever have a relationship, other than a business relationship, with the deceased, Sarah Scotty McDermitt? Or with her daughter, Linda Murphy? Do you know of any relationship between a woman named Alice Tyson and Linda Murphy, Scotty's daughter?"

"Is that your complete list?" Morehouse asked when Leslie fell silent.

"About it," Fischer answered. "Add, do you have any financial interest, either directly or via a shell company, in Able Security?

"Are you finished?'

"For now."

"Okay. No further business. Can I interest anyone in a cup of coffee? Or perhaps tea. Or something stronger if you wish. We have fresh-baked key lime pie for dessert. The best there is."

"I'm skipping dessert," Leslie said, having barely finished her chicken.

"I'll do likewise," Fischer said following her lead. "We've taken up enough of your time."

Both detectives dropped their business cards on the table and walked toward the door. The floor attendant met them and escorted them back down the spiral staircase and into the main lobby where the receptionist, a woman barely old enough to have graduated high school, said "Ms. Morehouse has asked if you would give her a few minutes before you leave."

Fischer responded, saying, "Tell her we'll wait with pleasure."

To Leslie, he lowered his voice. "If Morehouse has any suspicion her client is guilty, we would have already been escorted onto the elevator. You put the fear of God in Blair. If he's innocent of the murder then he'll be anxious to spill the beans on what he knows about the death to protect the rest of what's going on. He's up to his ears in something. We just don't yet know what that something is."

THIRTY

"FIRST OFF," MOREHOUSE SAID WHEN Hodges and Fischer were shown into her large corner office overlooking the Caloosahatchee River, "my client states emphatically he had nothing to do with the McDermitt death." The three of them were alone and Blair was nowhere in sight.

"Should we assume you are about to answer our questions?" Leslie asked.

"To the extent I can, yes. Sit down and let's get started. I have a busy afternoon." When everyone was seated, Morehouse said, "Of most importance, Mr. Blair has an alibi for the time in question. If needed, we will provide full details. But only if required to prove his innocence."

"Nature of the alibi?" Fischer asked, guessing at what was to come.

"He was with a woman. A married woman and I'm certain you know what difficulty this presents for him — and for her."

"I assume if needed down the line we'll be provided the particulars," Leslie probed.

"I trust it won't be required. Let's leave that for another day, shall we? You asked if the person you saw in the video was my client. He says no and has no idea who it was. His relationships with people working for the museum, or who worked for the museum are not your business. That is a direct quote." Morehouse studied the two detectives before moving on. "However, I am authorized to tell you he did have a relationship with the deceased. In his words, 'more than casual'. And before that, with her daughter. A few years back he had an affair with Gina Napoli and that's as far back as I can go. Have I answered your questions?"

"Mostly," Leslie said, not consulting her notes. "What about relationships between Linda Murphy and Alice Tyson?"

"That he knows nothing of. I can say this. A woman by the name of Millie Russo is part owner of Able Security.

That got a rise out of Fischer. "Say again? Russo owns the security company?"

"Part owner. Two holding companies own Able. Sling LLC and RiverRock Partners LLC."

"You going to make us track down the members of those LLCs?" Fischer asked.

"It'll take you a while if you try. I'll short cut it for you. Don't say I never gave you anything. Napoli is the sole member of Sling. Blair and Russo share RiverRock seventy-thirty."

Leslie digested what she had just heard, then asked, "When was RiverRock formed?"

"Before I knew Blair. Good ten years I'd say. Why?"

"Curious's all." Leslie stood in preparation for leaving. "You're meeting with Roland McDermitt in a half-hour I understand."

"I make it a point to never discuss who I meet with and when."

"He told us as much."

"Your point?"

"You rewrote Sarah McDermitt's Will. When was that?"

For the first time today, Morehouse hesitated. She covered her pause by saying, "If memory serves me, mid-January."

"Of 2019?" Leslie pressed.

"2020."

"According to what you told us earlier, Blair and McDermitt were...were in a relationship at that point. You represented her in changing her Will?"

"You crossed the line detective! Questioning my ethics! Get the hell out of here! Discussion is over!"

"You sure hit a nerve back there." Fischer commented when they were back in the law firm lobby. "It's 2:40. Roland and Linda should be here any minute. I have a question for them."

"Same question I have?"

"What's yours?"

"What changes were made in the Will by Morehouse?"

"And?" Fischer prompted.

"And when did you first learn of those changes?"

"Bingo!"

The problem with their planned ambush was that Sarah McDermitt's children never arrived at the lavish offices of Morehouse, Young and Cohen. As Leslie commented in the elevator going down after waiting over an hour for the no-shows, "Morehouse told us everything we could eventually learn from official records or from interviews. She gave us very little more. She redirected her clients knowing we'd ambush them in the lobby. Wanted time to brief them first."

"Get used to it, Leslie," Fischer shrugged. "We got more from her than I had expected. That only means she's dancing around something else."

"You believe Blair's involved?"

"In something. I doubt it's the homicide."

"What drives you there?"

"His alibi."

"Some married woman he's having an affair with? Won't give us a name. I'm calling it smoke."

"Think about it. How hard would it be for us to retrace his steps now that we know what we're looking for? If we eventually like him for the murder and he's lying about his alibi he'll have to find a married woman who's willing to lie to save him and screw up her own life in doing so. Not many things harder to do than that.

Morehouse is too good a lawyer to allow him to give us an alibi that won't hold up."

Leslie's thoughts were interrupted by a call from Allen. "This is business," he began. "I volunteered for the Silverado case and came up with major problems. Any chance stopping by and helping me get this thing back on track?"

Fischer, hearing Allen's question, nodded his approval. Adding, "I got a full plate back in the office. See you in the morning."

"I'm not far away," she said into the phone. "Be there in fifteen." To Fischer she said, "I can do without the stupid smirk. It's all business."

"That's what they all say when they work late. Just business, Honey. Nothing to see here. Have fun, partner. And, oh, don't work all night."

The urge to shoot Fischer was strong. Just not as strong as Leslie's desire to remain employed — and out of jail.

THIRTY-ONE

IT WAS 4:15 WHEN LESLIE walked up the steps of the Lee County Justice Center a few blocks inland from the river. She was surprised at how few people were moving about, most likely the result of the pandemic. Lawyers, clients, police, clerks, visitors, were mostly gone. The last time she was here, the line for coffee snaked out the door. Now a lone woman stood stirring her drink, the glass-enclosed pastry shelves empty, save for a single deformed bagel off to the side.

She walked up the stairs to Allen's office and found him at his desk, head buried in a mass of papers. Looking up, his smile was lopsided, forced. "Best thing I've seen all day. Thanks for coming."

"You look to be in pain. Some judge lay into you?"

"Prep day. Like most days. How'd yours go?"

"Talk later. What's up?"

"Silverado case. Lawyer's making the claim the defendant, that guy Weslo Custer, the guy you arrested in the storage unit with the Silverado, he..."

"Yeah, I remember him. Sleaze bag if there..."

"...isn't the owner of the truck."

"If he's not the owner then why was he there? If I recall, his driver's license address matched the vehicle registration."

"That's the thing, Leslie. It did. He claims he sold the truck the day before. Lawyer produced a canceled check to prove it. Guy by the name of Garso Lewis bought it."

"Did he tell you why he and the truck were there in the unit if he sold the truck?"

"Claims he left his phone in the glove compartment."

"How'd he find the truck?"

"Tracked his phone."

"You believe any of that BS?"

"Jury might."

"What can I do for you?"

"Need your statement as to exactly what you saw when you entered the unit. Where Custer was, what he was doing, what he said. Everything."

"Fuck you doin?"

Allen's eyes went wide. "What?"

"That's what shitbag Custer said when he drove out of the unit and I stopped him."

"He was driving?"

"Of course, he was driving. That's why I arrested him. Driving a truck with stolen material."

"That's not in the file."

"Then sorry, but you have the wrong file. Besides, we got a warrant to search his house and found most of the equipment stolen from three other break-ins neatly stacked up."

"None of that's in the file."

"You folks have a problem," Leslie told him. "A real problem."

"Or you folks have the problem."

"Ours is mostly electronic." She proceeded to punch information into her cell. A moment later she handed him the phone. "Scroll though there. Tell me what you see."

"Shit! You're right. It's all there. What's the number on that file? I'll order it, see what comes over."

"Something you just said struck a chord. But I lost it. Crap! Hate that."

"I was talking about our friend Custer and how he sold the Silver..."

"That's it! Glove compartment! Loose ends drive me crazy. In the McDermitt homicide there are several. Starting with two, maybe even more, foil recording cylinders missing. One of them is worth in the forty million range."

"You lost me. What's that to do with Custer's car title?"

"Not the title. The glove compartment! Those cylinders were in Scotty's possession in January and gone in August when she died. She didn't throw them away and whoever took the phonograph didn't sell the recordings."

"And you know that how?"

"The buyer told me."

"You spoke to the buyer of stolen property?"

"I believe I did. Yes."

"I didn't see an arrest report. You have him under surveillance?"

"Wasn't in Florida and I have no direct proof. FBI's had an open investigation on the man for years. I passed along what little I have. They essentially rolled their eyes."

"What other loose ends are troubling you?"

"For starters, Blair seems like a harmless ladies' man. I have a nagging feeling he's a con artist, using the woman for what they can do for him. His latest romance was with Scotty McDermitt and appears to have lasted just long enough for him to persuade her to change her will. Guess who the lawyer was who made those changes?"

"Morehouse?"

"Nailed it!"

"Isn't she the one who carried on about your warrant for the Edison's security footage?"

"One and the same. I've been asking myself why would Blair want McDermitt's Will changed? The only answer makes sense to me is he wanted the Edison phonograph, the real original one, for himself."

"Give him some credit. Maybe for the museum?"

"Perhaps, but I doubt it."

"That would explain Morehouse's involvement," Allen concurred. "I believe she represents the museum as well."

"Assuming, of course, the Will was changed in that regard. Thinking of that, if you're correct and Morehouse represents the museum then could she allow McDermitt's Will to cut the museum out?"

"Depends on what the original Will said. If originally, the phonograph was bequeathed to the Edison Museum then it's a conflict for her to change that. More likely, the original Will granted the phonograph to one or both of her children, or to some third party other than the museum, then Morehouse has no duty to the museum. Trust me, if Morehouse had an issue, she would have sent McDermitt to a lawyer pal of hers."

"Any thoughts on how I can get my hands on the new Will? I mean short of a warrant."

"I'm a criminal lawyer, Leslie. My knowledge of probate law is pure textbook — and what was required to pass the bar exam. If I recall right, the time for filing the Will with the court is ten days, give or take. My guess, if Morehouse had possession of the original, as you seem to be suggesting, then time is up and she filed it. Probate is downstairs on the second floor." He checked his watch. "They close in ten minutes."

Leslie took the steps down two at a time. The lights were still on, but the big glass paneled doors were closed. She pushed them open, saw the top of a woman's head bent forward behind a counter that ran the width of the room. Leslie hurried over and positioned herself directly in front of the woman who continued what she was doing without looking up.

After waiting unacknowledged for what seemed like an excessively long time, Leslie leaned over the counter. "Excuse me," she said in as polite a voice as she could muster.

"Oh, I'm sorry," the woman responded, still not making eye contact, and not bothering to pull up her mask, "we're closed for the day. Open at eight-thirty in the morning."

"This is important. I'm with the Lee County Sheriff's Department and need to see a newly filed Will."

"I said we're closed. Come back..."

Allen's voice, coming from behind Leslie, said, "Bobbie, that's no way to treat our detective friends. Take you a minute."

"Oh, hello, Allen," the clerk said, standing, her face coming alive at the sight of the Assistant Prosecutor, "I didn't know this was for you. What name is the Will under?"

"McDermitt," Leslie answered. "Sarah McDermitt. Do you need anything else?"

"Take me but a moment." She sat back down in her chair, hit a few keys on her computer and started typing. "Is that spelled M small c, capital D?"

"It is."

"Two t's?"

"You got it."

"This it?" She turned her computer to face Leslie.

"That's it!"

 Copy?"

"That would be appreciated," Leslie answered.

Looking at Allen, the clerk asked, "File number for the charge?"

"It's for me, not him," Leslie said. "I'll pay."

"Oh. I'm sorry but unless I have a file number..."

"How much in cash?"

"Cash drawer is closed."

"Bobbie," Allen said, "please make an exception. You can log the cash in the morning."

Bobbie hit a key, then stood facing Allen, her well-proportioned figure on full display. "Clerk's Office is here to serve. No charge today, Allen." She winked before turning and walking across the office to the printer, returning with a sheaf of papers. She laid them on the counter in front of Leslie. Turning to Allen she said, "Is there anything further I can do for you today?"

"Thanks, Bobbie. That's all we need."

"Glad I could be of help. See you soon." A second wink. "Bye."

"What was that about?" Leslie asked. "She all but came over the counter after you. Anything further I can get for you Allen? Anything you need? Anything at all? Oh, Allen."

"Let's just say, in a hospital doctors are the prize catch. In the courthouse, lawyers replace doctors."

"And just how far has this chase progressed?"

"Not my type. Nothing more to say."

For now, maybe. Leslie told herself, suddenly uncomfortable with her feelings.

Back in Allen's office, he reached for the papers. "Here, let me see the Will."

Leslie handed over the document and he immediately flipped through several pages. "Most of this is boilerplate having to do with taxes, her real property, her car. Oh, here it is." Allen read a paragraph, looked up and said, "Sorry to say, your assumption's correct. The Edison phonograph, identified as Edison One, and the original recorded foil cylinder are bequeathed to Edison and Ford Winter Estates. Everything else seems to go evenly to her son and daughter."

"Does that mean," Leslie asked, trying to sort it all out, "that the museum has a claim against the buyer of the stolen phonograph?"

"Yes and no."

"Typical lawyer answer."

"Hear me out. Technically, when the phonograph was stolen it belonged to McDermitt and not to the museum. Some court could change that. I think that's good law. More importantly, items of personal property usually don't carry titles with them. A buyer can buy items that are for sale so long as the seller is someone normally selling that type of merchandise. From what little you've told me, that phonograph is now owned by a guy who specializes in owning stolen property and is keeping that ownership very much hidden. If the FBI hasn't been able to crack him so far, I'll put my money on Edison One never being seen in public again. It's certainly not coming back to its rightful owner anytime soon."

"What about insurance? Could the museum have had the phonograph insured?"

"Great question. Yes, because while they don't own it, they did have an interest in it."

"Then the same goes for the recording cylinder."

"Certainly."

Leslie sat in a chair in the corner of Allen's office quietly digesting and reviewing the McDermitt case, paying particular attention to what she had learned in the last two days. Now that she had a partner, things were moving significantly faster. Or was it that the more facts they gathered, the more facts those facts led to? She heard Junior's voice from back when they first met, describing just such a phenomenon. She also recalled what he had often said about leads drying up and the hot embers turning to cold ash.

She looked up and watched Allen for a few moments while he sat, his head bent forward, concentrating on a file. In a lot of ways the two of them were similar. Both knowing themselves very well and both able to focus on the immediate problem. Physically, they were both solidly built. Junior was perhaps an inch taller at five eleven and because he spent at least an hour in the weight room every day, his body had been well-toned.

The vision of that Bobbie woman in the Clerk's Office with the enviable figure and long curly eyelashes making a play for Allen filled her with uncomfortable feelings. The beginnings of jealousy. "Hey," she called to him, "how about I buy you dinner tonight in payment for all this free legal advice?"

Allen looked up from the file, his eyes revealing nothing. "Need a raincheck. I pulled up your Silverado file and somehow my original information was, as you suggested, corrupted. Everything I've sent over to the defense is wrong. I need to correct it all before morning. Sorry."

"It happens," Leslie replied, trying, but failing, to control her disappointment. "Try not to work too late."

"This promises to be an all-nighter. File's a real mess."

"I'll bet," Leslie mumbled to herself outside Allen's office, jealousy making its way to the surface. "I'll just bet."

THIRTY-TWO

LESLIE SAT IN HER CAR and worked on a text to Great Southern Insurance Company.

JACK. WAS THE MCDERMITT EDISON ONE INSURED BY GSIC EITHER FOR HER PERSONALLY OR FOR THE EDISON MUSEUM? THANKS.

After hitting SEND she started home, her route taking her past the Edison Museum. Noticing Blair's car in the lot, on impulse she parked and tried the front door. It was locked. There was no answer to her knock.

She knocked again, this time pounding as hard as she could. Turning to leave, the door opened framing William Blair. "Why Detective Hodges. What a surprise. I don't recall an appointment."

"Just driving by. Learned some things. Have a few more questions for you."

"On advice of counsel, I won't…"

"Let's not go there, shall we. My questions don't pertain to you. For now, I'm accepting your story."

"As I said, On advice…"

"I'm not in the mood for bullshit! Understand this, you have an absolute right not to speak with me. But… and this is critical…I have a job to do. Part of that job is checking your alibi for the night of August 22nd. You're sensitive about who you were with that night, otherwise your lawyer wouldn't have been reluctant to give me the name. Could that mean the woman is married? Or perhaps it's not a woman. In checking your alibi I'll need to confirm that person's story as well. Who knows where that might lead? These things have a tendency to go south fast with you being a public figure and all. Get my drift?"

Blair stood his ground, his face tight, his eyes seething. The stand-off continued with neither of them speaking or moving a muscle. Blair was the first to blink. "Okay, detective, you made your point. Come in. We have a donor reception in an hour and the catering folks will be here any minute. That's who I thought was out here. Oh, here they are now." He nodded in the direction of two white vans pulling into the lot. One van headed to the far corner while the other one turned to position its back end toward the museum door. Blair slipped a bar into the ground to block the door open and followed Leslie into the office. "Now just what is it you wish to know?"

"McDermitt's Will left her phonograph to the museum. Was that a change she made at your suggestion?"

"I refuse…"

"I thought we were beyond that."

"She was a docent here at the museum for many years. That phonograph was given to her great-grandmother and passed down over the generations. Mother to daughter. She had…well…a falling out with her daughter as I think you know. Anyway, she wanted to do something nice for the museum. I suggested donating the phonograph."

"Was donating the phonograph to the museum her idea or yours?"

"Let's just say it was a mutual decision. You know, a lot of people donate valuable items to museums. It's done all the time."

"Did the fallout, as you called it, with her daughter result from you dumping the daughter and starting up a romantic relationship with the mother?"

"Nothing further to say on that subject."

Changing directions, Leslie asked, "When Scotty changed her Will to include the museum, did you insure the phonograph?"

"Tried to. But Jack Silver said he couldn't do it."

"Tell you why?"

"Not secure enough at her house, is what I understood."

"Did Scotty have it insured?"

Before Blair answered, several people came through the front door, looked around before heading directly to the corner where the bar had been set up.

"I asked her to do it," Blair said, obviously distracted by his arriving guests. "She said she would. I don't know beyond that point. Hey, I need to be out there. Get a bite to eat if you like. Heavens, do the museum a favor and don't flash your badge."

Leslie noted his sensitivity but said nothing. "One final question if I may?"

"You'll ask it anyway. So, shoot."

"By any chance did you, or anyone, ..." A voice within her cautioned her to stop. Listening to that voice, Leslie continued, "...skip it. Go enjoy your party." Left unasked was whether anyone had told Linda or Roland about the gift to the museum. She planned to spring that question on the son at the appropriate moment.

On the way out, Leslie took Blair up on his offer and helped herself to a plate of cold shrimp, several wheat crackers and a wedge of brie. She stood in front of Edison Two thinking what an incredible mind Thomas Edison must have had to even dream of recording human voice, let alone make it happen. She moved as close as she could to the display case to again see exactly what the tin foil recording cylinder looked like and to fix in her mind its relative size. Someone had likened the mechanism to a Coke bottle, but as she could now see for herself, it had less circumference and was not as tall.

"This is a party and you, my young friend, seem to be working."

She turned to face Susan Morehouse, her eyes alive above her mask. Beside her stood a man about half her age, shirt opened into a deep-V showing off his well-buffed chest. "Detective Hodges," she said, her eyes twinkling mischievously, this is my escort for the evening, Syd Prescott."

"Pleased to meet you, I'm sure," Prescott said, making a show of eying her up and down. "So, you're a detective. Something gone missing I can help you locate? I just love a good mystery."

"Not that I know about. Your…your date would know that better than I would. Just admiring the genius behind these phonographs." Looking down at her now empty plate, she added, "And having a bite to eat."

"Enjoy the night, then," Morehouse said, steering her escort in the direction of Blair, who was deep in conversation with Comptroller Gina Napoli.

Leslie's cell chirped.

MUSEUM REQUESTED INSURANCE. REFUSED FOR SECURITY REASONS. POLICY PENDING ON SIMILAR PIECE. REGARDS, JACK.

At least Blair's story matched Silver's.

In the parking lot her cell again sounded, displaying Fischer's name. "What's up," she asked.

"I saw your note on the phonograph being given to the museum in the Will. Got me thinking. I called in a favor and got a warrant for both the son and daughter's cell phone metadata from the 22nd and 23rd. Daughter's was off from 6 p.m. on the 22nd until 4:35 a.m. on the 23rd."

"That's a match to what she told us."

"And the son's never left Pittsburgh."

"Gives him a good alibi."

"Perhaps. Perhaps, not. Cell was on, but not one call that entire time.

"Just how was he notified of his mother's death?"

"Remains to be seen. See you in the morning."

THIRTY-THREE

LESLIE WAS IN THE SHOWER when her cell rang. She hadn't slept well and was slowly waking up as the warm water flooded over her body. The last thing she wanted to do was climb out to answer the phone, but she knew she had to. It wasn't as though she had a life independent from her job where people randomly called her. The probability of this being a business call even though it was only 7:10 was high.

It was Honker from the *U-Wreckum We-Crushum* salvage yard telling her about a message on his voice mail from a Mr. Roland McDermitt inquiring about his mother's 2019 Mazda. "I called him back and just got off with him."

"What did he want?" she asked, reaching for the towel to dry off the now dripping phone.

"If we still had the car. I told him we did. He asked if he could see it. I said he could."

"When will he be coming out?"

"Seemed like he was in a hurry. On his way now."

"Okay. Thanks for calling."

"You asked me to call if anything came up. Here's your call."

"Thanks. I owe you one. I'm on my way. Remember, the car's been impounded, nothing leaves without my permission."

"Know the drill, Detective."

Another skipped breakfast. This time without having time for coffee. She called Fischer from the car, and when he didn't answer she left a message telling him about Roland and asking him to meet her at the wreckers.

Pulling into the *U-Wreckum* yard, Leslie saw no other cars parked in the area designated for visitors. That was good news, she would have a few minutes alone to again look over the wrecked car.

"Hey, detective," Honker called when she entered the parts building, "that guy called a few minutes ago. Got himself lost coming over here. Guy's from up north somewhere. He's a good fifteen minutes out."

"How about showing me the car again?"

"Sure thing. Got it in the back lot. Give you a ride out there. Lookin' for anything in particular?"

"I need to be certain we have all of McDermitt's personal stuff."

"All's I can say is nothing's in that shell. Was a water bottle, a fancy lookin' one I have to say that, in the glove box. That's it."

"You have the water bottle?"

"I'll have to see about that. People don't usually come here lookin' for water bottles and stuff along those lines. One of the workers mighta taken it for hisself for all I know."

"Mind showing me?"

"Follow me," he called, snaking his way around table after table of salvaged parts removed from vehicles of all sizes and makes, from compact cars to massive tractors. "We have the largest selection of parts in Southwest Florida," Honker said proudly, pointing to several tables of what appeared to Leslie as transmissions. "There's more outside, you don't see it here."

They walked past axles, brakes, seats and items she couldn't hope to recognize. The further back they went the smaller the items became. "Water bottle'll be back here," Honker finally announced. "Over to the right we have electronics and navigation systems. It won't be there. Check out that area in the corner. Stuff that's non-car related, the likes of sunglasses, wastebaskets, cup holders, ornaments, be over in that area. Good luck. I'll be up front when you want me."

Leslie touched several items and was surprised how clean everything was. No dirt or dust, and particularly no grease, even on parts that were designed for grease. There were several crates of sunglasses, some prescription, some off-the-shelf. Another crate held reading glasses, another tissue dispensers. There were dozens of stacked cardboard boxes with names such as Chevy, Buick, Ford, Honda, handwritten in black marker on their sides.

Lying on their sides, mostly hidden behind large Happy Days mugs, were several water bottles. One appeared from memory to be identical to the one she had seen Scotty carry in one of the surveillance videos. Leslie snapped a picture of the bottle, pulled up the Coroner's photo of the water bottle found in Scotty's car and compared the two.

They were identical.

Its weight surprised her when she picked it up. Thinking it contained liquid, she shook it. Hearing and feeling nothing, she slipped it into her bag and started back to the front taking her time as she remembered how her father and her late husband had both enjoyed working on cars, rebuilding engines, tuning them, listening to them run smoothly. They would have been right at home in this giant playland of automobile parts.

Roland's voice broke through Leslie's thoughts. He was questioning Honker about his mother's car. In short order it was clear Roland also was looking for the water bottle. Leslie held her breath, hoping Honker had the presence of mind to not reveal that she had beat him to it.

This was confirmed a moment later when Honker replied, "Don't believe we found anything in the car, Mr. McDermitt. But, if you'll please wait here, I'll go back and look see what we have. This'll take a while. We have the largest collection of parts around here."

Leslie waited a few minutes before coming out from behind a pallet of car doors. "Good morning, Mr. McDermitt. You remember me I'm sure. Detective Hodges. We met..."

"You scared me. Popping up like that. Certainly, I remember you. What're you doing here?"

"Same as you I suspect. What brings you way out here?"

"My mother's car's here. I'm collecting her belongings."

"The car's completely wrecked. You have an insurance claim."

"I wanted to be certain nothing of Scotty's stuff remained in the car."

"I believe the coroner took everything they found. It's been logged in down there."

"Yes, I know. I picked it all up right after I filed the Will."

"And?"

"And my sister believes she had two water bottles. The coroner only had one. I was hoping the other one was in the glovebox or under a seat or someplace where the coroner didn't find it."

"Must be important to you to go to all this trouble."

"Something very valuable is missing and we believe… Anyway, no real trouble. Doing my job as Executor is all."

"Good luck with that. Oh, by the way, I understand the Will gives that phonograph, the one you were telling me about, the one your mother played for you back at New Years, to the Edison Museum. Do I have that correct?"

All pretext of his smile faded. "How the hell you know that?" he demanded.

"It's my job to know such things. I take it I am correct."

"That's private information."

"Actually, it's public information once the Will was filed. I take it that makes you unhappy."

"Wouldn't you be? Family heirloom and all that. And she gives it to the museum!"

"You're upset with her. Don't take it out on me! What about the millions of dollars that phonograph is worth?"

"How dare you insinuate we only care about the money?"

"Just stating a fact. Insinuating nothing."

"Felt that way."

"Sorry about that. When did you learn of the change in Scotty's Will? I mean about her giving the phonograph to the museum in her Will?"

"Yesterday. I think that's when I saw the new Will."

"That's when you first knew about the change?"

"That's what I said. Yes."

Roland's face, particularly his eyes, were inconclusive for signs of deception. "And when do you suppose your sister, Linda, first knew about the change that gave the phonograph to the Edison Museum?"

"I don't suppose. I know. She was with me yesterday when we both read it for the first time."

"And where was that? Where did you first read it? You told us you had an appointment with Lawyer Morehouse. Was it at her office?"

McDermitt seemed puzzled, a bit disoriented. Then he said, "Not exactly. She called and asked to meet us at the courthouse instead. Said, we could meet there and that way we could file it immediately."

"Did she tell you why the need to hurry the filing?"

"Something to do with it being beyond some time limit."

"Let me get this clear. You met Morehouse at the courthouse and..."

"One of the lawyers in the firm. Morehouse got called away on some business we were told."

"You read the Will at the courthouse and learned for the first time, both you and your sister, that the valuable phonograph, the one known as Edison One, was to be given to the Edison Museum? Do I have that correct?"

"How many times must I repeat this for you. Yes, that is correct, Detective."

"One last question. Just so I have my notes straight. Where exactly were you on the night of August 22nd when your mother ran off the road and hit that tree?"

"In Pittsburgh. Where else would I be?"

"And when Sheriff Deputy James called to inform you your mother had died in a fatal accident you were in Pittsburgh?"

"I was."

"Thank you, Mr. McDermitt. Hope you find what you're looking for. Have a good one."

"Great interview, Leslie!" Fischer exclaimed several minutes later when Leslie briefed him. "Couldn't have done it better myself. Need to be careful now. With the Will change we have motive for killing the mother and stealing the phonograph before the museum took ownership. We have opportunity in that Roland could have been down here. We're a long way from proving anything, but we now need to be certain all interviews include both of us.

"Got it," Leslie replied, bristling that Fischer had felt the need to remind her. Swallowing her pride, she asked, "If the son's off limits, I assume we can still talk to his wife."

"Yes, but let's be on the safe side for now. Only about things she knows from her own observation. Nothing about conversations between them. If you're uncomfortable with that, run it by your lawyer friend."

"Late breakfast?" Leslie asked a moment later when Allen answered the phone. She had planned on inviting him to lunch before realizing it was still only 9:45. "This is not all pleasure. Have a couple legal questions. Bring your law cap."

"I'm fried from the law stuff, but otherwise your timing's perfect. Just finished sending the revised file to the defense. I could use something to eat."

"Suggestions?"

"Oasis over on MLK Boulevard. Great waffles. You like waffles?"

"Happens I do. See you there in thirty."

"I'll be on my second stack by then. Use your lights — siren if need be."

Driving to meet Allen gave Leslie time to dwell on what had been troubling her during the night. It wasn't until she replayed in her mind the text from Silver that her agitation took shape. What did he mean by policy pending after saying they rejected the policy over security concerns?

"Jack," she said when he came on the line, "Leslie Hodges down in Florida. How are you?"

"Doing well. And you?"

"Can't complain, I guess. Have a quick question for you. On Edison One you said you declined coverage for security concerns."

"We don't, as a rule, insure objects in people's homes unless they have proper display cases and sophisticated security. Neither of which McDermitt had."

"That's what I gathered. What confuses me is your comment, policy pending. Sounds as if you were in the process of insuring it anyway. What am I missing?"

"The McDermitt woman was terminal. A month or less to live. Blair had a display case made for the museum and the whole nine yards. There's a fundraising event scheduled around the unveiling, so to speak, of the very first recording machine. Originally planned for early September, just after Labor Day, but because of COVID-19 they pushed it out two weeks and cut down the attendee list. Wanted to kick off the winter season with a bang. It was more of a whimper."

"Blair knew Scotty was terminal. Is that what you're saying?"

"Of course Blair knew. From the little I know McDermitt herself was involved in the planning of the event. Morbid, if you ask me. Who am I to judge? Planning your own testimonial isn't my thing."

"Thanks for taking my call."

"Anytime. Are you any closer to locating the missing recording cylinder?"

"You referring to the one Stratis offered five mil for?"

"Closer to fifty than five. One and the same. Price seems to be going up by the day. I wouldn't be surprised to learn that it fetches over a hundred million."

"Can't say as I am. What makes you ask?"

"Judging from your questions—and from the escalating price tag—it follows that's all."

"If I find it, you'll be the first to know."

"Check that. Put Stratis on your speed dial, he's the one with the interest. I only insure stuff, he buys it. Have a good one."

———⬥———

True to his word, Allen started into his second waffle order as Leslie put her fork into her first. He had coordinated timing and her breakfast was placed in front of her the moment she sat down.

"That coffee is just what I needed," she said, still processing Silver's comment about McDermitt planning her own testimonial.

"Okay, Leslie, spill it."

"What?"

"Look, I slept less than an hour last night, but even I can see your mind's working overtime."

"Speaking of work, you're not one to be lecturing. Hate to break it to you but you look like shit, sleeping in your clothes, no less. Don't go to court looking that way. Judge'll confuse you with the defendant. You'll spend a month behind bars before they get it all straight."

"You have a low opinion of the system."

"Says the guy whose files were corrupted."

"Forget me. What's on your mind? You asked for legal help."

"Seems like ages ago."

"Forty-five minutes by my watch."

Both of their plates were clean, and two cups of coffee were consumed when Leslie finished her briefing. "So, here's my first question. We're likin' the two of them, brother and sister, for the homicide."

"Motive," Allen said, "I suppose is that if the mother died of natural causes the valuable Edison would go to the museum. They wanted to steal it first but had no key to the house. Am I hot?"

"Need I answer that?" Leslie smiled trying to convey she was only joking about him being hot. "Close. There are easier ways to get Scotty's house key."

"So, what then?"

"They knew the recording cylinders were missing and thought maybe she had hidden them in the museum. It was her museum key they were after."

"Didn't you tell me the person in the museum was six-five or so?"

"That I did. Hence my mood."

"What's your question?"

"Miranda warnings. They are now both persons of interest. Can I talk to them without an attorney and without reading them their rights?"

"What do you think? You just graduated detective school top of your class."

"I say it's okay. So long as they're not under arrest. As long as we stop once they ask for a lawyer."

"That wasn't so hard, now was it. I think you just wanted to have breakfast with me."

"That's true as well," Leslie admitted. "Here's the thing. Fischer's risk-averse. You'd think for as long as he's done this he'd know where that line is. But..."

"He's been beat up by the best of them. As long as the person's not in custody you're okay."

"Same thing goes for a spouse? Can I call the son's wife and ask questions that may incriminate him?"

"Long as you're not beating her with a pipe in the back alley. Even that would be okay for Miranda. Might not pass muster for other reasons, but for Miranda it's a go."

"Our evidence to this point is mostly circumstantial. Scotty's son says he was in Pittsburgh at the time of the homicide. I believe he's lying about his whereabouts. I also believe they're both lying about knowing the Will had been changed and about Scotty's terminal condition. Fact remains, lying and proving one or both of them committed homicide are far apart."

"Pardon me if I'm slow, lack of sleep will do that. Didn't you like that guy Blair, the museum director, for the murder a few days ago?"

"In theory, he has an alibi."

"In theory? What the hell's that mean?"

"Means he was with a married woman at that time."

"That convinces you?"

"I suppose I'd be more convinced if I had a name."

"And if you knew she was still living with her husband. Maybe it's an open marriage situation."

"For a guy who's sleep deprived, you seem to have it together."

"Lot of practice in law school pulling all-nighters."

"You still look like hell. I've arrested guys look better than you."

"So, you've said."

"Then go home and go to bed. Or take a room over there," Leslie pointed in the direction of the hotel across the street. "But get some sleep."

"Was that an invitation?"

"You only wish. Besides, I have work to do."

"Sounds like an acceptance to me."

"Wrong time. Wrong place." She stood, leaned across the table, kissed him on the lips, and whispered, "I'll take a raincheck. Now, go get yourself some sleep before you pass out."

Instead of leaving the restaurant, Leslie sat back down across from Allen. "Get out of here. I have work to do and this is as good a place as any. Go. Get some sleep. Call me later. We'll have dinner and then see what life brings."

"Sounds like a plan. I have a few loose ends to clean up at the office and then I'll call it a day." He placed his hand over hers. "Can't wait." This time he initiated the goodbye-for-now kiss, lingering a moment, then stood and made his way to the door. Turning he said, "Thanks for breakfast."

"You'll get dinner," Leslie answered, turning her attention to her cell and the conversation she was about to have with Roland McDermitt's wife.

THIRTY-FOUR

A FEMALE ANSWERED ON THE second ring. "Is this Betsy McDermitt?" Leslie asked, thinking the voice was too young to be the wife. "I'm calling from the Sheriff's Office in Lee County Florida."

"No. This is Cathy. Is something wrong? My father…"

"Nothing's wrong. Is your mother available?"

"Is he hurt? Is my father okay?"

Thinking that's exactly what she was trying to determine, Leslie responded, "He's fine. I have a question for your mother."

"What's this about?"

"Your grandmother?"

"She died a few weeks ago. In a car accident. In Florida."

"That's what I have questions about."

"My mother's in the backyard planting."

"Can you please get her?'

"She doesn't like to come in the house when she's been gardening without showering."

"How old are you?"

"Twenty-two."

"Please ask your mother to call me when she can." Leslie spelled her name and provided the phone number. Then on a whim, she asked, "Tell me, were you home when you heard about your grandmother's accident?"

"No. We were with my grandfather at his lake house up on Lake Erie. August thing. Do it every year."

"Your grandfather? Your mother's father? Oh, mind if I record our conversation?"

"No problem. Yeah. Grandpa Henry."

Leslie tapped the recording icon on her phone. "Cathy, was your mother with you up at Lake Erie? I understand from your last answer that is where you were when you heard the news about your grandmother."

"Of course. Mother loves it up there."

"What about your father?"

"He was there for the first two weeks. Then something at work and he had to come back home."

"Do I then understand correctly your father wasn't in Erie when you learned of your Grandmother Scotty's accident."

"That's right."

"How did your father get back to Pittsburgh from Erie?"

"His car."

"What car does he drive?"

"An Audi. Why…is something wrong? Why do you want to know about his car?"

"Color?" Leslie asked, sensing the daughter was about to hang up.

"Gray. Listen, I'm not…"

"Please ask your mother to call me when she's back in the house. Thank you. Will you do that?"

"I'll tell her."

"Thanks. Bye."

Leslie texted Fischer.

LISTEN TO PHONE CALL WITH ROLAND DAUGHTER CALL ME.

It took fifteen minutes before Leslie's phone rang. In that time, she reviewed the facts she knew for certain and the facts she knew by implication and circumstance. She then formed a hypothesis about what it all meant. Her conclusion continued to point in the direction of brother and sister killing mommy-dearest for the valuable phonograph. Missing from the proof side of the equation was the money, which was easily hidden, and any actual evidence linking either brother or sister to any of the various possible crime scenes. The conversation with Roland's daughter about her father's whereabouts on August 22nd, coupled with his car being the same make and model as the car parked at the accident scene, was beginning to establish the required link.

"Apologize for not getting to you sooner, Leslie," Fischer said when she answered his return call, "but I had to brief Boots on where we were on the file."

"Boots? Aren't you getting ahead…"

"She has a good connection up in Pittsburgh. I wanted permission for you to fly up there. Get written statements, examine Roland's car, all before he gets back home."

"I have the daughter's statement. I can take the wife over the phone." Leslie felt as if she were being sidelined from the mainstream of the investigation. This was in keeping with what she had been told would happen when they got near an arrest. "I can do from here what needs to be done," she insisted. "I don't see the need to…"

"Maybe yes, maybe no. Fact is, you're on the next flight north. Leaves in two hours."

"But…but I need to go home, get my stuff."

"Use the overnight bag we're all supposed to keep in the car for emergency situations? Hope you did a good job packing. It'll have to do."

In fact, it was just this bag Leslie had planned to employ after dinner that night with Allen. "Why exactly am I going north?" she asked, still bristling at being moved off stage.

"The car is our best evidence. If we can place his car at the scene, we'll have him on first degree murder."

"What about the daughter, Linda? How do we tie her to it?"

"Working it. Banking and phone records. I'll cover that for now. Better hurry. I've arranged for you to work with a guy I know up there. Guy named Jakowski. Senior Detective Pete Jakowski. He'll meet you at the airport."

Southwest Air to Pittsburgh left on time and arrived fifteen minutes early. Leslie had no instructions as to where to meet Jakowski, nor had she been told what he looked like. From his official portrait on the Verona Department of Public Safety web site he appeared to be in his mid-twenties with a hard-set jaw and the shoulders of a Steeler defensive lineman. She held out little hope of spotting him.

How wrong she was.

One step into the airport and the massive hulk of Detective Jakowski loomed over her. The twenties were well gone. And so were the thirties and forties. The face and jaw were the same. A bit harder maybe. A few more lines. A couple of scars. But the same intense eyes. The man was large, but apparently without an ounce of fat. His movements were fluid as befits a man whose strength is clearly visible and who doesn't feel the need to prove it to anyone. Everything about this man screamed, "mess with me at your peril."

"Detective Hodges? Glad to meet you. Hear you're working with Fischer. Says nice things about you. Yinz getting along okay?"

"So far. This is the first case Fish and I've worked together, so it's too soon to know."

"He playin' nice?"

"I wouldn't say otherwise."

"Must be those great green eyes of yours got him snookered."

"I'd hope it was more than that."

"Least you're frank. I'm known as Jak in these parts. You got a handle?"

"Not to my face. Behind my back I suppose they call me lots of names."

"Les work for you?"

"As good as any."

"Les it'll be." Jakowski fell silent when they boarded the tram and remained that way until they were on the escalator down to the baggage area to claim her weapon.

"You can reload your weapon in the car. Captain's approved your carry request. Boots requested it. Anyway, it's done."

"I'm here to interview a wife and daughter, maybe collect some evidence from a car. Can't imagine…"

"That's the rookie in you talking. You, young woman, are investigating a first-degree homicide. If you have the right person, he's already gone and killed one person. Facing the death sentence, or life in prison, as it stands. Killing one or two more folks doesn't add a day to his life. In fact, taking out a cop gives him street cred in prison." Leslie had heard stories ever since she joined the force back in Mobile but had never been involved with a homicide investigation. Certainly, she had never arrested anyone for murder, premeditated or accidental. Her phone buzzed.

NAP TIME OVER. FEEL GREAT. LOOKING FORWARD TO DINNER AND …NIGHTCAP.

"Need to answer, I can wait for you over there," Jakowski said, nodding toward the exit door. "From your reaction I'd say that's personal."

"I can text a reply," Leslie said, already composing what she planned to say. Terse and to the point.

IN PITTSBURGH. SEE YOU WHEN BACK.

"Good to go," she said to Jakowski after tapping the SEND button.

"Special friend?"

She studied this perceptive giant for several seconds, finally deciding she hadn't much hope of fooling him. "Climbing the fence."

"On the up or on the down side?"

"Up, I'd say."

"Good for you. It's been over a year since Junior's been gone. Nobody'd fault you if you dip your toe back in."

Leslie was surprised he had taken the time to check her background, wondering if he was always this thorough. "What else did your friend Fish give you on me?"

"What makes you think I didn't research you on my own?"

"Did you?"

"I did."

"Why?"

"Because in all my years I've never worked with a raw rookie on a homicide. That's why. Sure, we send the babies out to round up this and that, to plow through bank accounts and phone records. Tedious stuff. From what Fish said, you're lead on this. Impressive."

"Don't know what to say."

"Accept the compliment and move on."

His car was parked at the curb between exit doors, an official looking Verona Police sign in the window. They got in and drove away, pulling into a fuel station on the airport grounds not far from the terminal. "Now would be a good time to reload."

When she was done, he drove out of the lot and proceeded to Interstate 376, heading east to Pittsburgh. "It's almost five. With rush hour traffic and all, even with the reduced COVID traffic, I don't suppose we'll get to Verona until six, maybe even six-thirty. Want to have dinner somewhere? Southwest is not known for their food service."

"Maybe close to where we're going. I'd like to get this behind me tonight if possible."

"I'd suggest morning."

"Why's that?" Leslie asked, hoping to gain knowledge from an experienced detective.

"Frankly, to allow me time to buy you dinner and get to know you better."

"I thought the restaurants here in Pittsburgh were closed."

"Most are. Some places are open at twenty-five percent and would love to have our business."

"I'm going home in the morning. In and out's the plan. How much do you need to know for a one-day visit?"

"Life's never what it seems. How do you know I don't plan to retire in your sunny state? Maybe get a security gig in Fort Myers. Maybe you'll be boss one day and hire me. One never knows. I learned long ago, be nice to the folks you meet on the way up 'cause you may need them on the way down."

"You win. We'll do the interview in the morning."

"What changed your mind?"

"For certain it wasn't your philosophy. Just being practical and viewing this traffic. At the rate we're going if I force the interview tonight, I'll end up eating something out of a machine in a third-rate motel. Doing it your way, I'll get a decent meal and perhaps learn something. I'd say that's a win-win if ever I heard one."

"Fish told me you're a practical woman. I see what he means."

"What else did Fish tell you?"

"You'll have to supply the alcohol you want that question answered."

THIRTY-FIVE

DINNER WITH JAKOWSKI WAS FUN. After his second
Scotch he confessed that his life's ambition, since grade
school, was to play pro-football. He played high school
quarterback for Peabody and in his senior year took the
team to the state championship, losing 24-23 when the
opposing team kicked a forty-two-yard field goal with
one second on the clock. "Average high school kick is
under thirty yards," Jakowski exclaimed as if he had just
replayed the game. "This bozo has his best kick ever.
Never did it again!"

Jakowski had been recruited by Pitt, converted to
a tight end and made All-American in his junior and
senior years. Drafted by the Detroit Lions, cut after one
year, picked up by the Steelers, played in three games,
and on the first play of the fourth game, "I blew out my
friggin' knee! Can you believe that? Had to rebuild my
knee. Never played again."

"I'm sorry about that."

"Not as sorry as I was, I can assure you that much.
Anyway, Pitt had given me a BA in something called
Administration of Justice. So, here I am. In case you're
wondering, still happily married to my high school sweet-
heart." He lifted his Scotch in her absent honor.

They spoke about his wife, his three children and
his two grandchildren. Leslie listened, fascinated by a
man who had spent his whole adult life around violent
people and who could turn it off and enjoy the softness
of family, watching children and grandchildren grow up
immune from his world.

———

Leslie didn't get into bed until after 1:00. She couldn't decide what had been better — the food, the drinks or the conversation. Conversation, she concluded, switching the light off. Her thoughts turned to Allen and the night this might have been.

Her alarm sounded at exactly 8:00. In the shower and out by 8:10. Dressed and ready to go by 8:20. Standing in front of the motel at 8:30, exactly as agreed between her and Jakowski. The only problem was the blue shirt, the only one in her bag. Now she had to wear Saturday blue on a tan Wednesday. Convinced nothing good would come from the day, she wasn't at all troubled that Jakowski was late, almost thirty minutes late, before he rolled to a stop in front of her.

"You have every right to be angry," he said, not bothering with a 'good morning' or any other kind of greeting. "Had a family emergency. Might not be an emergency to you, but today's my granddaughter's birthday and I had to deliver a present. Sorry."

"Thought I was being stood up. Isn't the first time, and not the last, I'm sure. Know the address?"

"So why so glum?" Jakowski asked the moment the door closed behind her. "If I didn't know better, I'd say you lost your best friend. Time to fess up. What'd I do wrong?"

"Heavens no. It's not you at all. It's…well it's a quirk of mine. A bit of OCD if you will."

"You gonna tell me or let my imagination run wild?"

"It's nothing much. Only I make my life easy and cycle my shirts each day by color."

"Neat. Never thought of doing that. So, what do you do? Like blue on Mondays, green on Tuesdays kind of thing?"

"You got it. Only for me it's red, green, tan, gray, aqua, blue, yellow. Running from Monday to Sunday."

"Got it. Let's see," Jakowski said, mentally cycling through the colors, "you're wearing Saturday blue and not…not tan. Got that right?"

"You do."

"Okay. Time for us to go catch us some bad guys. Or as my sainted mother liked to say, 'We're gonna reddup this mess.' You're a southern belle. What'd your mommy say?"

"Not to talk to strangers."

"Hey, we're not strangers, now are we? I meant about cleaning up the mess around you."

"She'd say to me and my brother when we made a mess, she'd say, 'Y'all think you might could clean that floor?' When one of us gave a lame excuse why that wasn't possible, she'd say, 'why bless your little hearts,' and walk away."

The drive up the hill to the McDermitt house took four minutes, during which neither of them spoke. The unannounced interview with the wife, Betsy, went as had been scripted in Leslie's head. She confirmed exactly what the daughter had told her the previous day. Leslie ended with, "You're certain your husband was here in Pittsburgh when he learned of his mother's death?"

"Positive."

"Why are you so certain?"

"That's the reason he came back from Erie. His sister Linda called to tell him Scotty's illness had progressed to the point where she didn't have long to live. Linda wanted her to go to hospice, but Scotty refused. She needed Rol's help and he was getting ready to fly down when he got the call."

"How can you be certain he was here and not in Florida?"

"I spoke to him on the phone."

"On his cell?"

"Yes, that how I always...no wait. Now I recall. Something was wrong with his cell. It was off or something. I called him here at the house. He didn't answer the first time. I was about to call again when he called me."

"From his cell? Or from the house?"

"I don't know which. I just know I spoke to him about ten the night before his mother passed."

"You're positive he was here at the house?"

"Where else could he have been?"

"Good question. Now mind if I look at his car?"

"It's in the garage. Right through that door."

"Is it unlocked, or will I need a key?"

"Unlocked."

"Mind giving us the key."

"You're not taking it anywhere are you?"

"Not without your permission. Certainly not, Mrs. McDermitt."

She went off to the kitchen and a moment later tentatively handed the car keys to Leslie.

"Okay. Detective Jakowski and I will go out and take a look. We'll let you know if we have any further questions."

The gray Audi was in the garage as promised. Jakowski started the engine. Using Leslie's phone, he took pictures of the gauges, including the mileage, then turned on the GPS and did the same. He brought up the About screen and photographed it as well. Nothing of consequence turned up in the glove box or in the door pockets. They examined the back seat and found nothing of interest.

"Don't know what you expected to find, Les, but there's nothing inside the car. Clean as a whistle."

"Let's do the trunk and I'll be out of your hair. Keep my camera rolling."

They popped the trunk and it was as clean and neat as inside the car, with the exception of two large blankets against the back wall. Leslie pulled on the blue one, but it caught on something and wouldn't budge. She tugged harder and it broke free revealing a canvas bag.

Her heart stopped.

She had seen that bag before in the video taken by good Samaritan Chris Wang. It had been in the hand of the person walking up the hill from the back of Scotty McDermitt's still smoking car.

"This is now a crime scene," Leslie announced. "Detective Jakowski hand me my phone so I can maintain the video. Please call your forensics department."

Jakowski did as instructed, then asked, "What do you expect they'll find in that bag? I know that look. Your reaction is more than mere speculation."

"Bag's identical to a bag carried from the scene of the McDermitt crash. Unless I'm totally off base, I believe we'll find a length of tubing used for connecting the tail pipe to the air intake. At the very least, trace evidence from the tail pipe."

"Then you'll need residue from the inside of the tube to see if you have a match to the McDermitt car."

Leslie's excitement rose as the adrenalin rush she had heard so much about began in earnest. She was close to breaking open a homicide investigation. All she had to do now was lock down the evidence.

"But," Jakowski's voice brought her back to the McDermitt garage, "may I remind you canvas bags like that can be found in every hardware store in the country. It's a staple for boaters."

Leslie began to respond when the door from the house to the garage opened. Betsy called out, "You two're taking so much time. How much longer will you be?"

"Most likely the rest of the day, ma'am," Jakowski replied. "We're waiting for forensics to arrive."

"I thought this would be fast. I need to go out in a little while. Have a dentist appointment at one."

"You can go. If we finish before you get back, we'll lock up."

"What's forensics doing coming out here for anyway? Is something wrong?"

"Found a bag in the car we need to check."

"Let me see that bag."

"Okay, but don't touch anything."

Betsy McDermitt slowly walked around to the back of the Audi and looked in the trunk. "I've never seen that bag before in my life. Whose bag is it? My father has one like it up at his boat house, but that's not his."

"If it's not yours or your husband's and you say it's not your dad's, then that's a good question. We hope forensics will be able to tell us who it belongs to."

"All that trouble to find out whose it is. Just open it and see if there's a name in it."

"Wish it were that simple," Leslie replied, steering the wife as far back as she could without being obvious about it.

"And those blankets. They're not ours either. Roland keeps his cars pristine. He never has anything in his trunk. Not even a blanket. And there's a box or something under that other blanket. Not like my husband at all."

"We're waiting on forensics to move anything. You're welcome to stay or go about your day. But, please, if you remain do not touch anything."

Betsy moved across the garage, took a chair from a hook on the wall, opened it and sat.

Forensics had just become a spectator sport.

"Mind if we use a couple of those chairs?" Jakowski asked Betsy. "This promises to be a while."

"Help yourself."

———————

When the forensics van pulled into the driveway two hours later the team of four found several neighbors sitting socially distanced in a semi-circle at the top of the driveway, their masks around their necks, an open cooler of beer on the ground in front of them. Betsy had pulled her chair out to join them in their vigil. Within five minutes, the flashing lights from the van brought folks from far enough away that they had to introduce themselves to Betsy. With them came rumors of dead bodies and mafia hits.

Leslie explained to the forensic captain what she expected them to find. The team meticulously began the slow process of documenting every square inch of the trunk space, beginning with dusting for fingerprints and vacuuming for trace elements, such as hair, skin, liquids, pollen, fibers, dirt. This process would be repeated for every object found.

Finally, it was time to open the bag. Leslie held her breath knowing this could now prove to have been for naught. What an embarrassment that would be. She could almost hear the laughter. Laughingstock of two cities. That's what an abundant supply of rope will get you.

The zipper slid back easily allowing the top of the bag to be pulled open. Leslie's direct vision was blocked, forcing her to hold her phone over the team heads hoping to capture what was inside the bag. The captain, knowing there was a high probability of him being called to testify, described for the recorder exactly what he was doing and seeing. "Zipper is now open. I'm looking inside the bag and it appears something is coiled in there. I'm now extracting a tube, appears to be vinyl. There appears to be a residue on the inside of the tube. The tube has a total length of…"

Leslie stopped listening. Her heart began beating faster and she wanted to jump for joy. At the time of the homicide, this car had been in Florida, not in Pittsburgh, and she now had the hard evidence to back it up.

She then heard the forensics captain announce, "And under the second blanket there is a metal case with a latch. The case stands…ten inches tall with a length of… twenty-four inches and a width of…eighteen inches. I am opening the case and inside I find…what is this? Something folded. I'll have to take it fully out of the case to open it. Never seen anything such as this before. There are two of whatever it is. Oh, I see now. Stilts! Well, that's certainly a new one on me. This stilt is set to lift a person, let's see, I'd say about nine inches off the ground."

Nine inches, Leslie thought. What would that mean? It came to her suddenly and the excitement pulsed through her body. It was all she could do to refrain from yelling, "Nine-inch stilts would make five-nine Roland appear in the surveillance video as being six-six. My God, killing your own mother! We got you!" Could anything be worse?

She couldn't wait to get back to Florida and put the guy in cuffs. Premeditated murder was now a lock. Then she remembered the story Sarasota Detective Craighton had told her about the potentially stolen stilts from the circus museum. Whether these were the same or not made no difference, the answer had been in front of her all this time. She mentally kicked herself for not making the connection.

To the forensics captain she said, "Impound the car. I'm looking for evidence showing this vehicle was in Florida within the past month."

"You got it. Mind if I clear the looky-loos? Don't want things getting any more contaminated than they already are."

"This is your scene, handle it your way."

The captain nodded in the direction of Jakowski who said, "Your wish is my command." He spoke a few words into his radio and within five minutes the driveway was cleared, beer and all. Two empty pizza boxes were jutting out of a trash can in the corner of the garage.

"How long a drive to the airport this time of day?" she asked Jakowski.

"With lights, forty-five minutes. Otherwise, a good hour, perhaps longer."

Leslie checked her phone for flight schedules. "There's a five-ten flight. Can we make it?"

"It's two-fifteen. See no reason why not. Get in the car, be there in a minute."

It was closer to five minutes by the time Jakowski pulled his door closed and put the car in gear, having handed Leslie a closed pizza box that was still warm to the touch. "Apologize for keeping you waiting. Ordered this especially for you. A peace offering. Pepperoni embellished with French fries. A Pittsburgh special."

"Fries? What's that about?"

"Pittsburgher's love their fries. All's I can say."

Halfway to the airport Leslie's phone buzzed. Looking down she exclaimed, "Shit!"

"I assume something on your phone and not the pizza."

"Shit! Your buddy Fish just arrested Roland!"

"This being your first homicide, I suppose you wanted that honor."

"I thought about it."

"You did more than think about it. You tasted it. Been there. Done that."

"I'm the one who broke this open. I should get..."

"Just thank your lucky stars, or whatever you thank, that it wasn't you making the arrest."

"You can't be serious! This is my investigation!"

"Hate to keep reminding you, but you're new at this game. From what I've seen so far, you're much further from an arrest than you can imagine."

"What are you talking about. Those stilts. The hose! What the hell more do we need?"

"I admit it looks to be a slam dunk. Not until the lab confirms residue in the tube matches Scotty's car can you tie the two together. And what the hell does a pair of stilts prove?"

"Proves Roland could be the one in the surveillance video."

"Exactly. Could have been. Beyond a reasonable doubt is the standard. Could have been isn't even in the starting gate."

"What are you saying?"

"I'm saying you need to prove his car was down there. That was a good move having them impound the car. Great instincts, I'll give you that."

"Can we get that from the GPS in the car?"

"That's why I took those photos of the system info. A contact's running it now. Might be morning before we know for certain."

Leslie didn't respond and Jakowski, his tone now lighter, said, "Let me say one other thing. A word of advice if you will. There is no such thing as your investigation. If you solve this — let me correct that, when you solve it — it will be due to the efforts of lots of folks, many of whom you don't even know and never will. Folks who designed the equipment you're using, folks who read and interpret the results, folks who make suggestions, bounce ideas around. I understand this all started because that highway cop, James I believe his name is, thought something was wrong and followed up. All I'm saying, there are a lot of people working with you. It's a team you're on. 'Nuff said."

Jakowski had made good time even without lights and siren, giving Leslie over an hour to cool her heels in the waiting area dwelling on the advice Jakowski had given her. Something else had been nagging at her, something to do with Roland. Something his wife had said, lost in the excitement of finding the hose in the Audi's trunk.

Roland and Linda, according to the wife, had known about Scotty being terminal. They had spoken about hospice, so they knew her time was limited. Then why asphyxiate her?

Mercy killing? What kind of mercy was that?

People were being called to board the flight and Leslie, being a late booking, was one of the last people to enter the aircraft. She took her seat far in back and a moment later was instructed to turn off her cell. Looking down she saw a message from Fischer.

SUSPECT ARRESTED AT RSW. GOOD WORK.

She started to reply when the flight attendant stood over her, saying, "Miss, you'll have to turn that off now."

Not worth making a scene, particularly when anything that happened would have a high probability of going viral on one or another social media platforms. Leslie quickly finished her message.

SUGGEST MOVING SLOW. MAJOR HOLES.

Thinking about what a defense lawyer could do with this note, she removed the major holes portion and hit SEND.

A few minutes later the hilly terrain around the airport gave way to deep valleys as the plane, which had taken off toward the north, banked steeply in a semi-circle to the west, and eventually to the south to begin its journey to Fort Myers. Below her, almost obscured by clouds, was the Ohio River beginning its own journey, only it was headed west toward the Mississippi.

THIRTY-SIX

THE SKY WAS DARK BY the time Leslie arrived at her car in the Southwest Florida International airport short-term parking. She had been in the terminal for over an hour, her eyes focused on her cell phone screen trying to keep the moving parts from tangling on one another. "Missed you last night," Allen said when she finally had a chance to call him. "What happened?"

"Nothing's changed, if that's your question. Had to fly up to Pittsburgh."

"Can I assume the McDermitt arrest came from that?"

"Good assumption. Stay tuned."

"What's that mean?"

"Better in person. Can't get into it now."

"Any chance of that being tonight?"

"Love to, but…text coming in. Gotta go. Talk tomorrow."

PRELIM GPS NOTHING SOUTH OF PIT. JAK

Leslie called Fischer. "We need to talk," she said when her partner picked up.

"That's an understatement," Fischer shot back. "Just saw Jakowski's report. Doesn't look good. Listen, I'm over at the main jail. ASA Henderson's here with me. He's agitated, to say the least. Lawyer Morehouse wants to talk. How fast can you get here?"

"Twenty at most."

"Make it ten."

"Do my best."

Driving with lights and siren is dangerous and demands full attention, especially when doing so alone, as Leslie was now doing. She knew full well that all it takes is one person not paying attention; one person being hearing impaired; one person too far into their music to hear external noise, and wham! It's over.

Fourteen minutes travel time and another minute to the conference room where she found Morehouse, Fischer, and an agitated man she hadn't met before, his tie hanging loosely from his neck. The three of them were parading back and forth on opposite sides of the table, masks nowhere to be seen. Morehouse and Fischer threatening each other with dire consequences. Leslie made the assumption that the angry-looking man was ASA Henderson.

As soon as Leslie opened the door, Lawyer Morehouse turned in her direction. "As I understand it, you're the cause of my client being arrested today."

"I don't know what..."

"Roland McDermitt was arrested and charged with first degree murder! Are you telling me you don't know about that?"

"I knew he was arrested, but..."

"Based on evidence you uncovered in an unlawful search of his personal car!"

"There was nothing un..."

Henderson broke in. "Please Ms. Morehouse, this is not the time nor the place to argue about searches and evidence. Your client was properly arrested based on evidence uncovered at his home. He had a flight reservation to Dallas prompting his arrest."

Morehouse shot back, "Only because there are no direct flights to Pittsburgh right now because of the virus. He booked to Dallas and then to Pittsburgh."

"He was fleeing the jurisdiction," Fischer replied. "We have every right..."

"That's pure bullcrap and you know it! Now set him free or..."

"Everybody please calm down," Henderson pleaded. "I'm certain we can work this out. The night judge is aware of our situation and once we work out a plan we can move forward."

Fischer stopped pacing and looked straight at Morehouse. "Detective Hodges is lead on this and I wanted her here before we move forward."

"Spit it out!" Morehouse barked. "You've wasted enough time already!"

"We're prepared to request the court to release Mr. McDermitt on his own recognizance with two conditions. First, he signs a statement agreeing to remain in Lee County for a week."

"And second?" Morehouse demanded, her voice reduced in temperature but not yet normal.

"Second, assuming you represent the museum and not Blair personally, you tell us what you know about him."

"I'm not his personal lawyer, that's true enough. I'm also not an informant. You can ask me questions and I'll answer if I think it proper to do so."

Fischer knew without a doubt that based on the GPS report the case against Roland McDermitt was on life support already. By arraignment time in the morning they would be forced to drop it altogether. "So be it," he conceded.

"Let's get this straight. I say nothing to you until McDermitt's on the street. And, I have your word you won't bring him in on some other charge?"

"That I can't do. If Hodges agrees, we'll notify you ahead of time."

Fischer looked over at Leslie who nodded her approval.

"I'll accept that on the condition his confinement to Florida is for two days, not seven."

"Four and we have a deal."

"Henderson, call the judge tell him we have a deal. Get his blessing," Morehouse said. "You two want to talk tonight or in the morning?"

"Tonight works," Fischer said. "Leslie, you wait here. I'll go with Lawyer Morehouse, expedite the process."

He looked over at Henderson who still had his phone to his ear.

A moment later, Henderson pointed his thumb upwards.

Following Morehouse from the room, Fischer said, "This shouldn't take but fifteen minutes."

In fact, it took almost an hour before Fischer returned with a now somewhat subdued Morehouse. "Just what is it you think I know?"

"When Blair sent Scotty to you to change her Will, did he have in mind the phonograph going to the museum or to himself?"

Morehouse sat quietly for a moment before answering. "My memory is he called me and asked if I could handle a Will for a friend. I know Blair well enough to know that friend meant a woman he was having a relationship with. I told him it depends on the situation. He said his lady friend wanted to give him a gift. I told him she'd have to come in and see me in person and talk to me directly. He didn't like that idea, but I told him there was no way around it if he wanted my services. I had met Scotty several times at the museum and at several fundraisers. So, I wasn't surprised when she asked me to do her Will."

"Scotty came to your offices or what?"

"Blair brought her, but I kicked him out. She told me about the Edison One. That was the first I had heard the story of the two phonographs and the part her great-grandmother played in the design of the recording pin. On the next visit she brought in the phonograph and two recording tubes and I heard Edison himself recite *Mary Had a Little Lamb* and I heard him give the phonograph to Sarah Davis Johnson, her great-grandmother. On the second cylinder I heard her relatives recite their favorite inventions. I must confess, I was moved. She instructed me to change the Will so the Edison One, and the cylinders, would go to Blair when she died. I asked her why she wanted them to go to Blair. She said because Blair promised to give them to the museum when she passed. I told her she could do that herself. I explained the tax benefits of doing it directly. Anyway, to make a long story short, she agreed to do it directly."

Leslie broke her silence. "Did Blair know the phonograph wasn't going to him on her death?"

"I didn't tell him, but Scotty might have. Now that I think about it, Blair did know. They were going to have a tribute to Scotty next week to announce her gift of the Edison One to the museum."

"The other day," Leslie said, "when we asked about Blair's alibi for the night Scotty died you said he was with a married woman during the hours in question."

"I recall that. Yes."

"Do you also recall the name of that married woman by chance?"

"I do."

"Is it too much to ask that you share the name with us?"

"This is one of those times where I would typically decline. But, seeing as though an alibi for Blair can prove detrimental to my client Roland, I am willing to divulge the name, yes. But it'll cost you."

"How much?"

"Drop all charges against Roland McDermitt."

Fischer looked the lawyer directly in the eyes and said, "Not prepared to do that."

Morehouse stood and walked toward the door. "Call me when you want the name. You know the terms."

The door closed behind her and Leslie asked, "With that GPS data we're dead in the water tying Roland to the murder and burglary."

"You know that. I know that. Morehouse doesn't know that."

"What will you tell the judge in the morning at the arraignment?"

"Part of Roland walking without bond is we agreed to no arraignment for two days. Keeps his name out of the system that much longer. We get to keep our powder dry another day. Never know what may turn up."

THIRTY-SEVEN

SOME SYSTEMS WORK 24/7. POLICE departments are one of those systems. While Hodges slept, the computers labored doing what computers do. It was 11:58 a.m. in the Isle of Man, 6:58 a.m. in Lee County Florida, when an Alert Message was generated signifying a strong possibility that an eighteen million dollar transaction originating on 23-08-2020 at 16:18 EDT (UTC-4) with an account associated with the Stratis organization had ultimately been deposited to the credit of an account in the Isle of Man owned by RiverRock LLC.

At 6:59 a.m. Leslie's Alert alarm went off. She sat bolt upright studying the screen, making certain she understood the full implications of what she was seeing. William Packard Blair and Millie Russo were members of RiverRock LLC. "We got you, Asshole!" she shouted to an empty bedroom. "We got you!"

Four minutes later "Fish" popped up on her screen. "Wake you?" he asked.

"Alert alarm did. We got him!"

"Let's not be getting ahead of our skis. Once is enough on this case. We can now tie Blair and Russo to Stratis. It would be great if we could link Stratis to Edison One, but I'm afraid that's going to prove impossible. He's about as smooth as they make them. FBI's been all over him for years. Blair's not far behind him. They tried to pin the loss of the Ginevra de' Benci at the National Gallery to him but could never prove a substitution had even been made."

"Suggestions?"

"See you in the office. We do what we always do. Put our noses back into the file and work it from the beginning. Hope like hell we find a thread we haven't already pulled on. I called Morehouse and offered to spring McDermitt in exchange for the name of the Blair alibi."

"So?"

"So, she didn't pick up. She's playing us."

"Or perhaps too much escort last night and she's sleeping late." Leslie said, mostly in jest.

"What's that mean?"

"Fill you in later."

Working the file, Leslie knew, wasn't going to help. Like Fischer, she had a photographic memory and she didn't believe there was a fact hidden anywhere she hadn't already considered.

Halfway to the office she replayed this morning's message for perhaps the tenth time. She almost rear-ended a stopped car as she mentally studied the message. Scotty's water bottle flew off the passenger seat, slamming into the dash, falling to the floor and rolling under the seat. Leslie turned into a shopping mall in order to continue concentrating on the message and its implications.

If their assumptions were correct, then Edison One had been removed from Scotty's home around one in the morning of August 23rd by a person or persons unknown. Yet eighteen million had begun its journey from Stratis to RiverRock that same day at 16:18 EDT. One further assumption being that Stratis would have inspected the Edison One before parting with the funds. Possibly, that inspection could have been by video, but Stratis didn't seem to operate in that manner. Holding it, touching it is what he lived for. That was why he bought Firsts, the excitement of uniting with the creator. Particularly with Seminal Society Firsts. It would be mandatory for him to personally see, touch, smell such a prize. Leslie concluded that for Stratis there could not be any other acceptable alternative.

If all her assumptions were correct, then how the hell did Edison One get from Fort Myers, Florida to Pittsburgh, Pennsylvania within a few hours. The puzzle was even harder to solve if she factored in the museum break-in at 4:15 in the morning. That would leave about fourteen hours to move the treasure north, inspect it and set up the fund transfer. Possible, but tight.

She called the Real Time Intelligence Center and asked the Investigative Assistant to rush a check on Blair, Morehouse, McDermitt, Murphy, Nikolson, Napoli, and Russo, to see if any of them took flights that day.

Leslie was already at her desk when the results of the flight check were returned with no hits. All local airports were checked, including Punta Gorda, Sarasota and Tampa. Nothing.

All local airports? What about Page Field, where she had boarded Silver's plane for a flight to Pittsburgh? She called the airfield and was put on hold. Ten minutes later she was still on hold. "To hell, with this!" she announced to no one in particular, "I'll haul my butt over there and see for myself."

Pulling into the mostly deserted looking airfield Leslie realized she enjoyed using lights and siren more than she was willing to admit. "Who keeps the log for daily flights?" she demanded of the first TSA person she saw, holding her badge high.

"Flight controller's office. Down that hall to the left. Door's locked. Need to knock."

A few minutes later she had photographed the several computer screens listing the tail numbers of all flights in and out of Page on the 22nd and 23rd of August.

Leslie painstakingly entered each tail number in a database and copied down the owner who was associated with that number. Many of the numbers belonged to leasing companies and the planes were used on a time-share basis. She didn't believe Stratis would do that, but he very well could own the plane through a shell company. From what she had learned over the years about shell companies, they were typically used to avoid taxes and hide income. Business aircraft were expensive to operate and a great tax deduction causing Leslie to maintain hope she'd recognize a Stratis-owned tail number if she saw it.

An hour and fifteen minutes into her search she yelled, "Voila!"

There in front of her was the name of Stratis Industries.

Back to the log to concentrate on landing and takeoff times for the Stratis-owned aircraft.

Type: Bombardier Global 5000
Landed: 08:31 EDT 08-23-2020
Departed: 09:28 EDT 08-23-2020
Destination: PIT

Leslie, now armed with exact times, went back to the flight office. Flashed her badge, and said, "I'd appreciate seeing any footage you have on file for 23 August from 08 hundred to noon."

"Any particular camera. Or all of them?" the attendant, a young man barely out of his teen years, asked.

"Give me all. I don't know what I really need."

"You'll have to give me a few minutes," the young man said. "I need to get permission to enter the database. If you'll sit over at that desk, I can set it up for you."

"If you need help getting permission, I can…"

"Won't be necessary. It's just a formality. Be right back."

It's never easy, Leslie said to herself. But this promises to be easier than most. She took the time to upload into the case file what she had found so far.

While waiting for the footage, she made a calculation beginning at the Bombardier departure time of 09:28. Three hours to Pittsburgh and some slack time puts the Edison One up there at around 1 p.m. Drive from airport to Stratis' house, call it two hours. Time is 3 p.m. Time to inspect: an hour or so. Plenty of time to accept and start a payment of eighteen million on its way.

"Okay," the kid called, "here's the video you asked for. I'll insert the drive in the machine, and you can use the space bar to toggle it on and off. Go for it. Let me know if there's anything more you need."

The camera marked RUNWAY showed planes landing and taking off and was of no use. The one labeled SHOP was likewise useless as was WESTSIDE. She hit pay dirt with SOUTHSIDE. The Bombardier she was looking for rolled to a stop at 08:38. Steps were lowered at 08:46. The figure of a man, his back to the camera, appeared at the base of the steps at 08:50 and started tentatively up. His right hand held the same metal stilt box as Leslie had seen in the trunk of Roland's car. His left hand carried the zipped canvas bag. No hint of Edison One. Other than the man appearing to be over six feet tall, she had no way of identifying him.

Nothing happened for several minutes. Then at 09:05 Leslie sucked in her breath as the man who had carried the canvas bag and stilt box onto the plane appeared in the doorway. There, clearly framed in the arch at the top of the steps was William Packard Blair.

He started down the steps and stopped halfway. Leslie had been concentrating on Blair with such intensity that she had missed the woman carrying a small suitcase who had come out of the terminal to join him. Blair took the suitcase, said something to the woman, and proceeded back up to the plane. The woman turned and retraced her steps, disappearing in the direction of the terminal, but not before Leslie identified her as Millie Russo.

At 09:12 the stairs retracted, the door closed, and the plane began moving toward the runway presumably taking off at 09:28.

"See what you needed to see?" the young man called from across the office to Leslie.

"Everything I had hoped for and more," Leslie replied. "Thank you for your help." In fact, the only thing more Leslie could have hoped for would have been if Stratis himself had appeared at the doorway.

"If you need a copy just say the word and I'll get it for you."

"That would be nice if you could."

"Be but a minute."

"You made my day," Leslie called after him.

"Pleased to be of help, detective. Be right back."

While she waited, Leslie again viewed the few minutes of video showing Blair going up the stairs with the canvas bag and the metal stilt box. Then Blair meeting Russo midway on the stairs and retrieving the suitcase from her. Blair was on his way to Pittsburgh. Only this time Leslie had her phone video running with Fischer watching live.

"We'll never know what was in that suitcase, but for our purposes," Leslie, said to Fischer when the video finished, "at least as to how I see it, it's irrelevant. Now we know how the stilts and hose got in Roland's car. Blair managed to break in and put them there to frame him if need be."

"I agree with you. Great work thinking of his plane. They overthought the whole thing. The stilts were a nice touch. Threw us off bigtime. Shows you, even undoctored video lies. They must have rented a gray Audi as part of the framing of the brother if need be. Now that we know what we're looking for we should locate that as well."

Leslie fell silent, thought about all that had happened. Then, almost to herself she mused, "But Scotty was terminal. She was going to die anyway. Guy's sick to kill her and deny her the only pleasure she had left in her life, turning the Edison One over to the museum."

"When Scotty refused to bequeath the phonograph to him, Blair panicked. If he waited for her to die naturally then the insurance policy would have kicked in and I suppose he was more afraid of Silver's investigators than he was of us. Good job Leslie. Great way to begin."

"Are we ready to arrest them, or should we tie up the ends?"

"If we hadn't arrested Roland, I'd say wait. But Roland's about to be cut loose. Once he's out, Blair and his woman, Russo, will know what's coming and slide into some hole or another."

"I suppose eighteen million buys a lot of comfy holes in faraway places. To think they left perhaps a hundred mil on the table."

"How do you figure?"

"Silver told me bidding's going up for the missing cylinder. It wouldn't surprise him if the price is over a hundred. I'm thinking that's the only reason those two, Blair and Russo, remained around. They wanted the cylinder as if eighteen mil isn't enough."

"Cylinder belongs to the museum now. It's their problem to find it."

"What a great problem to have," Leslie quipped, thinking about where she would start if she was available for hire.

Fischer snapped her out of her reverie. "Who do you want to take? Blair or Russo? We need to arrest them simultaneously."

"Mind if I take Blair. You do Russo. That okay with you?"

"It's your case. Your call. Go get lunch. I'll arrange a takedown team, locate both Blair and Russo and coordinate. Be a few hours. Relax. Savor the moment."

———◆———

Back in her car Leslie was still playing the case in her mind when she drove out of her parking spot and slammed on the brakes to avoid hitting a mail truck she hadn't seen. Scotty's water bottle, which had been under the passenger seat, flew forward and was now lying under the dashboard, its top open. Something had slid out from inside the thermos and rolled into the far corner.

Leslie stretched herself across the seat and retrieved the device with the tips of her fingers. It took her a moment to realize that she now held in her hands the missing original Edison recording cylinder.

It took another minute to process her options which were: 1) log it in as property belonging to Scotty. In which case it would go to Roland as the Executor of Scotty's estate; 2) same as 1 but encourage Roland to call Stratis. In which case, if Roland sold it Leslie would get between four and ten million dollars; 3) keep it and call Stratis directly, netting her between forty and a hundred million.

She reached for her phone, found the name she was looking for and hit SEND.

Allen answered on the second ring. "You okay? Been worried about you."

"Doing fine, now. That dinner invitation still open?"

"It sure as hell is, Leslie. In fact, I can knock off at lunch and call it a day, if that works for you."

"I wish. Need to handle two matters first. May take until dinner. Sorry."

"What the hell you up to?"

"Make an arrest in the Scotty homicide."

"Thought you did that."

"Long story. Didn't take."

"What's the second?"

"Log in an item belongs to Scotty."

"The missing Edison cylinder?"

"One and the same. Gotta go. See you later."

"See you. And Leslie."

"What?"

"Congratulations. Not many rookies solve homicides."

And not many rookies forego a massive payday either. "Thank you, Allen. You don't know how welcome your words really are."

END

THE SEMINAL SOCIETY — CHLADNI

CHAPTER ONE

Second Book In The Series

The coded message transmitted to two Seminal Society collectors as they flew high above the earth in private jets was simple:

EUPHON CARNEGIE PITT 1-12-211.

To them, as well as to a third Society collector, the meaning was profound.

It was New Year's Day and Sanjay and Riya Kumar had taken off from New Jersey's Teterboro Airport; destination, Cannes by way of three nights in Paris. Riya looked forward to a long-awaited shopping trip, while Sanjay planned to enjoy the Folies Bergère and all that Paris has to offer in after-hours amusement.

Alexandre Colton's official destination was listed as Anchorage, Alaska. The message reached him as his leased jet passed just south of British Columbia heading northwest. His actual destination was Saint Matthew Island in the Bering Sea. With a change of appearance, aircraft, and new travel documents, he would make his way to Magadan in Russia as Dmitri Volkov in the employ of the Russian government.

The third collector, Dexter Morris Stratis, one of the world's richest men, was in Peru in quest of a recently unearthed Inca gold statue believed to be the long-lost Inti. The artifact was originally housed in the Temple of the Sun at the Qorikancha, the sacred complex at Cuzco, and Stratis had his doubts as to the statue's authenticity. Until he ruled it out with his own experts, the hunt was on.

Within minutes of the message's delivery, both jets set new headings. Colton to 40.4919°N, 80.2352°W, Pittsburgh

International Airport. Kumar to 40.3524°N, 79.9270°W, Allegheny County Airport. Both airports not far from the Carnegie Museum in the Oakland section of Pittsburgh.

Stratis, after carefully considering his options, remained in the Peruvian Andes. His decision not to abandon his hunt for the gold statue that at one time held the burnt vital organs of Inca kings was not made lightly. He knew from a trusted employee, a man known as Esquire, that delaying his return home by a few days would not compromise his ability to secure for himself the long-lost euphon, a musical instrument that produced unique sounds.

Stratis, an avid collector of Seminal Society Firsts, was especially anxious to secure the euphon which was invented by Ernst Chladni, primarily because Chladni was the acknowledged father of acoustics. And acoustics fit perfectly with Edison's love of sound and the creation of the First phonograph which Stratis had recently acquired. Stratis often thought how wonderful it would have been if Edison had predated Chladni so that the sound of the euphon, as played by Chladni, would have been preserved forever.

Chladni, Stratis knew, was born in Wittenberg, Germany, in 1756 into a long line of preachers and lawyers. Chladni was trained as a lawyer, but when his father died, he followed his real passion and switched to physics. Educated at Leipzig University, Chladni spent his life researching the speed of sound in various substances, including glass and wood.

Stratis was especially excited about the euphon because Seminal Society collectors like himself believed Chladni was the spirit bridge linking Sir Isaac Newton and Thomas Alva Edison. In their minds all three men shared the same soul; a soul which has been passed on from a relatively unknown fourteenth century song writer named Wolkenstein through Leonardo da Vinci to Galileo to Newton to Chladni. From Chladni, the seminal soul passed on to Edison who invented sound recording.

Seminal Society collectors have always known of Chladni's musical invention and the fact that the renowned scientist often played the euphon to evening sellout audiences as he toured Europe giving science lectures in the Universities by day. No records were known to exist as to what had happened to the euphon at Chladni's death. Over the years many of the collectors, including Stratis, had commissioned investigators to locate the euphon, all to no avail. That had all changed recently when a prominent eighteenth-century forensic historian and European art expert, Dr. Sigmond Fuller, located the Chladni euphon. Fuller's extensive authentication report, the contents of which had been shared with Stratis, as well as with several other motivated collectors, had just this week been validated by the Polish Government. The Poles, upon authentication, declared the euphon a national treasure and further declared that it could only be displayed at the Polish National Museum.

In anticipation of this action by the Polish government, Stratis, using Esquire as the negotiator, made two large contributions. One to the Polish museum to allow the euphon to go on a limited exhibition in the USA. And the other to the Carnegie Museum in Pittsburgh to host the euphon. All transportation and other incidental costs were to be borne by Stratis.

If events played out as Stratis now believed they would, he'd soon have the ability to hear the euphon played live for him whenever he wanted to hear it. His head swam with the intoxication of that thought, even knowing that there still remained several steps before the euphon would be his. One thing he knew well enough; anything could happen in an environment where money is of little concern.

Thank You

A great big Thank You to my editor, and wonderful daughter-in-law, Brenda Goldberg Tannenbaum for her excellent editing and thoughtful comments and suggestions. Editing a book is never easy. COVID-19 didn't help the situation. If characters didn't wear proper masks or touched each other in ways not sanctioned by the CDC, blame that on me, not on Brenda. She tried. I wouldn't always listen.

First readers are critical to an author. Ronald Slusky, who remembers my first manuscript some forty or so years ago (which, under his guidance in 2016, became Out of the Depths), is a perfect first reader. Thank you, Ron, for being there for me all these years.

Last eyes, as I call the final review before publication, is also important. Lori Mercier, the daughter of a good friend, did a masterful job in a compressed time frame. Thank you Lori.

Thank you to all the early readers. Richard Cohen, John Charnes, Richard Conrath, James Mercier, Marnie Monheim, Dr. Deodutt Patel, Kathleen Possai, Charles Ryan, and Marion Wikes. Their comments, critiques and plot-fixing suggestions are much appreciated. My friend, Dr. Patel, went far beyond the call of duty and I commend him for his patience with me and with my murderous treatment of the King's English.

Special thanks to Sgt. Russell Park, Lee County Sheriff's Office, for his invaluable and patient help in correcting my faulty police procedures and terminology. Hopefully, I have now mastered the world of POI, BOLO, ASA, SOV, CIA, DFU, ROR and RTICs. I claim literary license for those instances where I have tripped over a procedure or have used an improper acronym. Hopefully, Sgt. Park will forgive me for my transgressions.

Thank you also to Susan Peterson for introducing me to the Edison's Last Breath test-tube exhibit at the Ford Museum. Thanks to Henry Ford, some aspect of Thomas Edison remains with us to this day, making a perfect aspirational target for collectors focusing on the Seminal Society.

Book publishers are a special breed. They see half-completed manuscripts and are able to, as the British are wont to say, separate the wheat from the chaff. Joyce Faulkner, an award-winning author in her own right, took time from her busy schedule to listen to the outline of The Seminal Society series and encourage me to move forward. I thank Joyce and Red Engine Press for their hard work and dedication to authors across the country.

My deep appreciation goes to my wonderful wife, Mary, who makes my writing life possible. She untiringly spreads green fluorescent marker ink over the manuscript — draft after draft — always asking tough questions and making the story better in the process.

About The Author

David Harry Tannenbaum and his wife, Mary, have a home in Miromar Lakes, Florida. When David isn't writing, he enjoys swimming, model train building and walking Franco.

Communications

David can be reached at *author@seminalsociety.com* and followed on website: seminalsociety.com.

Other Books by

David Harry Tannenbaum

General Fiction

STANDARD DEVIATION

OUT OF THE DEPTHS

ADVENTURES IN THE LAW

Mystery / Thriller

(UNDER THE PEN NAME: DAVID HARRY)

JIMMY REDSTONE / ANGELLA MARTINEZ SERIES

THE PADRE PUZZLE

THE PADRE PREDATOR

THE PADRE PARANOIA

THE PADRE PANDEMIC

THE PADRE POISON

THE PADRE PHANTOM

THE PADRE PHONY

THE PADRE PIRATE

THE PADRE PUPPETS

You can also follow him on Facebook: (patentguru or David Harry Tannenbaum) and on twitter: david1harry.

www.ingramcontent.com/pod-product-compliance
Lightning Source LLC
Chambersburg PA
CBHW050925030726
47503CB00007BB/2471